Her
A Pacific W
Jame

Arnold Schwarzenegger

**THE TERMINATOR**

Michael Biehn
Linda Hamilton
and Paul Winfield

Make-up Effects by Stan Winston

Executive producers
John Daly and Derek Gibson

Written by
James Cameron and Gale Anne Hurd

Produced by
Gale Anne Hurd

Directed by
James Cameron

An Orion Pictures Release

*Also available:*

**TERMINATOR 2: JUDGEMENT DAY**

# THE
# TERMINATOR

A NOVEL BY
**Randall Frakes & Bill Wisher**

Based on a Screenplay by
JAMES CAMERON WITH GALE ANNE HURD

WARNER BOOKS

A *Warner* Book

First published in Great Britain in 1991
by Sphere Books Ltd
Reprinted by Warner Books 1993

Copyright © 1984 by Cinema, a Greenberg Brothers Partnership

The right of Randall Frakes and Bill Wisher to be identified
as authors of this work has been asserted.

*All characters in this publication are fictitious
and any resemblance to real persons, living or dead,
is purely coincidental.*

All rights reserved.
No part of this publication may be reproduced,
stored in a retrieval system, or transmitted, in any
form or by any means, without the prior
permission in writing of the publisher, nor be
otherwise circulated in any form of binding or
cover other than that in which it is published and
without a similar condition including this
condition being imposed on the subsequent purchaser.

ISBN 0 7515 0634 6

Printed in England by Clays Ltd, St Ives plc

Warner Books
Little, Brown and Company (UK) Ltd
165 Great Dover Street
London SE1 4YA

*For James Cameron, who first saw* Terminator *coming out of the fire.*

*Thanks to Fred Klein and Dave Stern at Bantam for their forbearance and good taste.*

# THE
# TERMINATOR

# DAY ONE

Los Angeles California
Griffith Park Observatory
March 9, 1984
Friday—3:48 A.M.

"History Is Dead" had been scrawled on one of the stucco walls girding the moonlit observatory. Perhaps it had been put there by an undergraduate with a bad case of whimsy, or maybe it had been spray painted by a *barrio* gang member who interrupted his usual ritual of marking territory with a literary conceit. Or maybe it had been put there by someone who knew it was the truth.

The triple-domed building was silent, lit only by a pale yellow globe above the copper-and-glass entrance. The grounds surrounding it were neat enough, trimmed with smug precision by the city park gardeners, but there were little eddies of trash swirling across the vast parking lot and flattened by the March wind against the defaced wall.

The observatory had once been a working window on the cosmos. Since it had first been built, astronomers had pondered the centuries-long ticking of the cosmic clock in the sky from high atop the hills. This was now a near impossibility because of the city's glowing spiderweb that illuminated the LA basin at night and blotted out the stars. The exhaust of industry and freeway traffic created an almost opaque and constant cloudcap that further hampered the use of the now mostly dormant telescopes.

Over the years, the observatory had become a planetarium, the ceiling of the domes now reflecting "stars" projected from a machine, as if only it could remember their patterns. Once academic, now it had become, like Disneyland, a place for tourists to get lost on their way to, a mecca for high school science-class field trips, and since the "Laserium" had been added—laser beams streaking complex shapes across the curved ceiling to the beat of blasting rock music—a hangout for school kids looking for alternatives to drive-in movies and rock concerts. The other attraction was the view of Los Angeles from the parking lot. On the thirty or forty days in the year when the air was clear—and it could get mountaintop clear with shadows like the edges of razors—couples would stay after the last Laserium show to admire a more static but nonetheless spectacular light show until their car windows fogged up and senses other than the visual became more important.

Even if you didn't have a date, the view was worth the long climb. That is, when the road was dry and it wasn't raining over the city, the technicolor matrix of streetlamps and neons subdued by black clouds coming in low and wet from Santa Monica and the brooding dark-green expanse of the Pacific beyond. Then it wasn't worth the careening, bumpy trek. So, before the impending storm, the only vehicle moving on Vermont Canyon Road now was an orange-and-yellow behemoth, a GMC city trash truck.

Del Ray Goines groped in the right hip pocket of his navy pea coat for the tiny volume control on his Walkman. B. B. King's fingers were urging his guitar strings into a righteous blues chord. Del loved this part, but his truck was losing ground. He had to gun the howling diesel engine, and in the noise B. B. King just went away. The lightweight earphones that had come with the cassette player let in too much sound. He reminded himself to buy the older style that covered the ears completely. It was illegal to wear headphones while driving, doubly so for a city employee, but fuck it, a man's got to maintain his sense of priorities. Music before trash, Del thought. If they found out he smuggled the Walkman on the job, he'd be on the street. Again. Not that he loved the job. Far from it. But he had to eat, and there was Leanna's alimony and the snot-nose landlord and his dog Boner.

Course, he had a decent paycheck now, and the Great Dane ate well, no doubt about that. Then, no one would accuse Del of being a lightweight, either. During the leanest times he could bounce the scales past two fifty. Still, hauling garbage from one end of the park to the other wasn't exactly his dream occupation. Twenty-two years ago he was doing it as he wanted—linebacker for the Houston Oilers. Two good seasons, about the only good seasons the Oilers ever had; then he hit a brick wall of bad luck. Knee injury. Divorce. Cut from the team. Most of his salary had gone into a better poker player's pocket. Since then he'd ridden the roller coaster. There were a few ups, but mostly that sucker took him down. And now he was a garbage man. 'Scuse me . . . city sanitation department, field engineer. Fucking slop hauler. An old teammate recommended him, and he was hired on.

Up at two A-fucking-M. Stagger into this metal moose and wrestle it up narrow gravel roads to collect the half-eaten remains of somebody's picnic. That rotten, orange-rind stench of slime-soft garbage rode with you, see. Always. Like a foul living thing.

He grabbed the shifting lever in his broad brown palm and double-clutched violently. He was cresting the last rise and had to drop a gear to make it. The jimmy diesel rattled the engine mounts, and the gut-throbbing vibrations traveled through the frame, into the steering column and up Del's beefy arms. He wheeled the truck into the observatory parking lot and blinked when he saw a primer-gray '68 Chevy Malibu sitting like a blockade right in his path. In the two seconds his brain required to fully register amazement, fear, and then hurt that someone would make his job any more dangerous, any more difficult, he glimpsed a white kid urinating on the vehicle's front grille. He wore a black leather jacket wrapped with chains, purple hair teased straight up into spikes, reminding Del of Buckwheat from the Little Rascals, and gray jump pants with high rockets tucked into combat boots. A punk rocker, they called him. Del braked hard and spun the big wheel around. The kid—maybe he was seventeen or eighteen—didn't move a muscle as Del's truck roared by. Del looked in his side-view mirror to see if the kid would jump back. Instead, the boy calmly faced the passing garbage truck and continued to piss, the stream splattering the rear tire.

Prickly explosions of anger replaced Del's fear, and he slapped his palm against the center of the wheel. The blast from the air horn above the cab could have startled the dead. *That* would make the kid's hair really stand on end. Del eyed the mirror but could only see the dwindling figure of the punker flipping him off.

Punker, hell. Asshole. If he tried that when Del came back, he'd give him something to piss over.

There was a sticker on his truck bumper that read, "This Property Insured by Smith & Wesson." And he was packing, all right, even if it was only a seventy-dollar HR .22 pistol he bought off his brother-in-law a few years back. Maybe the only thing he ever killed with it was a can of Budweiser, but he could aim and pull the trigger okay.

B. B. King came back, swimming into his consciousness as he drove the big truck across the asphalt toward the dumpsters.

Del Ray tried to calm down. But then he remembered why he started packing the gun. It wasn't the dozens of knifings and gang fights that littered the park's recent history. It was more personal than that. The night of the third week he began driving for the city. About this time, in another section of the park. He was running the lift, moving a dumpster over the cab to empty it into the back, when something thudded on top and rolled onto the hood.

The police said it was a drug-related murder, but all Del knew was that the eighteen-year-old boy had been gutted and a lot of what he'd eaten had spilled onto the windshield. So Del started carrying. Everybody knew LA was full of whackos. And white kids *were* getting strange these days. He looked in the side-view mirror again, but he was too far away to see anything now. He drove around a curve in the wall and pulled into a cul-de-sac where the dumpsters huddled like metal derelicts. As he angled the truck so he could hook on to the first dumpster, he began to relax a little. *Getting to be a real old lady, Del,* he thought. But he took longer than usual to get the job done because he kept absently glancing in the side-view mirror—just in case.

Mark Warfield was in mid-piss when the monster roared into the parking lot. Like a kangaroo frozen in the glare of a hunter's headlights, Mark stood his ground. It was fate coming now, challenging his mettle. Fate with half a load of garbage on its back, rumbling toward him like a juggernaut. Fuck fate. And piss on it, too.

As it passed, he did.

A moment later, as he was routing his nozzle back into his pants, the air horn caused him to jerk, pinching himself painfully in the teeth of the zipper.

Then a primal revelation misfired through his wired brain cells, and he realized that fate was fucking with him. Blowing his ears out, mangling his meat. He raised his fist and pointed his middle finger in the air. He'd take on fate. He'd taken on worse. Like the ground. It was fucking with him, too. Undulating under his feet like a snake attached to a wall socket.

Although he rode it like a surfer, a real pro, sensing its movements, fighting it for supremacy, the ground won. It reached up and smacked his face, hard. He saw a flash of white, heard his own distant grunt, and then felt the swelling on his forehead where the parking lot had hit him. He laughed. He heard his buddies laughing, too, probably at him. Johnny, short, fast, and dirty mean. They usually called him Kotex. And Rick, tall, bony, like a ghost in a torn trench coat. His friends. He loved them. He hated them. They were assholes. Maybe he'd cut one of them tonight. He saw a few unopened bottles of beer at the base of the coin-operated telescope around which Kotex and Rick were dancing. They were on an observation platform at the edge of the parking lot, a million miles away, but he could hear them as if they were only ten yards off. Their ghetto blaster was playing "Let's Have A War" by Fear.

The three of them had started at the Cathay, slamming near the stage, arms whirling, cranking up the dynamo. The energy of the adrenaline had spilled over onto the street when they left, into the parking lot where some rockabilly assholes had braced them.

Kotex put one guy's head through the side window of his truck, and the others had faded. The dynamo spun faster, the adrenaline and coke mixing in their blood, creating a freezing hot rush of exhilaration.

Piling into Rick's Malibu, they set out to cruise, sharklike, hungry, directionless, until they found themselves in the hills.

Mark dry heaved, or maybe he laughed. Sometimes they felt the same. Kotex and Rick were fighting now. Or maybe just taking a long time to fall on one another. They were going to break the bottles. And he was thirsty. That was a cutting offense. He began to crawl.

Lightning flashed under the vast expanse of rain clouds as they moved toward the observatory. There was no way Del wanted to get wet going down Vermont Canyon, so he sped his pace, working the hydraulic that controlled the lift, slamming the last dumpster onto the pavement. He backed away to clear the lift fork as another streak of lightning flashed overhead. That time it had come close, right above the truck. He saw the headline: "Sanitation Worker Killed by Lightning." He wanted none of that. So he slammed the shifting lever into first. As his foot pressed the accelerator peddle, the engine sputtered and died. At the same time, his headlights winked out, and B. B. King faded away.

*Not this shit again,* he thought, broken down in East Jesus four steep miles from a phone.

He tried the key. Nothing.

"Son of a bitch."

Again. Not even a click from the starter solenoid.

The coarse hair prickled on the back of his neck. Maybe it was the small voice that told him his Walkman ran on batteries and there was no sane reason for it to cut out just because the truck was acting up. Maybe it was the strange *charged* feeling to the air. He slammed a fist onto the dash.

"Goddam son-of-a-bitch truck ain't worth a nickel in Chinese money—"

All this was a subvocal growl, and Del was just getting wound up when something happened that was beyond the pale of the mechanical pool's sloppy maintenance. Lights were flashing alongside and above the truck, like a thousand Instamatics popping off in his face. He turned the key in the ignition. It wasn't going to happen. No juice. Then a huge bolt of energy tore through the atmosphere and snaked along the rim of one of the dumpsters. Whatever it was, it was getting worse. Instinctively, Del let go of the metal keys, yanked off the metal headphones, and jerked his elbow off the metal armrest. He was wearing rubber boots. Were they good insulators? Did insulators stop electricity or pass it along? *Oh, mama, don't let me fry now!* The air crackled and howled like a radio stuck between two stations, the music all twisted into a dissonant squeal. And the crackling revved up, like a slow-starting seventy-eight RPM turntable, building into a heavy hum in the bristling air next to the truck; the scary, don't-touch hum of a powerful transformer.

Del wanted to get out and run, but if he moved, he was certain he would die. This was no regular lightning. A chaotic crisscrossing of arcing purple-white lines of energy licked at the truck, their fiery tongues lashing out like a lizard's, caressing the metal of the cab.

He watched the frenetic dance of power as it snarled into a thick ball of whiplashing light. The ball of light was brightening as the bolts of energy seemed to coalesce. Del's hair began to rustle, as if caught by a breeze, even though his windows were snugly shut. Then his hair stiffened and rose straight up. Like that punker. But it wasn't because he was scared, although he had screeched past scared thirty seconds ago and was now overtaking terror; it was because static was everywhere, filling the cab with the pristine, tingly odor of ionized air.

Then Del's ears blocked up as pressure increased on them. The ball of light exploded into purple slashes, and something erupted into existence with a sound like a gargantuan Mean Joe Green slamming into the Rocky Mountains.

Del ducked as the pressure leaped, slapping the window and pulverizing it into tinkly fragments that sprayed Del's back. The backwash of the explosion sucked air out of the newly vented cab with a crack. Then things seemed to settle down.

Del slowly sat up, gingerly feeling for cuts. He was okay except that his ears had something in them. The concussion.

Trying to pop his ears with the palms of his hands didn't help, either. His throat tightened, but he couldn't swallow, because the deafness didn't matter, because he was looking at the vapor cloud where the explosion had been, rapidly dissipating in the chill wind, like steam. And something was in there. Where there hadn't been anything before. Del didn't want to look.

But he knew he had to see what was going to kill him. There was no doubt in Del Ray Goines's mind that this was something supernatural and that it was for him, and since he was basically a rotten bastard, it was here for his death. And you must always look your executioner in the face. So Del turned his head and saw the white lump in the clearing mist.

It had come from nowhere and now was there.

He could see it breathing. Then it slowly and gracefully unfolded into a naked man. The military-short hair was smoking. The skin was covered with white ash that fell away like fine flour, revealing baby-pink skin beneath. But this was no infant.

Del had seen bigger men on the scrimmage line when he was with the Oilers. Maybe even some who were stronger. But not as perfect. The muscles bunched and loosened in smooth fluid motions, rippling the beautifully sculpted torso. The arms were a study in powerful symmetry, the angry curve of the biceps narrowing with precision at the elbow, then expanding with awesome mathematical balance into thick forearms that flowed into almost gracefully thin wrists. The fingers on the massive hands rolled out and flexed.

Put this man on a football field and he could have gone anywhere he wanted. Not even three Del Rays flinging their entire weight would bring him down. And Del realized why that was. Not because of the body. It was the face. Implacable. Alive yet dead. Taking in, not giving out, and more than the face, it was the eyes. There was death in those cobalt-blue eyes. Unimaginable. Pitiless. Relentless. The kind of death people never dream about because it is too real. Straightforward, without emotion, and therefore without mercy. He could plainly see the man was staring at him. If he was close enough to see the man's eyes, Del knew, he was close enough to be killed by him.

One of Del's worst problems on the playing field was now his only hope. His legs. His heart was racing now.

Del slammed his shoulder against the door and spilled out onto the cold pavement. His foot took the shock badly, sending the old familiar pain through his weak knee. *Move!*

Del took off, running along the length of the truck away from the man whose eyes turreted after him like artillery on a destroyer, tracking the fat man as he broke into a respectable sprint.

Del ignored the jabs of pain roaring up his legs, reverberating off the soft knee, and pistoned his thighs. That scary dude was right on his ass, and he knew it. He didn't have to look, and he wasn't about to. His stomach was a sack that bounced and whipped down over his belt, then rippled back up his chest, but he kept his balance.

It wasn't his gut that would bring him down.

He was halfway across the parking lot when he saw the punkers on the observation platform. Got to warn them.

Then he remembered the kid pissing on his truck, and he cut them out of his life. Take care of themselves. Besides, they might slow that guy up. The Man from Glad. Ready to wrap your soul in cellophane. Freeze it for later.

He ran like a son of a bitch.

The run of his life.

Past the primer-gray Chevy Malibu.

Past the punks.

Down the winding driveway.

Then plummeting down the mad incline of Vermont Canyon Road. Now he couldn't stop if he wanted to. The momentum lifted him along as if he were caught in a giant's hand until his knee did fold and the earth caught him on the ass and slid him off the road and down the steep incline. He rolled, passive to the forces of gravity and inertia, content in his agony to let where he wound up be decided by them.

He came to rest in a clump of wet weeds about two feet from a chain-link fence, on his back, body limp. And then someone turned up the volume on the world. His heavy breaths became audible, and he sobbed. Welcome back, B. B.

Del sat up slowly, the world wavering as he did so. The road above was empty. No footsteps. No demon Man from Glad. Touchdown. His mind babbled every prayer of gratitude he had ever been forced to learn. He was sitting on something that dug into his hip. He groped down there and felt the body-warmed metal of the .22 pistol.

His deepest and most sincere prayer was that he had forgotten to use it. He didn't know why he sensed it wouldn't have stopped the man. And Del didn't care. He clambered to his feet in the moist earth and continued limping along the fence, away from the observatory. Unemployment was beginning to look very good to him.

He was one of the few who survived Terminator.

Terminator had lost a beat for a microsecond. Something overwhelming had caused him to black out. Then awareness rapidly ballooned outward again. The static in his mind ebbed, and images swam into focus. There was an occulting mist around him, but he could see through it. The chronoporting had been nominal. He took in a breath and analyzed it. It was the same Here as There, with minor exceptions regarding pollutants and nitrogen content. He was curled into a fetal ball to increase the efficiency of the discontinuity envelope. He slowly rose up, maintaining perfect balance as parts of his body adjusted. The carbonized conduction jelly had successfully buffered his epidermis from flash burn. The coating of white ash created a resemblance to classical sculpture, in white marble or alabaster, as awesomely perfect as any Bernini or Rodin.

Terminator scanned the area for activity. A large metal object rested on asphalt four meters away. He locked onto the outlines and immediately recognized it as a GMC diesel refuse truck, circa 1975. The building beyond he identified a half second later as the Griffith Park Observatory. Within another second—as all his senses began to function at optimal—he took note of the grounds, the weather, and the general geographic fix on this location, referencing against a map in his memory. He was on target.

He turned his attention to the man in the truck. He was Negroid, approximately fifty years old, massing close to 150 kilos. His facial expression suggested fear, confusion, and temporary shock. Evidently, he was the operator of the vehicle he occupied. The temporal displacement had concussed the glass and burned out the ignition system. Terminator focused on the man. By observing isolated and subtle body movements, he could estimate the subject's behavior and immediately determined that the level of threat potential was extremely low. Just before the man lunged out of the cab, Terminator predicted that possibility by calculating the direction of muscle contractions in the upper torso.

While the rest of his brain and body came up to speed, Terminator observed the man run across the parking lot. He could have overtaken him easily should he have thought it necessary, but the subject was neither a target nor a hostile. The naked man took a tentative step and found he was in complete control of all motor functions.

He walked to the edge of the parking lot and looked out on the city below. A map from his memory overlaid itself on the scene below. Los Angeles. He became aware of streets and their names and began accumulating options. Terminator reviewed the events since his arrival in minute detail and caught an error. He was naked. He needed clothes. The black man had clothes. He should have taken the black man's clothes. Options crowded his thinking now, and he realized that this was a city filled with people. He would find one of suitable size and configuration, and then the error would be corrected. He turned back to the cityscape below, a powerfully built man with a near-perfect physique, naked in the forty-two-degree wind, and studied the relief map of Los Angeles, planning a hundred strategies, charting a thousand pathways, and accumulating valuable environmental data before setting off on his mission.

Mark was on his feet now, the chemicals in his blood fueling him like a hydraulic puppet to walk toward Kotex and Rick. He wanted to grab the world by its balls and yank with all his strength. Settling for Kotex, he grabbed the chain epaulets of his jacket and spun him in a frenzied arc, slamming him into the steel railing that ran along the parapet. His fists and feet swung with the backbeat as Kotex came off the rail and they slammed together in a fraternal frenzy.

They spun together in a sweaty embrace and crashed into the coin-operated telescope that had been absorbing Rick's attention. Rick laid his half-empty beer bottle across the back of Mark's head, and he went down in a spray of foam and glass shards. Then a judiciously applied combat boot sent Kotex reeling off balance onto the tape player, which crunched and stopped cold, echoes of Fear slapping back off the observatory building, diminishing to silence.

Rick glanced up from the eyepiece of the telescope that he had trained across the empty parking lot. His slack, astonished expression changed to a leer of malignant good humor.

"Hey," he said, calling jovially for their attention as if he hadn't just cracked a beer bottle over anyone's head. "Hey, what's wrong with this picture?"

He made a frame with his hands as movie directors wearing ascots and porkpie hats always did on TV, and Mark looked to see what he was framing.

And his face went slack, too.

Kotex looked for a long time as if his eyes weren't focusing; then he giggled.

It was one of those guys whose bodies you don't believe wearing lots of sunscreen and a little speedo bikini down at Muscle Beach in Venice. Except this guy didn't have the speedo, and it was forty-two degrees and raining and the middle of the night.

"He's walking right up to us, man," Kotex said, closing ranks with the other two.

Rick moved forward from the telescope, letting the soles of his GI boots drag with a laconic, dull sound, as he did when he was feeling gnarly.

"Let's fuck him up," he hissed over his shoulder.

Mark saw the grin and knew they were about to mainline trouble.

The naked man was striding straight toward them, his gaze unwavering. Mark felt a premonitory chill, and so, apparently, did Kotex. He said, "Hey, Rick, cool your jets, man. This dude's really fucking enormous."

Rick turned to him contemptuously. "These guys are fags, man. They pump for the mirror. They can't fight. Trust me. Watch this."

Kotex grinned. He was buying it, but Mark sensed something in the stranger's deliberate stride and expression that made him uncertain.

Rick's hand went into the pocket of his artfully ripped overcoat.

That was the signal, and Mark and Kotex gripped their knives surreptitiously. Mark's hand was sweaty, and his brain buzzed with fear and electric exhilaration. If he backed away, there would be no rejoining. He would be out.

He didn't want to be out.

He stepped forward.

The naked stranger's bare feet slapped on the wet asphalt.

Rivulets of rain had washed down the white ash in a pattern of streaks as complex as wood grain, giving him now the appearance of Renaissance statuary that had been exposed to the elements for centuries.

He stopped in front of the three punks, arms at his sides. Parade rest.

They sauntered apart, flanking him, casually threatening.

Rick's death's-head grin appeared.

"Nice night for a walk," Rick commented.

The stranger glanced calmly from one to the other, taking in, giving nothing out. He looked directly at Rick and said, "Nice night for a walk."

But Mark got confused, because it sounded a lot like Rick. Only Rick wasn't talking now; the stranger was.

The trouble with drugs was that you were never sure if something weird was really happening. So far, this shit was high on the weirdness scale.

Rick was shifting his weight jauntily.

"I got it," he said, a sudden light-bulb idea. "It's washday tomorrow, huh? Nothing clean tonight? Right?"

Mark had to laugh then despite the ice-cold snake that somebody had dropped down the back of his shirt. Rick was too much.

"Nothing clean tonight, right?" the big guy echoed.

Mark thought dully, "Is he fucking with us?"

What if he's a martial-arts guy and this is his idea of fun? Take off all your clothes and go kick some ass.

Mark gripped the pearly handle tight. I got your pearly gates, pal.

Kotex, with a droolly grin, reached out and snapped his fingers several times in front of the stranger's face.

The intense gaze remained unbroken. He didn't blink.

"Hey," Kotex ventured, getting into the spirit, "I think this guy's a couple cans short of a six-pack."

"Your clothes," the stranger said flatly, "give them to me."

This was so unexpected that even Rick was caught off guard. His grin faltered, then came back, spread all around his face.

"Now," the stranger commanded, his stare rigid.

Rick's grin dropped like a door slammed shut by a cold wind.

"Fuck you, asshole!"

*Shit, here we go,* thought Mark.

Rick's blade snapped out, glinting in the fluorescents, under the big guy's chin before Mark's hand could move.

Then he and Kotex had their switchblades out, snapped with drill-team precision and brandished.

Very clean. Very scary. Guaranteed.

Except the weight lifter wasn't registering quite the degree of slack-jawed fear they had hoped.

In fact, he merely glanced from one to the other without expression.

Mark felt something was really wrong.

Then a baseball bat smashed him in the face, and as the world spun around, he knew that it had been the stranger's fist, moving impossibly fast.

He hit the railing and slumped but looked up in time to see Kotex catapulted backward by a second pile-driver blow. Then he flopped to the ground, unmoving. Broken, Mark knew. Dead.

Rick feinted and lunged, piling his weight behind the point of the blade. It sank to the hilt in the man's belly, but it seemed to hit something hard, like a rib, maybe. Except how could there be a rib just below his navel?

Rick jerked back, hand and blade bloody, to try again when Terminator's fist blurred into him.

*Into him.* Mark saw the naked forearm sink up to the elbow just below Rick's sternum.

Rick's eyes bugged as the wind was driven out of him, more in amazement than pain.

Terminator lifted his arm like a hydraulic jack.

Rick's boots dangled off the ground, swaying like a hanged man's for one dilated instant. There was a muffled crunch of bones, and Terminator's arm jerked back.

Rick dropped, dead before his face smacked the concrete. *Reached in and ripped his spine out*, a voice screamed in Mark's brain.

Then the stranger turned to him, gaze riveting. Looking into those eyes was like looking up the muzzle of a gun.

Mark stumbled, backing up as the stranger advanced.

Mark couldn't tear his gaze from the man's arm, coated with blood to the elbow—Rick's blood. *Punched into him and—*

Mark was blindly moving backward, smack against a chain-link fence. He turned to go in another direction and saw he was in a corner on the far side of the observation platform. The man stepped up to him.

Mark had the sense to start ripping his clothes off. He held out the coat as an offering, as a shield, as a desperate plea that maybe he could get a little more time . . . time to get away . . . get down off this mountain . . . get into bed . . . pull the covers over his head and wake up. He was right. The offering did buy him time. About fourteen seconds.

### Downtown Los Angeles
### 4:12 A.M.

Twenty-four minutes later, in the linear progression of time as we know it and almost eight kilometers away, the air took on that *charged* quality again.

It happened in a fetid alley running along behind Broadway at Seventh, and the first of the alley's denizens to notice were the rats. They paused in their unceasing patrols of the trash heaps and dumpsters to sniff at the air uncertainly. They could sense something at the threshold of perception, a tension, an urgency in the air. Reluctantly, they abandoned their forages and darted for concealment just as a faint, unearthly illumination lit the alley like moonlight on the sea floor.

In a scramble to flee, one of the rodents skittered noisily across the wet cardboard under which Benjamin Schantz huddled in an alcoholic stupor. He swore and batted clumsily at it, then hugged himself and subsided back into his trackless mumbling.

Through a gap between buildings Schantz could catch a glimpse of the ethereal chrome cylinders of the Bonaventure Hotel. It seemed a vision from a utopian world and time inconceivably far removed from his own, although the distance was less than four blocks.

In rare moments of lucidity Ben reflected on the pinball workings of fate that bounced him through life on a bum's rush to this urban-decay purgatory while his best high school buddy had become the CEO of a major film studio.

However, this was not one of the lucid moments. In fact, the sourceless wind and the oppressive buzzing noise had been growing for some time before he noticed them at all. The purple glow intensified into a spotlight glare as the wind kicked bits of paper and pieces of things that used to be whole into the air. The buzzing became the static of a vast transistor radio searching frantically for a station. The storm of papers, boxes, and refuse swirled into a blizzard.

Schantz's cardboard shelter was snatched away. He cringed, squinting at the glare, covering his ears. Fingers of purple chain lightning began to dance around the wet brick walls, hissing, sputtering, seeking anything metallic, then crawling along it like a living thing.

It licked the rusting fire escapes, raced up and down the drainpipes, undulating like St. Elmo's Fire. The static rose in pitch to a piercing whine. Painted-over windows exploded inward, showering glass into darkened buildings. A burglar alarm added its strident clamor to the din.

Ben had seen some pretty weird sights, but he'd never seen anything like this before. There was an explosion of light and sound in midair—a strobe flash and a thunderclap followed by a back rush of imploding air.

When Kyle Reese came blasting through, he was high and off-center. His body stabilized in this temporal continuum a good two meters above the ground. He hung there for a microsecond; then gravity took over and slammed him into the alley floor with a loud, flat whack.

He lay there, naked and trembling, eyes shut tight against the searing light, fists clenched against his chest, knees drawn up like an overgrown fetus. Spasms wracked every muscle in his body. After the explosion the wall of sound had ceased, leaving only the rustle of papers settling back to earth.

The sickening odor of singed hair filled Reese's nostrils, choking him. Pain was shooting through every fiber of his body. They didn't tell him it was going to be like this, he thought. Maybe they didn't know. But oh, fuck . . . it hurt.

He took it slow, marshaling his resources, sipping at the ozone-filled air until he could draw real breaths. The feeling of having his nuts kicked up into his chest cavity was abating. A little. He opened his eyes and saw ghosts; afterimages of sights that had yanked at his sanity like saltwater taffy.

The sensations were fading. Memory could not hold that kind of intensity—the high chroma. What had it been like? Falling down an elevator shaft with a high-tension cable tied to your balls, lighting you up like a thousand-watt bulb, pumping napalm down your throat and lungs.

Reese let the sensation of the rain running down his back help him focus. He dragged his knees under him, steadying both hands on the ground, and stayed that way, like a bent-over supplicant, until the pavement ceased its dizzying movement. He felt sharp pebbles between his palms and the asphalt. Wherever he was, it was real. Solid. Not like that banshee maelstrom he'd just ridden.

Reese glanced up quickly and saw two eyes peering at him from a pile of cardboard debris. Schantz, his grime-blackened face and stringy beard molding him into the substance and texture of the alley, except for the eyes, which blinked uncomprehendingly.

Reese saw no immediate threat from the man, recognizing him instinctively for what he was—a harmless scav. For the moment, he could be ignored.

*Okay, move it, Reese,* he thought to himself. *Off your ass and on your feet, soldier. Let's go.* With a supreme act of will, he staggered up and reeled dizzily to a stairway railing, melting into the safety of shadows. Only minutes had passed since his arrival, he knew; still, he cursed himself for having lain there, exposed and helpless, for so long. He scanned his surroundings. Buildings. Brick or concrete. Glass windows. Unbroken. Electric streetlight. Movement at the end of the alley, passing red-and-white lights—automobiles. Definitely prewar. Good.

He rubbed his arm unconsciously—a bloody scrape where he came down. The techs had brought him in high. With so little time to familiarize themselves with the displacement-field equipment and its calibration, they must have erred on the side of safety. Better than materializing knee-deep in pavement. Right.

Looking down, Reese noticed he was covered in a fine white ash, although some of it had been washed away by the rain. He brushed at it, realizing that it was the carbonized residue of the conductive jelly the techs had smeared on him.

He had questioned nothing. They said strip; he stripped. You're going alone, they said. Fine. No weapons? No. *Shit*. Metals won't displace. *Fuck it*. Okay, he wasn't a tech. Just a soldier. He wished he could have brought something, though. His fingers unconsciously clenched the remembered shape of the stock of his Westinghouse M-25 plasma rifle.

He glanced upward. Nothing but sky above the tall buildings. No hunter-killers, of course. Not in prewar. But to look was a reflex, a reflex that had saved him more than once. Didn't they have something like Mark Seven aerials, though? Helicopters? Yeah, I think. But he wasn't sure. History was a blur to him. What was invented when? Who could keep it straight? Prewar was a jigsaw puzzle spilled on the floor, and he'd lived his whole life among the pieces. The charred pieces.

He realized with a start how stunned he must be to have stood daydreaming in one spot for so many seconds. He forced himself to think clearly. Strategically.

First, clothing. For warmth and camouflage.

Second, weapons. Third . . .

"Say, buddy . . ." The words were a slurred croak, but Reese turned, remembering the old scav.

"Hell of a shit storm here a minute ago," Schantz ventured. Reese identified the words as English, probably American, though the inflections were unfamiliar. Good news.

He sprinted to where the derelict lay, sprawled in a doorway.

"Get your clothes off," Reese said, already tugging at the old man's jacket.

"Whaa. . . ?"

"Just do it," Reese hissed, "now." He drew back a fist to expedite cooperation, but the old man caught the intensity in Reese's voice and began to comply.

"Don't hit—don't hit me," Schantz mewled, slumping back into a stupor as his grimy fingers fumbled futilely with the unassailable complexity of his zipper.

Reese pulled the filthy trousers rapidly off Schantz's spindly legs. They smelled—urine and caked-on grime. Reese barely noticed and didn't care.

To Schantz, Reese was a figure going in and out of focus. He seemed to be a young man, maybe twenty, twenty-five, but there was something about him that was older. The eyes—yeah. Old man's eyes. Seen too much, said a particularly cogent Schantz mind bubble, like me.

But not exactly like Schantz. Something in Reese's gaze sent a chill into the old man's belly. He kept quiet and hoped he would live.

Reese had the trousers on and was reaching for the jacket when he felt, at the edge of his consciousness, trouble. His senses had been fine tuned by years of hunkering down, listening, waiting, and watching, sipping at all the little sights and sounds that tell you death is in the neighborhood, hoping to drop by and smother you with a cold, wet good-bye kiss. Reese pivoted and crouched, eyes instinctively focused on the street at the alley's end.

A brilliant white light stabbed toward him, sweeping across the walls, then caught him in its beam like an insect. For a microsecond Reese stared intently into it, through it, past it, to its source: a black-and-white LAPD cruiser, searchlight mounted on the window frame, two men sitting inside. Reese knew instantly what they were. Police. Hostiles. If he'd had more time, he would have cursed himself again for his slowness; where he came from he'd be dead already.

Reese was on automatic now, decisions coming in instant flashes. He needed what they had, transportation, weapons, radio, but they would be armed, and he was not. There was no question of a fight.

*Evacuate.* He twisted away from the beam and dissolved into the shadows.

*Evac. Evac.* The words echoed urgently inside Reese's head. How many times had he heard them before? A thousand, maybe? In how many voices? And as you shouldered the wounded and turned to run, the words were always followed by other sounds behind you, closing-in-for-the-kill sounds. This time he heard the chirp of tires as the black-and-white cruiser came to a halt. Reese was halfway to the other end of the alley before the sound faded and died.

Sgt. Michael Nydefer futilely swept the searchlight around the alley, trying to spot the young man he had pinned only a second before. *God, that kid's fast,* he thought.

"He's rabbiting," Nydefer said. "Take the car around. The alley comes out on Seventh." His rookie partner, Lewis, nodded and threw the black-and-white cruiser into reverse. As Nydefer jumped out, drawing his .38, the cruiser was already tearing away, siren blasting, throwing out a red-and-blue light show.

Nydefer caught sight of Reese flashing through a patch of light, heading toward a junction where the alley intersected with another. He took a deep breath and ran after him.

Reese had heard the cruiser race away and the single pair of footsteps behind him, and he knew what they had done. He had gotten lucky. Only one of them was behind him. One was better. He could take out the one and have a weapon. He concentrated on that single goal, ignoring everything else. Broken glass was scattered all along the alley floor. He felt pain as some of it cut his bare feet. Reese pushed the pain back, away from his consciousness. The effort helped him clear his head.

A pile of tumbled garbage cans loomed up, blocking his path. Reese cleared them and ran on without slowing, a hot-wired rat in an urban maze.

Reese whipped around a corner and disappeared.

Nydefer instinctively slowed his pace. Fifteen years of bad coffee, Taco Bell, and cigarettes made his lungs wheeze. But that wasn't why he had slowed now. Fear made that decision.

Nydefer muttered a curse. He had let him get out of sight. Now it would be more dangerous. Son of a bitch. Inside his stomach, condors were flying around. *They don't pay you enough for this. No way.* He cocked the hammer of his revolver, stepped to the center of the alley, and slowly walked to the intersection.

Nydefer peered down the side alley, one hand holding the gun before him like a shield, the other hand unconsciously covering his belly. He saw no one. Carefully, he made his way down the near-black corridor, pausing as he came abreast of two large Dempsey dumpsters. They were spilling over with flattened cardboard and wooden boxes. No room in there. But there was space between them. Enough space for a man.

Nydefer put both hands back on his weapon and raised it to chest level. He peered into the gap intently. Nothing. Just some wooden slats thrown haphazardly away.

But Reese was there, waiting. Nydefer was staring right at him but saw nothing. Just the wall and the boards. Reese was staring at Nydefer's revolver the way a starving man stares at food. It was an old design but in mint condition, probably new, and Reese recognized it immediately: Smith & Wesson police special, caliber .38 super. He had actually fired one several times. The kick was light, and it was accurate. It wasn't a serious gun like a .44 mag. But he'd had to use worse weapons before.

Then Reese turned his attention to the man in front of him. He was middle-aged, paunchy, short of breath, and he was scared. Reese couldn't have asked for more.

He came flying out of the darkness like a high-speed whisper, with the full weight of every solid ounce of matter in his being focused into a point at the tip of his shoulder. He aimed that point at the center of Nydefer's back and slammed into him like a freight train. Reese's right hand grabbed onto the wrist holding the revolver, and as Nydefer started to go down, there was a deafening concussion and glare from the muzzle flash. Twisting fiercely, Reese pulled the weapon free. With his other hand, he controlled his roll and came up on both feet.

Pulling the stunned officer up and slamming him against the alley wall, Reese stepped back, raised the weapon, cocked the hammer, and aimed it directly into the officer's face.

Nydefer stared past the barrel of his service revolver into the eyes of the oldest kid he'd ever seen. The eyes were flat, too. Not really angry. Just intense. Spooky.

Reese had a thousand questions that needed answering: his exact location, the location of the target, the number and condition of vehicles in the area. Endless. He saw "Los Angeles Police Department" written on Nydefer's badge, and he knew he was in the right city. But there was one question whose answer could render all the others as irrelevant, and Reese knew he had very little time before that other police officer would come screeching around the end of the alley.

"What time is it?" Reese barked.

"About four-thirty, uh . . . A.M."

"What day?"

"Friday," Nydefer answered, hoping it would somehow calm the lunatic down. It didn't.

Impatiently, Reese snapped at him. "The date!"

Nydefer was a little unsure. He stammered, "Uh, the ninth . . . March ninth," Reese glared at him viciously and asked the million-dollar question.

"What year?"

Nydefer felt blind terror crawling up from the center of his belly and clawing away at the edges of his brain. *He wants to know what year it is? This is all I'll ever see,* he thought. *This insane kid's face. Goddamit!* Nydefer closed his eyes and waited for the bullet.

The howl of brakes on wet pavement echoed across the walls of the buildings. Reese turned and saw the flashing blue-and-red lights of the cruiser as it came to a halt at the mouth of the alley. Lewis jumped out, his weapon drawn. Reese spun around and began to race toward the street exit at the opposite end when he saw another flashing cruiser roll up in front of him.

He was flanked. Cut off. Sealed.

Reese scanned the terrain with lightning-fast precision. The padlocked steel door was just a few meters away. He lunged for it, focusing himself like a battering ram, intent on the point just beyond the lock. The force of impact almost knocked the air out of him, but the door gave way and beckoned into the darkness beyond.

His eyes strained to adjust to the new darkness. Beneath his bare feet, he felt the smooth, cold surface of a tiled floor. He bolted forward, twisting, turning, crashing through the mazelike hallway, bouncing off stacks of high boxes until, ahead, there was the horizontal crack of a dim light that meant a doorway. He hit it at top speed, punching it open.

He was in a vast shadow-and-light–streaked room, running through a gridwork of open channels between islands of tables and shelves. He was trying to get a fix on the terrain, willing his irises to open up and work.

The air smelled familiar. Antiseptic. Filtered. Like the air he had breathed in subsurface bunkers a second before his sapper team put the torch to them. He didn't like that smell at all. His ears picked up the distant, amorphous hum of air-conditioning ducts cycling atmosphere throughout the building and then, behind him, near the door he had come through, the unmistakable sharp echo of pounding feet that told him he was no longer alone in the dark interior.

Reese kept going, faster, nearly flying through the black space surrounding him, navigating on instinct, the sound of his own movements bouncing back to him.

Then his vision came on line. Stretching before Reese were rows and rows of fantastic treasure. Clothes, furniture, tools. Even half seen in the darkness, it was incredible. A gluttonous horde of sparkling multicolored merchandise.

He was in a department store.

Reese flashed off the aisle into the shadow of a rack of long coats, held his breath, and put out the radar. Above the thunderous roar of blood crashing through his ears, he locked onto the sound of the threat force. Three of them. Separated. Moving toward him in a loose sweep.

By quadrants, Reese scanned the room, hunting for an evac route. The northwest wall was plate glass. Intact. Facing the street. Beyond it, a black-and-white police cruiser slowly prowled past, then was gone.

*Camouflage.* Silently, Reese reached up into the rack above him and pulled one of the raincoats free, slipping it on, realizing only then that he had been cold. The footsteps were slowly converging toward him. The flicking finger of a probing flashlight hit the tiled floor on the next aisle. *Move, move, move.*

As silent as a wisp of smoke, Reese left the shadow of the rack and ran low, like a crab, along the edge of the aisle toward the plate-glass window. A display of well-dressed mannequins filled it, staring emptily into the street. Reese moved among them, scooping out the window, hunting for an exit. He looked up. A paper banner hung above the display. "THE LOOK FOR '84." Perfect. He was right on target.

Suddenly, the searing arc of a police cruiser's searchlight swept through the glass. Reese froze. *No good,* Reese thought, and backed away toward the center of the building. He could hear muffled voices and the careful padding of feet all around him now. He was halfway past a table of leather-and-canvas shoes before he slid to a halt. *Scan. Movement? Nothing. Empty. Where are you fuckers?* he wondered. Silence. *Good,* Reese thought, and grabbed a pair of shoes from the table, slapping them against the sole of his foot. *Too small.* Another pair. *Very close. Good enough.*

Reese hurtled down the aisle. Ahead, more flashlights darted in approach. He recon'd the immediate area. Where to go? A metal booth, its curtain drawn open, squatted in the darkness a few meters away. The words "Passport Photo" were painted on the side. Reese ducked inside, pulled the curtain shut, perched himself on a little stool, and quickly slipped into the shoes.

Every foot soldier since the dawn of history has known that a good pair of boots is as critical to survival as the best of weapons. Reese laced the shoes and tested their feel. They seemed light and insubstantial, with a thin sole, which would be bad for broken terrain, but they were well made and fit passably. The word "Nike" was stitched on the side. A type of obsolete ballistic missile, he knew.

Beneath the curtain, a finger of light dashed in, probed around, then retreated. There was a pause. More muttering. Reese tensed. Then, slowly, the voices faded. Reese released his breath and quietly slipped out of the booth.

An escalator sat impassively in the darkness. It had been shut off hours earlier, reducing it to a mere flight of metal stairs. Reese took the steps two at a time, flying up them to the second floor. Housewares. And ladies' lingerie.

On the southwest wall, Reese found what he was hunting for. A fire-escape exit. The smooth metal door was closed. A wire ran down the length of its edge, forming a crude alarm circuit, and a sign, painted on a bar spanning the door's width, warned that it was to be used only in case of an emergency. *No shit?* Reese punched the bar, and the door flew open. There was no sound. The alarm must be silent or burned out by time-displacement overload.

He perched quietly on the open grille of the fire

escape and scanned the alley beneath him. A black-and-white LAPD cruiser was parked directly below, lights flashing, empty.

Reese dropped to the asphalt like a cat and crouched beside the vehicle's door. *Empty street. Activity around the corner.* He tried the door. Unlocked. Amazing. They must have been in a hell of a hurry, Reese thought. He opened it up and reached to the ignition. No keys. He needed transportation. He thought of hot wiring the car. Fuck it. Too conspicuous. He dismissed the vehicle itself and focused on what lay inside.

Sitting in its mount, leaning against the dash, was a factory-fresh Remington 870 pump shotgun. Reese was in awe. He had seen and carried several of these weapons, but they were battered museum pieces. This one, like most of the wonders around him, looked new.

He lifted it free and into the safety of his raincoat. Holding it there, under his arm, it could not be seen. It would not get wet. It would be his friend.

Then Reese spun around and stepped quickly away from the car. After rounding the street corner, he strolled unhurriedly down the sidewalk. Three and a half minutes ago he had been as naked as a newborn infant. Now he was armed, clothed, and blending into the population. He would need money and supplies and transportation. But there was plenty of time for that.

Goddamit, he was here. He made it. A surge of adrenaline passed through him. Reese was almost giddy with the intense pleasure of being alive, pulling it off. He looked up, blinking against the rain falling into his eyes, and scanned the miraculous landscape that surrounded him. He was standing on the corner of Sixth and Olive. Across the street was Pershing Square. He realized he'd been born less than a mile away. He had even played here when he was a kid. But it never looked like this. Buildings, five and six stories high, surrounded the small park. And the light. Everywhere light poured down on him. Reese hovered in the shadow of a doorway, awestruck by the amazing scene before him.

How long ago was it? Reese wondered, just minutes from his point of view, when he was running down that steel corridor with the rest of his sapper squad.

Deafening explosions echoed behind them, tearing the corridor, and its equipment, apart. His people were zapping the place. Torching it. Killing it. The sense of victory was humming like electric current through the team members.

And then this.

It didn't seem to bother John. Nothing did. That was part of what made him what he was. He ran alongside Reese, his hand reassuringly gripping the young man's shoulder, shouting terse instructions into his ear. It was John's decision that Reese should be the one.

Then he was standing with a group of techs who were making last-minute calibrations on a vast array of equipment. Reese rapidly stripped off his uniform and handed his pulse rifle to one of his teammates. The techs poured over him like ants, taking bioreadings, pumping chemicals into his system. John stepped back, quietly fixing his eyes on Reese.

Things were happening really fast now. The techs sprayed him down from head to toe with a thick, bluish superconducting jelly. Its foul smell choked Reese. Then the techs lead him into a small chamber and backed away. Reese and John locked eyes. There was something unusual in John's face. An expression that Reese had only seen once, a few years before, when John pulled him from the 132nd and placed him in his personal Recon/Security team.

Reese gazed back into the staring faces of the people before him. His people. Then there was a horrible, unending flash of light and pain. And then the alley floor.

Now Reese, in the rain, gazing at Pershing Square, never felt so lonely in his life. Or so exhilarated. This place. It was the same place but so vastly different. He knew it would look like this. But he didn't know it would *be* like this.

*Don't think*, his mind commanded. *Do not feel this*

*place*. Reese shut it all out—put it in a tiny room and bolted the door.

The mission was everything. The mission was all that mattered.

Reese walked directly to a telephone booth a block and a half away and lifted the heavy directory to the narrow metal shelf. He opened it to the Cs and began scanning the pages. Seconds later, his finger stopped beside a name: Sarah J. Connor.

**Palms District
656 Jasmine Street
8:28 A.M.**

Sarah Jeanette Conner walked from her second-story apartment down to the entrance. She had forgotten to check the mail yesterday afternoon, and her roommate couldn't be relied on in that department. Anything else, maybe, but mail was not high on Ginger's list of priorities. With Sarah, it was like a duty. It was a rare occurrence when she'd get a letter. She never wrote anybody, so that was no surprise. But there were bills. Bills that she would pay religiously, always depleting her meager bank account at the beginning of the month and scrimping by on tips the remaining weeks, satisfied and secure that all her debts were promptly paid.

Her roommate was the other way around. But fortunately Sarah and Ginger had managed to find more things in common than not in the last eight months as roommates, like their exuberance and affection for a simple, uncomplicated, good time, although Sarah had to admit sometimes she was a little more conservative than Ginger—well, maybe a lot. Although Ginger was twenty-four and Sarah was only nineteen, sometimes it was hard to tell who was younger.

Sarah paused by the security gate. Someone had propped it open with a rock. A small and feeble anger stirred within. Somebody didn't want to hassle using their key.

When she reached the entrance alcove and the mailboxes, she was assaulted by bright sunlight and the smell of wet grass cooking in the morning heat. The storm had passed. It was going to be a great day for riding her Honda. The sky reminded her of a turquoise ring her first boyfriend in junior high had given her. What was his name? Charlie . . . Whatever. She still had the ring somewhere in her jewel box, along with the other mementos of the few relationships she cared to remember.

Palms was a quiet community of apartments and condos, with a healthy mixture of old and young, black and white, Jewish and Protestant. It was surrounded on all sides by Los Angeles proper, Beverly Hills, Santa Monica, and Culver City and was the unofficial hub of the eclectic patchwork of unlikely demography that made pollsters' heads hurt. Because there were so many multiple-unit complexes, the curbs were always bumper to bumper with parked cars. One of the reasons Sarah picked this complex was the underground garage. And the fact that it had a security gate.

As she unlocked her box, she examined the thick wad of envelopes that spilled into her hands—two bills, a letter from her mother, the rest for Ginger.

No love letters from passionate and wealthy men overwhelmed with grief that she had turned them down. No matter. Who cares? It would do, because tonight Sarah had a date. This was a day she had been looking forward to all week. A day she would remember for the rest of her life. *Well*—Sarah chuckled to herself—*let's not get carried away*. He wasn't prince charming, or even an especially wonderful man, but he did have tickets to the Julian Lennon concert at the Bowl.

Sarah folded herself into a diaphanous daydream, filled with ardor that began politely with romantic possibility, then rose to a crescendo of ecstatic—

Ginger Ventura jogged up the sidewalk and crashed

into Sarah's fantasy, smiling as if reality were actually more fun.

The tall brunette was out of breath but not energy. She ran in place as they talked, her shoulder-length ebony curls bouncing like electrified licorice as she hopped from one leg to the other. The headphones blasting Bruce Springsteen into Ginger's ear at a volume Sarah could easily hear were held on by a sweat-soaked headband. Sarah smiled broadly at her roommate. If Ginger could act and they were auditioning for Wonder Woman, Sarah had no doubt she'd be living with a star. Ginger was five feet seven inches of Amazon, without an ounce of fat or flab. Ginger could never be static, but even standing still, she would turn heads. She was a live wire snaking and coiling around an inexhaustible power pack of optimistic enthusiasm.

"Anything for me?" Ginger puffed.

Sarah handed Ginger the bulk of the envelopes. Her eyes went wide when she read one.

"Oh, my god, today is the day!"

Ginger grabbed Sarah's arm and led her back up to their apartment, absently kicking the rock out from under the gate.

"What is it?" Sarah asked.

"My test results. Gulp!"

"Test results? For what?"

"Pregnancy, silly. Didn't I tell you?"

Sarah stopped Ginger outside their door.

"Ginger! Of course you didn't."

"Must have slipped my mind," Ginger said flippantly as she entered the living room. Sarah was stunned, groping blindly to shut the door behind her as she followed Ginger into their apartment.

Sarah stammered, "But you use birth control, Ginger. How could you get pregnant?"

Ginger started to open the letter from the clinic, then hesitated. "You know organic me. I hate the pill. And foam does have a twenty percent failure rate. So I missed a period last month. So . . ."

Sarah stared at the letter. "Well, uh, what's the verdict?"

## 32 · THE TERMINATOR

Ginger covered her worry with a sly grin. "Bet you five bucks it's negative."

"Ginger, open it!"

Ginger looked down at the paper. "Right," she said, sounding brave and macho and unwavering and scared shitless. She opened the letter. Sarah watched her friend's eyes as they rapidly scanned the contents. Then they looked up at her with a kind of dull acceptance. "What name do you like? Maybe just Junior, huh?"

Sarah's heart sank. "Oh, no, Ginger. My god . . . what are you . . . I mean . . . are you going to . . . Ginger."

Ginger grimaced, then crumpled the letter and tossed it on the coffee table. "You want to know what I'm gonna do? Have a drink." And Ginger stood up like a criminal about to walk the last mile and trudged into the kitchen.

Sarah watched her go in shock. What a mess. Ginger never got into messes like this. Ginger had all the handles on the world figured out. Ginger led a charmed life. Ginger was—

Sarah narrowed her eyes with a sudden growing suspicion and walked over to the coffee table. She unwrapped the letter and read the results.

. . . a real funny girl.

Sarah shook her head, simultaneously burning with both embarrassment and anger. She stalked into the kitchen, fuming.

"Okay, Ginger, very funny . . ."

Ginger leaped out from behind the refrigerator and sprayed Sara with a bottle of shaken Perrier. Sarah shrieked and batted the air before her blindly.

"You bitch!" Sarah cried, but she was laughing now despite herself.

"Why do I let you do this to me?"

Ginger winked at Sarah. "Real question?"

Sarah nodded.

"Real answer. You love it, kiddo."

"Fuck you," Sarah said, smiling.

Sarah shifted gears, going into a half-serious pout.

"You knew it was a Pap-smear result all along, didn't you, you rat?"

"I sure as hell didn't think I was pregnant. I haven't missed a period since I was thirteen."

"Okay. Then why do you do it to me?"

"You're an easy target."

"I might surprise you one of these days."

"That would be nice."

Ginger's teasing was beginning to take on that "I'm kidding on the square" tone. Sarah shook her head in exasperation. Ginger thought her karmic duty in life was to guide Sarah through the rough waters of each day. What Ginger and Sarah's mother and just about everyone else didn't realize was that little Sarah was doing just fine. She was working, going to school, and even managing to put a few bucks into a savings account.

Sure, she had some problems, but nothing overwhelming or out of her control. Nothing anyone else wasn't suffering from. Except Ginger. Ginger seemed to carom off bad times as if gaining momentum to pile drive even more quickly into the good. And Sarah had a rare thought. Had Ginger even been thrown for a loop?

"Hey, Ginge?" Sarah began, uncertain of what she was going to blurt out but caught up in the impulse just the same. "What would you do if you *had* been pregnant?"

Ginger snorted. "Have a good yuk over the expression on Matt's face when I told him about it."

The few times Sarah ever seriously considered being a mother, she had shuddered. It brought back the memory of all the years, after her father had died, her mother had had to improvise a rule book for her: guide but not dominate, love but not suffocate. It must have been like crossing the Himalayas on a drunken goat. Besides, Sarah wasn't especially a fan of herself. She was all right as most people go but certainly no unique mold from which great men and women would be made.

But to Ginger she merely said, "Yeah, well, I'll settle for visiting yours."

Ginger patted her knee. "Don't kid yourself. You've got those maternal instincts, too."

"I can keep them suppressed, believe me."

*Yeah*, Sarah was thinking, *I can love. If anybody gave me half a chance. If I knew they would love me back.*

But finding a man you could trust to do that was like finding a vanilla malt in the middle of the Mojave Desert. And now the comforting circle of friends she had grown up with had all gone off to other schools or marriage. She had to fend for herself. Blind dates. Chance meetings at college. Somehow the ones she wanted were already taken or simply not interested.

With a small grin, Ginger was watching her roommate go into the static pool of herself. Sarah was as sweet a girl as they come. Maybe a little too sweet. Sometimes she wore her innocence like a shield against the real world. So Ginger liked to give Sarah a little goose now and then. Wake her up from the dream most people tended to wallow in. The dream of what should be as opposed to what was. So instead of hugging Sarah, as she wanted to, as she knew Sarah wanted her to, she used her usual shock therapy, as she had done with the clinic letter.

Ginger was hesitatingly checking the bottom of her running shoes.

"I think I stepped on Pugsly."

Sarah quickly shot a glance to the far end of the room. Pugsly was sitting like a stuffed leather dinosaur in his plastic terrarium, his unblinking eyes gaping at her with the cool aplomb of a reptile in low gear. He was a three-foot-long green iguana Sarah had inherited from her last boyfriend. She and Pugsly had formed a lasting relationship, one of mutual respect and love that far surpassed the one she had had with Pugsly's previous owner.

Sarah put her hands on her hips and scowled down at Ginger, who was now winking up at her with a blatant smirk. "Got your juices going, eh?"

"That's it! You die, Ventura." And she leaped on top of her and ruthlessly went for Ginger's most vulnerable spot: the belly button.

The intercom buzzer startled them both with its high-pitched sneer.

Ginger vaulted up and slapped the button.

"Good news or money?" she said enthusiastically.

The answer came through the tiny speaker like a mouse going through the eye of a needle—somewhat diminished.

"How about sex?"

Ginger grinned down at Sarah and winked. Then she spoke into the intercom again. "Sure, pal. Come on up. Leave your clothes outside the door." She buzzed the gate open.

Matt Buchanan didn't take his clothes off outside the door. He wasn't wearing much, anyway. Just a tank top and cutoffs that left his weight lifter's body well displayed. He wasn't arrogant about his powerful physique, or anything else, for that matter. Sarah could never get over the fact that the guy looked as if he could bench press a Winnebago and somehow had the sweetest, most un-jock-like personality of any man she knew.

Sarah was gathering her school books from her bedroom when she heard them crashing against the couch. She grabbed her purse and walked into the pandemonium.

"Three falls out of five, pal!" Ginger was yelping as she wriggled out from underneath Matt, pulling his index finger back and spinning him onto his butt. "Sarah, help me with this animal!"

"Sorry, I've had enough for one morning," Sarah said, and sat on the couch while she brushed her light brown shoulder-length hair into a ponytail and tied it off with an elastic band.

Ginger and Matt were embracing now, smiling at one another in that momentary and very private way that two people in love always do. There was so much puppy-dog adoration in Matt's eyes that Sarah felt envy rush through her. She hadn't had too many boyfriends. Some of them really liked her. But she had never managed to inspire the kind of passion that was going on in Matt's eyes. Sarah knew one day she would. Maybe even tonight.

As they walked to the parking garage underneath the apartments, Matt slipped his arms around Ginger's and Sarah's waists and hugged them both.

Sarah kneeled by her Honda Elite scooter. After securing the chain, she turned to her roommate. "Pick you up after work?"

Ginger nodded. "Hey, why don't we all go over to Stoker's and have a pizza afterward?"

Sarah was only partly successful in suppressing the nervous anticipation in her voice. "Sorry. Got a date tonight."

Matt mock punched her arm. "All right, Sarah!"

"No big deal, Matt. Just a guy I met at work."

"You mean that guy with the black Porsche?" Ginger wanted to know.

Sarah nodded but then grimaced. "Aw, I don't know. He's probably a member of the "Schmuck-of-the-Month Club."

Matt put his arm around Sarah's neck and led her off a few paces. "You need anything, Sarah?"

Sarah was genuinely confused. "Like what?"

"You know. A little money for emergencies. In case this guy gets the touchy-feelies before he springs for dinner. I mean, what do we know about this man? He could strand you in some god-awful place like . . . Anaheim. Huh?"

Sarah gave him a wry smile and lifted his arm off her shoulders. "No thanks, Dad. I've gone on a date before."

Sarah described her faint and deeply buried voices of reason the "little Sarahs" as a joke, because that's what they sounded like—little versions of herself sitting inside, watching and tsk-tsking her whenever she started boiling over with an emotion she suspected might be inappropriate. Sometimes she relied on the little Sarahs. Sometimes she felt like choking them. Now they reminded her that Matt and Ginger cared about her, and she relaxed into a smile. "I can take care of myself."

Matt lunged at her and gently bit the end of her nose. "Yeah, but what would you do if he tried that?"

Sarah unhesitatingly rabbit punched Matt's rigid stomach. It couldn't have hurt him, but he staggered back, gasping for breath, and clutched at Ginger.

As he writhed theatrically, Ginger ignored him and kissed Sarah on the cheek. "See you tonight."

Sarah hopped on the scooter and pressed the ignition button. The 125-cc engine whined a protest. Sarah looked back to wave good-bye and saw Matt leap to his feet like a ballet dancer.

"'Bye, Sarah," he said, grinning.

What a clown. She loved him. And Ginger. She gestured a good-bye and gunned the Honda up the concrete ramp into the warming sunshine.

Her mind did not detect anything out of place, any clue whatsoever that this was to be the last normal day of her life.


## Miracle Mile District
8:31 A.M.

There had been times during the predawn hours, as Reese was scurrying through the labyrinth of back alleys and forgotten byways of downtown Los Angeles, when he wasn't sure he was actually in prewar at all. Some of these little pissed-on and left-for-dead corridors were still standing even in his time. He would rush to an intersection, slide the shotgun up, slip a scan around the corner, just to make sure, and there it would be, a dazzling, carnival prewar boulevard, as unbelievable and exotic as a dream.

It had been like that all morning.

He couldn't completely shake the spooky sensation of being in two places at once. He knew he could anchor himself if he just stayed on the street, but that would have been a tactical error. The street was empty; it was hard to blend into the crowd when it was in bed. Suddenly it occurred to Reese that maybe his brain had been scrambled by coming through. Or the amphetamines that the techs had pumped into him were putting out a disastrous side effect. If anything fouled the mission objective, it would be checkout time for everyone. He did not even want to imagine fucking up. A little spasm of panic tested the waters inside his head. Out of habit and the instinct to survive, he strangled the life out of it.

There was still a lot of time, plenty of time. John had briefed him that target acquisition would take place at 20:19 hours at 656 Jasmine in Palms. Sarah J. Connor would be there, leaving the location. How John knew, Reese couldn't even begin to guess. But if John said it, it was true. You could bet your ass on it.

He decided to keep moving on foot, getting a feel for the place, checking out primary and alternate routes. He went over his mental shopping list. If he was going to pull this one off, he would need more ammunition, for one thing. A lot more. The fear of death that he had often felt going into combat was completely overshadowed this time by the fear of failing. His death would be insignificant. Sarah J. Connor was another matter. Her death would be important.

Reese was moving along the wall of a particularly nasty stretch of alley behind Gajewski's Foreign Auto Repair on Wilshire—"Guaranteed to put the bite back in your bug!"— when the roar of an engine behind him erupted from his rear. *Cover! Cover! Cover!* Reese's body was moving before his brain kicked in. He leaped to the far side of a pile of trash cans stacked against the decomposing brick, and rolling, burrowed his way behind them. A delivery truck had tumbled into the alley's entrance a little too fast, tires screeching on the wet pavement as the half-asleep driver jumped on the brake to avoid the wall. Reese chambered a round into the shotgun, his nerves jangling like high-wire tension cables, and brought it up as the delivery truck heaved and groaned past. Slowly, he released the pressure building up on the trigger and lowered the shotgun. The sleepy driver never saw Reese and would never know that he had been only a hairbreadth away from having his wife raise their children alone.

Reese's heart was pumping loudly. He glanced up at the tiny slit of sky beyond the rim of buildings surrounding him. It was light.

*No good staying in the alleys anymore,* Reese thought. *Got to blend with the population.* He had been carrying the long shotgun under his raincoat, held between his arm and side, but that wouldn't pass with the natives in full daylight. Time to adapt the weapon to street-fighting mode. He rummaged through the trash bin beside him—dead auto parts, bits of tubing, and greasy splinters of metal. Then he found what he was looking for, a rusty but usable hacksaw blade. Reese couldn't understand why so much perfectly good material was thrown away here. He could have built a combat carrier out of what he found in one trash bin.

Reese put the blade to the shotgun's stock, just behind the trigger housing, leaving enough wood to act as a makeshift pistol grip. He dug deeper into the bin but ran out of luck; nothing to make a sling with.

It was on the fourth try, in one of the bins farther down the wall, that he found a fraying piece of rope. Tying one end to the weapon's shortened stock, Reese made himself a sliding shoulder rig. When the time came, he could bring the weapon up smooth and fast. And the concealment was excellent. He'd have to be searched before anyone would notice he was armed. But by then they'd already know.

Reese buttoned his raincoat all the way to the top even though the sky had come up cloudless and bright, unseasonably warm for March.

He had never been so lonely in his life—the point man in an army that wasn't born yet. Rolling cautiously up to the mouth of the alley, he slipped a quick feral glance at Wilshire Boulevard, and as casually as possible, stepped onto it. His nerves vibrated on maximum alert as he began to recon the acid-trip terrain around him.

People were already coming out into the street. A few were denizens of the alley world. But most of them were working-class, waiting on the corner for a bus or stepping off one with a purposeful rush in their walk and a cup of coffee that was going cold fast.

Reese couldn't begin to comprehend the rhythm of prewar urban life; he was tuned to an entirely different scale of intensity. Casually strolling around in the daylight simply wasn't the way to keep on living in his world. *They* controlled the day. You had the night to play with. Though Reese's rational mind told him it was safe, his instincts were screaming at him. He had to force himself to step away from the safety of the building's shadow into the multi-colored swirl of activity going past.

With his raincoat on, hiding the puckered laser-pulse scars that dotted his compact frame, Reese didn't look a lot different than anyone else on Wilshire, but he was out of sync. Too feral and serious even for the mean part of the city, like an untamed panther dropped into the center of a bright, gaudy, decadent zoo.

He moved cautiously down the sidewalk, scrutinizing the faces that bobbed and weaved toward him. There was a quality there that he had never seen before. A kind of virginity, or innocence, a lack of information that made even the older ones seem young. A boy in a pair of faded denims, perched atop a two-foot board with wheels, weaved gracefully between the obstacle course of pedestrians. His body was moving and shaking to the beat of Springsteen's "Born in the USA", the music blasting into the street from a huge stereo the kid held on his shoulder.

The sidewalks were a Babylon of display windows, each hording an incredible amount of treasure. Radios, lamps, stereos, TV sets—rows of them, stacks of them, three and four high. One window held nothing but TV sets, all of them tuned to the same station. Bryant Gumbel and Jane Pauley chatted to each other simultaneously on forty screens. Reese was transfixed by the shear vulgarity of the display.

Everywhere he looked, his eyes were threatened with visual overload. A grotesque jack-in-the-box clown leered across the street at the pink-and-yellow Pussycat Theatre marquee. Billboards with the gargantuan faces of beautiful men and women smiled down on him, extolling the wonders of Caesar's Palace and the Golden Nugget. A rugged-looking fifty-foot man in a sheepskin coat invited Reese to come to Marlboro country, where all the flavor is.

Reese had never heard of the place. But the sign got him thinking about food. He realized he was hungry.

Down the street was a grimy little hole-in-the-wall take-out stand. A faded sign proudly boasted that you could get pizza by the slice there twenty-four hours a day. Reese didn't know what pizza was, but he could tell by the smell that it was all right to eat. He hovered near the place, scoping it out, trying to figure out how the system worked without giving himself away. Reese watched as an overweight man in a loud plaid shirt stepped up to the window. "Gimme a slice with everything. Hold the anchovies," he said. The man behind the window handed a steaming triangle to the plaid-shirt man. The plaid-shirt man then passed some green bills to the man behind the window and walked away. Reese watched the transaction intently.

He knew about money but had none. Quickly, he searched the pockets of Schantz's trousers. Nothing. The smell of the pizza was doing things to his stomach; it rumbled demandingly. *Fuck it,* Reese thought, and stepped to the window. Slowly, the man behind it glanced up from his newspaper with a look of annoyance.

"Yeah?" the counterman asked indifferently. Reese repeated the litany.

"Gimme a slice with everything. Hold the anchovies," he said.

The man laid a slice of the hot steaming stuff on the counter, just inches away from Reese's nose, then turned to his register. "That'll be a buck sixty," he said over his shoulder. When he turned back, Reese was gone. Enraged, the counterman jumped halfway out the window, eyes searching up and down the street. But Reese wasn't there. "You son of a bitch!" he shouted to no one and everyone.

Reese tore down the sidewalk, ducked into the first alley he came to, then crouched out of sight behind a pile of discarded boxes, wrapping the shadows around him like a protective blanket.

He glanced around furtively, still hiding the steaming pizza inside his coat. The exotic, spicy smell of it had taken possession of him, the way the scent of fresh blood consumes the mind of a wild animal. When he was sure that he was alone, he brought it out and wolfed it down, reveling in the taste, barely noticing that the cheese burned the roof of his mouth.

He hadn't even swallowed when he heard the low growl of a dog behind him. Reese whipped around. A nasty-looking mongrel was crouching in the shadow of a doorway, staring longingly at the crust in his hand.

Reese started to raise the crust to his lips, then paused. *Goddamit*, he thought, and lowered his hand. To turn down a hungry dog was a crime. They were partners in survival. Slowly, Reese extended his hand toward the animal. The mongrel cautiously trotted out of the doorway, and keeping his eyes glued warily on the man, seized the crust.

For good luck, Reese gently ruffled the fur between the dog's ears until the animal's tail began to swing back and forth as it settled onto the asphalt at his feet.

Leaving the hungry mongrel to its breakfast, Reese walked back to the edge of the street. The pangs of hunger within him had subsided now, and the sun was rising well up into the morning sky. He hovered at the edge of the alley wall and surveyed the parade of passing cars. He would need one soon. And many other things, as well.

*Time to move out*, he said to himself.


**Silver Lake District**
**Panama Hotel**
**10:20 A.M.**

It was a four-story firetrap that smelled of disinfectant and stopped-up toilets. In the winter it was a refrigerator, and in the summer, an oven, chilling or baking the human contents mercilessly. But it was cheap. Back from the main street. With a fire escape he could climb out of and into an alley, unseen by the desk clerk.

Therefore, he selected it, threw a wad of bills onto the counter, and refused to sign the register. The steel-blue eyes fixed the big-eared, tiny-framed fifty-year-old clerk like a bug on a board. The clerk muttered something about writing Mr. Smith in the book for him, then handed him the keys to the small room up the stairs.

He scanned the interior in minute detail as he strode purposefully up the steps and down the narrow hall. Rotted wood floorboards. Lumpy walls, like parboiled flesh where the third layer of hastily applied paint was peeling back.

The sounds. Voices in the dank cubicles. Suppressed rage. Lonely wails. Sexual cooings. Silence. Many of the rooms were vacant. Good.

He walked into his room and paused, taking it all in at a sweeping glance. The window that led to the fire escape. The small table. A desk. A rusty-springed bed. An alcove with sink and toilet. An outlet. AC 110. Good.

He began setting out his tools.

He had come down Ventura Canyon Road in the dark, seeing no cars or people. He had to walk because the chronoporting had fused electrical circuits in a hundred-meter circumference.

So he came down the mountain like an implacable god descending Olympus, the ornamental chains on the dead punk's heavy boots clanking with each step. Searching.

He had an indeterminate time to locate and terminate the target and therefore could be thorough in acquiring the proper equipment. His clothes were ill fitting, but he would get more later, if necessary.

First, orientation.

As the lip of the horizon began to bruise with daylight, Terminator encountered a woman in her late forties walking from her front door to her BMW sedan, dangling keys and carrying a huge leather purse. He stood at the edge of the driveway just out of sight behind a bush and watched for signs of life in the large house from which the woman had emerged. No sounds or light or movement. Good.

He considered his options and decided to wait. And watch.

The woman opened the door of the vehicle with a key from the chain and then slipped behind the steering wheel.

She put another key into a slot beneath the wheel and turned on the ignition. The starter motor whined and whirred until the gas was fuel injected into the firing chamber of the engine and ignited. The woman pulled on a lever, and the transmission clanged as it went into reverse. She pulled another lever, and a light went out on the dash. Then she let her foot off the pedal on the floor and backed out of the driveway.

Simple.

Terminator calculated possible alternatives as he continued walking into the city.

Ten minutes later he found a suitable vehicle. A station wagon. Ford Kingswood Estate. Circa 1978. No one was around. The suburban street was still in the gray-and-pink blush of early morning. He walked up to the yellow car and rammed his fist through the side window. The glass crystallized from the force of the blow. Unmindful of the crinkly shards strewn all over the seat, Terminator reached in and unlocked the door. He slid behind the wheel and scanned the interior. The dash controls. It took a moment for him to recall data on this particular model, but in a moment he saw it in his memory with precise detail.

He leaned down, and using the heel of his hand, smashed the ignition assembly on the steering column. It broke open like ripe fruit. He ripped the plastic steering-column cover away with one motion, tearing the lock cylinder out of its setting in the process. Using his fingers like pliers, he reached in and turned the tiny exposed shaft by hand. The engine turned over twice and caught. He recalled the woman in the BMW and adapted her movements to this vehicle, backing the car into the street. He paused for a brief moment, reexamining the gearshift, then pushed it into drive and sped off down the street. Total time: eleven seconds.

He noted the layout of the city. The streets matched the map in his memory—his perfect and nearly boundless memory. Each street name and corresponding landmark was duly noted, never to be forgotten.

He cruised Los Feliz Boulevard until it knifed into

Sunset, then turned southeast. A few blocks later, he found what he was looking for. A hardware-store owner just opening up for the day.

Terminator was his first customer. And his last. Afterward, on his way to secure weapons, he located his base of operations, renting a room at the Panama.

He looked down at the tools he had raided as they lay on the bed.

X-Acto blades. Tweezers. Pliers. Penlight. Metric set. Screwdrivers. Several files. And other odds and ends. He had also taken a pile of work clothes and the owner's black leather jacket as backups to the clothes he had on. There wasn't much money in the register, but then, Terminator didn't need much. This would be a short mission.

He went out the fire escape to test it as an alternate route. No one saw him leave.

## Garrett's Gun Shop
## 10:23 P.M.

Rob Garrett, behind the glass counter, looked up into the steel-blue eyes of the customer.

He looked like a weight lifter, but he was dressed like those crazy kids on Melrose. Probably a nut. City was full of them. They came in all sizes here. Rob had first gone into the drugstore business in Bangor, Maine, fourteen years ago.

Rob was the adventurous type, he thought, so he packed his bags and headed West. He'd always collected guns himself, so he had taken over this shop on Sunset Boulevard. At first he had been wary of dealing with the serious-issue low-lifes who came into the shop, but in the last few years he had learned to spot the dangerous ones and mostly avoided trouble. This guy was not especially dangerous looking. His expression was slack, blank, except when he looked up at the rack of weapons behind the counter. Then his face drew into a focused cone of concentration. His eyes paused on each gun as if he could identify every one.

Rob's attention was peaked. Maybe a fellow collector? The desire to make contact with one of his own kind caused Rob to ignore the man's weird clothes and look at the man. Hell, gun collectors come in all packages.

"Can I help you, sir?" he said hopefully. Gun collectors also spent a lot of money.

Finally, the man lowered his unblinking gaze to Rob, only now reacting as if he existed.

He began asking for the heavy artillery, the semiautomatics, the military stock Garrett didn't want to carry but did, anyway, because it was beginning to sell very well.

They were all perfectly legal guns, unless you knew how to file the pins off the semiautomatics to make them steady fire.

*Shit,* Rob thought, *this guy does have good taste.* He trundled back and forth, pulling a formidable arsenal off the racks.

In a voice that sounded as if the man were buying razor blades, he said, "I want to see the SPAS-12 autofeed shotgun."

"That's both pump action and auto, you know," Rob interjected. The man kept his eyes on the racks.

"Armalite AR-180 semiauto assault rifle," he requested.

As Rob pulled it from the rack, the customer continued, "The Desert Eagle .357 Magnum semiautomatic gas-operated pistol with ten-round magazine. The AR-15 5.56 carbine with collapsible buttstock."

Rob was panting a little trying to keep up.

The man was continuing in a dull voice. "Phased plasma pulse laser in forty-watt range."

Rob froze in confusion, trying to reconcile the request with his in-store stock, then narrowed his eyes at the customer. Phased plasma. Very funny. "Hey, pal, just what you see. Anything else?"

Rob was thinking that the guy must have been in the service. The way he was selecting the weapons, and his manner, cried out marines. Or, who knows? Maybe this bird was a real mercenary. The customer picked up a Colt .45, two inch over long-slide automatic, eyeing the laser targeting device mounted on top. It looked like a scope, but it actually was a small laser generator with internal battery power. When the man depressed the trigger slightly, a bright, nail-thin beam of red light shot out of the end of the device.

"That's a good gun," Rob said. "They just came in. You aim the dot where you want the bullet to go. You can't miss." The customer was aiming the beam at the walls. At the display rack behind Rob. At Rob. Wherever the beam met a surface, it made a tiny, intense ball of light.

It was beautiful to watch the customer. He was moving the bolt back and forth, over and over, almost as if he could become an extension of the weapon itself. Fascinating.

The man moved his eyes carefully over the shelves again all the while working the actions of the growing pile of weapons, seeming to familiarize himself instantly with their operation. Then he turned that steady gaze on the owner again.

"UZI nine millimeter."

Rob went to get it, saying, "You know your weapons, buddy. Any one of these is ideal for home defense."

Rob watched for a smile, but it didn't come. *Screw the jokes. Better tend to business.* "Which ones do you want?"

"All," the taciturn man said, toneless and certain. Rob raised his eyebrows.

"I may close early today. There's a fifteen-day wait on the handguns, but the rifles you can take right now." Rob began wrapping them up but turned when he heard the rattle of shell casings on glass.

The man was calmly ripping open a box of twelve-gauge cartridges and sliding them rapidly into the autoloader.

"Hey! You can't do that—"

The man faced Rob and raised the shotgun to his face. The customer said, "Wrong."

Rob thought for a moment that it was another stupid

joke, and then, a second before the shotgun blast, in a quiet revelation, he realized that he should have stayed in Maine.

Terminator carried the weapons and the sacks of ammunition to the station wagon and put them in the back. They were primitive killing mechanisms, but he estimated his firepower was comfortably above the minimum requirement for the situation.

After he'd first stolen the station wagon, it had taken him about sixteen minutes to adjust to the random patterns of city traffic. Twice he had run cars onto the sidewalk, and once he had plowed through an intersection and sideswiped an RTD bus. But then he learned to calculate the ebb and flow of the vehicles and through memory and analysis of contextual activity piece together the rules of the road. He was learning his way around.

**Panama Hotel**
**11:19 A.M.**

Terminator sat at a small table, carefully filing away the welded plate that prevented the UZI from firing full auto. He had finished converting and loading all the other weapons within thirty minutes by working in a steady, tireless rhythm. The plate dropped out with a quiet clink. A squeeze of the trigger would now unleash nine-millimeter bullets at a cyclic rate of fire of over eight hundred rounds per minute, the secret of the UZI's legendary firepower.

He loaded a full magazine into the auto pistol, then placed it on the bed alongside the other weapons.

He had carried them in through the fire-escape window. This was his base of operations. It had to be secure; therefore, he could not bring attention to it by any overtly aggressive behavior, such as outright life denial. He knew enough about this society to avoid doing anything that would jeopardize this neutral zone. That was why he paid the desk clerk for the room. That was why he had needed a back entrance to the room. But away from the room he could do anything he wanted without concern, because he would be constantly on the move, constantly driving forward until he reached and terminated his assigned target. After that, nothing mattered.

Terminator stood up, gathered extra magazines, filling his pockets, and selected the UZI, the laser-sight .45, and the nickel-plated .38 pistol. For his first run he wanted to go light. If there had to be a second, he would have ample backup firepower.

Then he slipped out the window and crawled easily down the fire escape to the alley and his car. It was time to access the target.

**Silver Lake District
Sunset near Fountain Boulevard
11:42 A.M.**

The Canadian never knew what hit him. He was a bear of a man, weighing in at 245 before lunch, his broad face, with its thick features, fringed with a beard. Carlyle Leidle was a carbide-steel tool and die maker working on a green card and studying for citizenship. Twenty minutes ago he had hopped on his Harley 900 to run an errand for his boss. Two minutes later, the muffler from a rust-smudged 1968 Dodge van fell into the road in front of him. He was making a turn and sideslipped on the muffler, going over before he could get his legs down for support. His injuries were minor—a small gash on his wrist and a slightly gouged kneecap. The Harley was trashed. So he parked the chopper on the sidewalk and sauntered in low-boil frustration half a block to a phone booth. Cursing under his breath with impatience, Carlyle waited while the phone on the other end rang twelve times. His old lady sure as hell loved her fucking beauty sleep.

She finally came on and was in the process of wondering who had the balls to wake her up after a long,

hard night when someone with a powerful grip lifted
Carlyle off his feet and swung him like a rag doll into a
nearby parked car. He slid onto his massive butt with a
bone-crushing thud. He was about to bellow his rage and
leap on the interloper when he saw the man's eyes. There
was nothing in them. No anger or meanness. Nothing but
defocused zip. He was grabbing the phone book and leafing
through it, as if Carlyle had ceased to exist. He was a big
man. Carlyle was bigger. He pulled himself to his feet and
said to the other's back, "You got a serious attitude problem,
man!" But this had no seeming effect on the man in the
phone booth. The receiver was swinging back and forth at
the end of the cord. This was too much. Carlyle started for
the man, but just then he saw the back stiffen and noticed
the man's finger, which had been running down the column
of names, lock into a frozen position over one, then jerk to
the next and then the next. Abruptly, the man turned to
leave. Carlyle considered getting in his way until he saw
the eyes again. They were looking right at him but seeing
something else entirely—something in the near future that
might have been of interest but certainly not here and now.
He pushed past Carlyle and jumped behind the wheel of a
station wagon and sped away. Carlyle swallowed. It was
only now that he realized the man had frightened him. He
had never been looked at like that. He never wanted to be
again. Sighing, he stepped into the booth to redial his
house. His eyes went down to the open page of the phone
book the man had been looking at. There was an indenta-
tion alongside three names, a depression caused by the
man's finger digging into the paper. The three names were:
Sarah Anne Connor, Sarah Helene Connor, and Sarah
Jeanette Connor. Carlyle stared at them as the phone rang
at his house. For a moment, a mere fraction of time, he
considered dialing the numbers and warning the women
that someone very spooky was looking for them. But the
notion was fragile and easily crushed into forgetfulness
when his wife came on the line and he began to explain his
own problems to her.

Eleven and a half hours later, he would be sitting in his

ratty easy chair in front of the TV, watching the late news. His wife would be startled by the expression of horror that would make his face an alien sight. For a little while, all he would be able to say was "I should have called. . . . I should have called. . . ."

## West Los Angeles Junior College
## 11:53 A.M.

The flat was the last straw. Sarah marched up to the Honda and nodded fatalistically at the deflated rear wheel. It wasn't even close to fair. There was no reason for this to have happened to her. Okay, maybe she'd find a nail in the treads, sure. But why today? Why not tomorrow? Or yesterday? In either case, she had a light schedule and could have easily accommodated disaster. But today? Why?

Things had begun well enough. After leaving her apartment, she'd had an uneventful and dreamy ride to school. Traffic was surprisingly mild, and the drivers had been uncommonly alert and gracious. So she had allowed herself to do something very suicidal when riding a two-wheeled vehicle in Los Angeles city traffic: daydream.

She was thinking about Stan Morsky and their date that night. She hadn't planned on it, but the images welled up over the vision of the road before her and simply washed reality away. She remembered his dark blue eyes, and his smile. It wasn't especially sincere, but it was smooth, and it was inspired by her. Okay, she had to admit, it wasn't anything like the expression Ginger could inspire in Matt. But it reminded her of a smile she had been able to inspire two years ago. Senior year. Standing in the hall after school with Rich Welker. A supersweet smile marred only slightly by a chipped tooth that he was quick to remind everyone he had won in a knockdown victory game with the former football-league champs. He was varsity letter, class president, and a class act with his wardrobe. His parents were wealthy, of course. She had managed to get into the cheerleading squad just so she could be near him. For months he was polite and available to everyone but her. Finally, one day, in the hall, he *saw* her for the first time, framed by her open locker. No one was around. He kissed her. And then he smiled for her.

They had three dates before he told her he was marrying the homecoming queen.

Hurriedly, Sarah clicked that thought off and went back to Stan. He was a lot like Rich. Classy, handsome, drove a Porsche, with a dreamy expression and a gorgeous smile. He was funny and polite. And when he had asked her out, she had been surprised. There was no warning. She was waiting his table, and he would make amusing comments from time to time as she made certain he was being well looked after. When a customer in the next booth started giving her a hard time, he had bailed her out with a joke that defused the situation. As she was thanking him for coming to her rescue, he asked her to go to the concert with him. The only major problem she faced now was what to wear. This guy was really upscale. Maybe Ginger would help her decide.

Then her scooter began to stutter and cough. It was dying underneath her. It rolled to a stop in the middle lane. Cars on all sides began honking, the drivers quickly turning vicious as their deepest hostilities burst through the thin veneer of patience to find a convenient target.

She somehow was unsurprised, and that was what surprised her as she walked the dead scooter to the curb. Then she realized why she was not surprised. She remembered forgetting to put gas in the Honda last night on her way home from the library. Lame.

Okay, just a few minutes behind schedule so far—no big deal. She walked the scooter a block to a gas station, and that was that.

Her first class on Fridays was a real adventure. Linguistics. Professor Miller kept her after class for her increasingly frequent tardiness.

Sarah's next major crisis was in Psych 104.

Rod Smith was one of the few men on campus who had discerned that the most beautiful women took psych classes. The letch had been hitting on every girl except Sarah. Today was her lucky day.

He was two seats away, glancing out of the corner of his eye at her bare legs. Sarah cursed herself for not wearing jeans, but it was such a nice day, and she loved the way the wind felt on her skin when she rode the scooter in her shorts.

Rod was reminding her, unconsciously, of course, about the unwritten law of the civilized jungle. If you wear something sexy, men have a right to stare. She decided to ignore Rod, and although he did not exactly go away, he did shrink in her mind to a small nuisance. Until class was over.

He followed her outside and walked with her across the quad, striking up an amiable conversation. She wasn't listening to the words; she was hearing the tone, which was urgent and hungry. He probably wasn't listening to himself, either. He concluded with "We haven't talked much. I think we should. There's a lot we could learn from one another."

Sarah stopped walking and faced him. There was no sign in his eyes that he was capable of distinguishing her from any other female on campus. She wasn't Sarah; she was simply a romantic target. It would be especially nice if he vanished, so she said, "The only thing I want to learn from you, Rod, is what you look like when you're walking away."

She was amazed to see the effect this had on him. Suddenly humbled, his face reddened, and with much embarrassment, he sauntered off. It was an act, she thought. Wasn't it? God, she didn't mean to come off so hard. Maybe this poor guy did have some feelings for her.

Then she reached her Honda and saw the flat.

She called Rod back. It was an impulse that would haunt her later. She went into her pretty smile, and Rod brightened up. In a few minutes he was grunting at her feet, patching and repairing the tire.

She realized she would have to repay his generosity, and so did he. When Rod finished, he wiped his hands on his jeans and slipped an arm around her waist. He pulled her to him and said, "I knew you'd come around."

There was the Look, mutating his face into what

suddenly seemed to Sarah to be a textbook example of slack-jawed lust. She couldn't help herself. She laughed.

As she watched Rod stomp off in anger, she realized she had made an enemy. *Wonderful*, Sarah thought, and mounted the scooter. *Not too bad a day so far.* As Sarah rode off to work, she allowed herself the feeble hope that she might only be a few minutes late. Surely this morning, which would live in infamy, was enough to appease the gods.

But sometimes the gods are never satisfied.

**Studio City
12856 Hatterass St.
12:02 P.M.**

Mike and Linda were standing on the curb, arguing over the toy truck. He held the opinion that it belonged to him. She held the truck. She was nine, and two years older than him. It was a plastic model, with realistic details, of a dump truck, and he had been using it to excavate Mrs. Connor's flower garden. Linda had come up behind him and snatched the truck up. "Mom said you couldn't play over here anymore."

Mike clutched at the truck. "You're not Mom, butt face!"

"She said I was in charge while she went to the store," Linda answered haughtily. But Mike lunged and knocked the toy out of her arms. When it struck the dirt, he dived for it. The truck bounced into the street and rolled to a stop.

"Real smart move, Mikey."

Mike shrugged and started to go get it.

A car was coming down the street. The driver was methodically scanning houses for the addresses.

Linda saw it coming and ran after Mike. She yanked him back. "Wait for the car, stupid."

Mike squirmed impatiently as the station wagon approached. "Come on, come on," he commanded the driver. Mike and Linda stood at the curb and watched the car slow suddenly, swerve in their direction, then skid to a stop, crumpling the toy truck into a plastic pancake.

The children froze, Linda stepping back with apprehension, Mike blinking back surprise and swelling outrage.

Mike and Linda looked up at the giant man as he unfolded himself from the car and stomped up to them. He was someone from a beanstalk, Mike was thinking. Linda was just scared, holding Mike around the neck.

The man just walked past as if he couldn't see them. "Hey!" Mike called out before Linda could clamp her hand over his mouth.

Terminator ignored the children and walked up to the Connor house. He rapped on the door. A little Pomeranian yapped ineffectually at his heels. It meant nothing to him. He was waiting for Sarah Connor.

She came to the door and opened it to the length of the chain lock.

"Yes?" she asked cautiously, staring through the crack at this huge, bizarre-looking man.

"Sarah Connor?" Terminator asked blandly.

"Yes."

He punched the door. It snapped the chain and swung inward, throwing the woman off balance. She screamed and fell back. In an instant, Terminator pulled out the .45 and activated the laser sight. It streaked across the room and locked on her forehead as Terminator aimed. She was blinded for a second by the red glare; then her vision was shattered as a bullet exploded from the gun and struck her two centimeters above the right eyebrow.

She collapsed on the carpet, and Terminator brought the beam down and centered it on her chest. He fired the weapon until it was empty. The staccato blasts echoed over the high-pitched yaps of the Pomeranian on the porch.

Terminator leaned down, and using an X-Acto knife, made an incision from the ankle to the knee.

Mike had run forward after the man before he went into the house, and now he was standing on the sidewalk, looking through the open door at the violence inside. He had no scale for this. He loved cartoons. Especially Tom and Jerry. He laughed when Tom would topple something on Jerry and the cat would flatten, like his truck, and then bounce back to normal. Mrs. Connor wasn't bouncing back. Instead, she was reddening the carpet beneath her. He had never seen anyone lay so still. Linda came up just as the man inside started to cut Mrs. Connor open as calmly as carving a roast.

Linda grabbed Mike's hand and pulled him next door to their house. She slammed the door behind her and locked it.

Terminator stood up over the body of the dead woman. He had not found what he was looking for. Target identification negative. He considered his options for a moment, then pocketed the weapon and strode to the door.

They watched from the window as the man walked back to his car and got in. As he drove away, Linda was crying.

All Mike could think about was how flat his toy truck looked out there on the asphalt. He murmured quietly, "He wrecked it."

The whole thing had taken maybe two or three minutes. Already it was becoming unreal. There was no drama in it. Only death. Abrupt and without apparent meaning. But there *was* a very deep meaning to these events, a meaning very few would ever decipher and certainly a meaning far too sad and profound for the children pressed to the window to comprehend.

In the next few years, Mike and Linda's parents would spend thousands of dollars on psychotherapy.

But it wouldn't do any good.


## Big Jeff's Family Restaurant
## 12:17 P.M.

Sarah buzzed through the gradually thickening haze, the heated smog shimmering the horizon into a mirage of loudly hued roadsigns and billboards. She guided her Honda into the parking lot of Big Jeff's. She hastily chained the scooter to a light pole near the plaster and fiber-glass icon of Big Jeff himself wearing a cocked chef's cap and an obscenely jolly grin. The freckled imp was perpetually lifting a sculpted hamburger—mustard drooling down the sesame-seed bun, always moments from dropping to the pavement—in homage to whatever deity watches over fat kids.

The smell of Big Jeff's wholesome atmosphere roiled up and enveloped her in a sickly sweet miasma of stale cigarette smoke, half-eaten, slime-cold hamburgers, and the "special sauce" coagulating and turning as dark as molasses.

The lunch rush was just welling into full chaos. Busboys hovered conspicuously, buzzardlike in their patience, clearing tables of culinary debris moments after the perpetrators of the mess departed. Waitresses jogged, customers wolfed, and even the older patrons rushed to restrooms.

A video camera assessed the dining-room area from over the Staff Only door. Sarah grimaced as she passed under it, not seeing and therefore colliding with Nancy Dizon, a robust, dark-skinned waitress who was half-Filipino, half-Irish.

"Sorry," Sarah breathed.

Nancy waved her off. "No, my fault. Rushing 'cause I'm late."

"Me, too," Sarah said to Nancy's rapidly receding back.

In the service corridor Sarah slowed down to forage in her purse for her time card, in the process dropping her books. As she knelt to pick them up, a tinny voice called her name.

She looked at the ceiling camera just above a door marked: Chuck Breen, Manager.

"Sarah, would you come to the office, please."

Biting her lip, Sarah slipped her card into the time clock and winced at the loud, accusatory clunk it made as her tardiness was processed and immortalized. Then she heaved the pile of books under her arm and pushed the door open.

Chuck Breen was sitting at his desk behind a console lined with monitors. All he needed was a uniform to look the part of a security guard. He wore no badges—except perhaps in his heart.

Sarah tried her brightest, bravest smile. "Hi, Chuck. Guess what, I'm late."

She said it as one word, but Chuck picked it apart and figured it out.

He leaned into the underglow of a monitor, and the moonscape of his pimple-pocked face went into bas-relief. Charming.

"This"—Chuck indicated the computer on his desk—"is an Apple Macintosh 128K with a multiplan spreadsheet. It's my organizer. I record wages, tips, work schedules, and . . . most importantly, the time clock. You're exactly eighteen minutes late, Connor. Excuse?"

"I had a flat."

"Why is it, Connor, that so many people's tires seem unable to hold air when I haven't had a flat in ten years?"

"For the last ten years you've taken the bus," Sarah answered evenly.

"As everyone without reliable transportation should."

"My bike is usually reliable. I haven't had a flat in—"

"Excuse me, Connor. I don't want to hear the history of your moped."

"It's a scooter, Chuck," she said.

*What are you doing*, the little Sarahs chided. *You need this job*. For a moment Sarah tried to throw off the cautious voices; then she gave in.

"Listen, Chuck . . . I'm sorry. It won't happen again."

Simple, humble, reassuring. With most people it would have been enough. Not this guy.

"Look, Sarah, someday you're going to have to learn that you have basic responsibilities you must fulfill as an adult. Care for yourself, your family, and honor your commitments to others. Namely, your employer. You must not be late again."

*Why do people have to act like this*, she thought. The urge to tell Chuck how relevant his cosmic view was to her right now rose to a peak, but it was beaten back by the little

Sarahs, who counseled job preservation. This was strangling time. It seemed to another part of Sarah that she should have been able to say something more than she had. But she didn't. And that was a little sad. But it was the decision she made. And Sarah was not about to sit on her hands and yell about the pain.

"I'm docking you half a unit."

He motioned her over and pointed at her name flashing like a miniature neon in a ghostly electronic limbo.

"See? It's entered."

Chuck was back into the black-and-white fishbowls, his eyes scanning independently, reminding Sarah of Pugsly as he contemplated a chunk of lettuce.

"Ain't life grand," she murmured to herself as she went out the door.

Outside, Sarah felt herself stiffening with rage. She hurried around the corner, and just outside the dressing room she whirled around and flipped a "bird" in the direction of the manager's office.

Chuck's voice came over a speaker.

"Bad attitude, Connor. That's not the kind of thing a Jeff's girl should be doing. Remember, you *are* a Jeff's girl, at least for the time being."

Sarah had forgotten the camera at the other end of the corridor.

"Don't forget to push the Jeff's salad today, okay?" Nancy strode down the hall toward her. "Come on," she said. "Big Jeff is watching you."

Inside the dressing room, Sarah tiredly dropped her books on the floor of her locker. "I'll bet he has one of those cameras hidden in here somewhere."

"Oh, yeah?" Nancy murmured. She lifted her Jeff's skirt and yanked her panties down and mooned the room. "This is for you, crater face."

Sarah laughed, releasing the last remnants of the anger, then started to undress.

"Careful," Nancy warned, smacking her ever-present wad of five sticks of gum.

Sarah faked paranoia and faced the wall, hiding behind

the locker door as she got out of her clothes and into the purple-and-pink blouse and skirt.

Nancy dawdled, goldbricking, waiting for Sarah to finish, using the time for her favorite activity—gossiping about their fellow waitresses. Today she was blathering happily about Sue Ellen, the new trainee with the sloppy habit of sneezing wetly on the food just before serving it.

Sarah hurried her makeup, applying a little liner and a touch of blush to bring herself back from the dead. The day was taking its toll, that was for sure.

When she was little, her mother used to tell her she had eyes that would one day drive men crazy. She studied them now. The lower lids drooped slightly. Her mother said women would envy that sexy look. But Sarah only thought it made her look as if she just got up after a long night. And the color. Her mother had raved about that, too. Mahogany, to match her chestnut hair. Sarah smiled to herself, then tossed her head back and tightened her face, studying the effects a few dabs of mascara made. The usual. Sarah saw only dark brown eyes and light brown hair. *Nice try, Mom.*

A moment later she stood before the full-length mirror and put her hair into the official Big Jeff's net.

"Hi," Sarah said, adopting a vacuous smile. "My name is Sarah, and I'll be your waitress." She pinched her cheeks for good measure. Peaches and cream.

"I'm so fucking wholesome."

That put Nancy on the floor.

## Big Jeff's Family Restaurant
**4:34 P.M.**

Sarah was gamely running the gauntlet of rabid customers, weaving between tables like a road-company ballerina, deftly balancing three full dinners on her outstretched arms and gripping a Jeff's salad in one hand. A beefy middle-aged man with a bear's face and a look of indignation reached out and tugged her apron. With practised aplomb, Sarah shifted the weight to avoid sudden disaster and faced the man, who pointed in vexation at his plate of fries.

"How about a bottle of ketchup, huh?"

Sarah put on her vacuous grimace and burbled ingenuously, "You mean in addition to the one you already have on your table?"

The man followed her eyes to the bottle of ketchup tucked behind the menu rack. Marching on, she unloaded her culinary cargo at a booth filled with impatient men. As she started sorting out who got what, an old man a few tables away shouted that he wanted his coffee *now*. She tossed a "be right with you" over her shoulder, then faced the immediate problem.

"Okay, who gets the Burly Beef?"

One answered, "I ordered barbecue beef."

Another cut in, "I think that's mine, but I didn't order fries."

Another overlapped, "Mine's the Chili Cheese Deluxe."

Sarah was falling behind the whole thing. Her feet had already gone half-past pain and agony and were quickly heading into fallen arches. Generally, she could easily handle the job, but this was not one of her better days.

More than usual, the personal hauntings and nagging little conflicts were stacking up on her, piling unbidden one atop the other, until she began to lose her concentration. And now, at this moment, the whole world was becoming an agonizingly simple and focused question: "Okay, then, who gets the Burly Beef?"

A fat blonde woman shepherding two hyperactive girls into the next booth touched Sarah's sleeve insistently. "Miss," she said, as if Sarah had nothing better to do than hang on every one of her words, "we're ready to order now."

"Yes, ma'am, I'll be right with you, if you'll just—" She was going on autopilot and put the last plate on the table. As she stood up, her arm brushed a water glass, and it spun onto the man at the end of the booth, dousing his jacket. He threw his arms up in dismay.

Sarah hastily patted his jacket and dabbed unthinkingly at his lap with a napkin, babbling, "I'm sorry, sir. That isn't real leather is it?" Of course it was, and the guy's expression left no doubt.

Meanwhile, one of the little girls in the next booth scooped up some ice cream and maliciously dropped it into Sarah's tip pouch. Sarah suppressed an amazed cry. The little girl chortled in triumph. Sarah fixed the child with a forlorn stare, and the little Sarahs yanked on her reins, barely controlling the exasperation.

The man whose jacket Sarah had drenched muttered, "Nice going, kid. Ought to give you the tip."

Sarah just stood there, the sense of malevolent forces whirling around her increasing. Nancy, passing behind her in the aisle, patted her shoulder, tilting her head sideways with an impish grin.

"Look at it this way, Connor. In a hundred years who's gonna care?"

**Century City**
**5:41 P.M.**

Reese's nervous system started pouring out the sweat as, one by one, squeaky clean men and women, their hair sprayed perfectly in place, their clothes spotless and unwrinkled, began to crowd around him on the curb at Pico and Doheny, waiting for the light to change.

The people seemed like an alien race. He hadn't expected that. They laid a hungry fear on him that sent his antenna up and sharpened his edge. After six hours, he still wasn't used to them. But outwardly Reese was doing the statue number, putting out stillness, like a skid-row Buddha, one hand clutching a brown grocery bag, the other reassuringly wrapped around the handle of the .38 in his coat pocket. All the eyes around him were glued to the red light twenty meters away.

Reese sniffed at the scent they brought to the air—that terrible smell again, the acrid-sweet chemical lie of perfume. He hadn't found the comforting, pungent aroma of a human being all day.

Eventually, the signal across the street went green, traffic changed direction, and the group of pedestrians, in their Calvin Klein camouflage, charged forward into the crosswalk. Reese hung back, letting them pass, keeping them in front of him, downwind.

He reached the southwest corner of Doheny, alone now, and surveyed the cars parked along the street. All day he had been hunting for one that fit the mission profile. He was after function, not form. It had to be heavy, with a large chassis to absorb incoming fire, and have a good-size engine to move something that big, fast. And it had to be inconspicuous.

His search had been confined to back streets and parking lots. The dealerships were of no use to him; he was gonna buy his car with a coat hanger. A couple of times he came close; right vehicle type, in secure terrain, clear of civilians.

He was halfway into a mud-splattered Cadillac on Spaulding when the owner's kids came home from school. An hour later, in the bowels of a concrete parking garage beneath a glass-and-girder office building, he was actually inside a light blue Chrysler and reaching under the dash for the wiring harness when an alarm, tuned to maximum nerve shatter, started screaming at him. He spent about six seconds hunting for it, couldn't find it, and decided to evac out. Fucking machines. He hated losing to them.

The sun was almost gone when Reese finished the block from Pico to Alcott. The tech's amphetamines had worn off hours ago, leaving in their wake a jagged, hollow edge to his fatigue.

*Move it soldier*, he ordered himself. *Scope the terrain. Stay busy.* His eyes were probing by polar quadrants, starting at his rear. East—paved street, no moving vehicles . . . SE to SW—two-story structures, apartments probably, no detectable movement inside or out . . . N—more street, nothing moving . . . NW to NE—construction site. Maybe 20,000 meters square. Chain-link perimeter. Two tractors, a crane, and a crew of six, seventy-five to eighty meters away in open terrain. . . .

Suddenly, the hair on Reese's skin turned to needles and stood straight up. He froze. Sweat beaded on his palms—there was a bad taste in his memory. Silent alarms went off in his head. Something about this place. What? There was fear in it . . . and . . . yeah, but more. Shit. What was it? Surreal image fragments of bodies and night fire frenetically clicked in and out in front of his eyes, trying to overlay themselves on the landscape before him. Reese took a deep breath and willed his mind to calm itself. *Think.* It wouldn't come. *Maybe I'm going Echo Delta,* he thought.

Then he remembered.

Reese didn't move for a second. Then he calmly adjusted the shoulder strap on the shotgun beneath his raincoat, shifted the grocery bag to his other hand, and continued down the sidewalk, wishing it had been Extreme Delusion, slamming that door in his memory shut and trying to lock it, and checking out the cars that he passed. Reese saw the LTD and walked around it, looking at the tires—tread's okay—checking out the body damage—negligible—and the paint—going dull, nonreflective, better.

He glanced around the street, then casually popped the hood and raised it, allowing streetlight to spill into the engine compartment. Underneath a lot of smog-control crap he would have liked to pull off was a 351-cubic-inch motor with a four-barrel carb. Plenty of torque. A good mill. He strolled to the driver's side and pulled the folded wire coat hanger from his pocket. Keeping the area scanned, he straightened one end and slipped it down the door panel, above the handle. By feel, Reese was searching for the lock release. Still no intruders. With a click, the lock came open. He slipped into the car, set the bag on the floor, and quietly pulled the door closed.

The wire harness was beneath the steering column. From memory, his fingers went right to the ignition line, stripped it, and touched the bare copper to the "hot" lead;

the engine purred to life. Two minutes had elapsed since he'd approached the car.

He depressed the pedal, running the RPMs up a little. The engine pitch rose evenly. No lifter noise or postignition. Tuned. Good.

Letting the engine idle to warm up, Reese untied the shotgun's shoulder strap, slipped the weapon from beneath his coat, and laid it on the seat. There was reverence in his eyes as he slowly scanned the luxurious interior of the car. A thick carpet covered the floor. The dash radio had come on when he started the car. He flipped through the dial until he zeroed a broadcast. The somnambulistic tones of Jim Morrison—("Take the highway to the end of the night . . .")—floated out of the speakers, filling the small, plush compartment. On another station, a pious baritone was denouncing his flock of sinners for not sending him enough money to keep denouncing his flock of sinners. Reese roamed the dial like a banquet guest who hadn't eaten in weeks. He found a news station and hung there for a while. Not much happening. Just eleven brushfire wars around the globe and three murders in town. He checked his stolen digital watch against KFWB's newstime. Sync'd.

Taking a deep breath, Reese reveled in the faint factory-fresh smell that still emanated from the car's upholstery. *So that was what it was like once,* he thought, and reached over to turn up the radio. He listened with wonder to the fatuous lyrics of a song about a young girl's broken heart.

Reese sank into the seat and leaned his head back. He felt his muscles, knotted by tension and use, begging to relax. A wave rolled up to the shore of his conscious mind and offered to carry him to a warm, peaceful place for a few hours' sleep.

No way. He sat up and emptied his pockets; three boxes of Super .38 ammo and four more of .00 buckshot. That would hold him for the time being. He had broken into a sporting-goods store at 9:15, and by 9:16 his pockets were full, and the guard dog there was sorry to see him go.

Reese reached down and retrieved the grocery bag at his feet. The things inside it were from a tiny liquor store on Crenshaw, run by an old Korean woman whose eyes were glued to an eight-inch TV screen behind the register.

Reese upended the bag and spilled its contents onto the seat. A copy of *Cosmopolitan* fell onto the cushion, along with two bottles of Perrier and fourteen Snickers bars. Chocolate. He'd had some when he was a kid; hoarded it till the last tiny precious flake had melted and disappeared like a dream on the end of his tongue. Now he had handfuls. He stuffed one into his mouth, whole, and chewed, letting the taste of it consume him and thinking about the kind of crap he was used to eating. He imagined Willy, a long-dead Tac-Com kid on his fire team, looking at him, eyes going bigger than the rest of his head and saying, "Oh, man, oh, shit, sarge. You really had fourteen of 'em?" Reese swallowed and unwrapped another one, for Willy.

He picked up the magazine and flipped through it. A few articles. He skipped past them to the ads. Oh, God, what a window they were. He was fascinated, spellbound. The women he'd seen on the street today seemed incredibly beautiful, so clean and delicate. He'd had a hard time connecting them up to anything he had known before.

But this was on an altogether different plane. These were fantasy women. Svelte, seamless, unreal, with glossy faces devoid of expression, save for a calculated pouting of lips or a seductive smile painted on by the precise brush of a makeup artist. Their long necks and slender arms looked weak, their nails as impractical and decadent as a mandarin's. He reminded himself how none of these haute-couture fawns would last more than minutes in his time, and it eased the ache a bit. Still, he found his scarred and calloused fingers tracing the lines of their porcelain-figurine beauty, a beauty made all the more painful for him by its fragility. A fragility that could never survive in his twilit world, with its razor-sharp rules of survival.

His head sagged against the door. The cushion beneath him was a seductress, pulling him deeper into her soft body, telling him to rest, just for a moment. He thought about all the things that he could never have and the one thing he wanted most of all, that he dreamed of all his life, that was so near now, and that he must not have.

He gazed dully out the windshield, past the chain-link fence, at the heavy steel tracks of a caterpillar as it slowly, systematically, chewed through the plowed-up earth. The roar and clatter of its treads echoed loudly in Reese's head as his eyes . . .

. . . were focused on a pair of enormous, gleaming treads, forty meters away and closing, hungrily grinding through a field of moonlit ferroconcrete, spitting out dead girders, splintered wood, bits of clothing, and bones.

Thousands of bones. Mountains of them.

The bones were blackened and charred by fires that were memories even when Reese was born. They lay about in dismal heaps that were so ubiquitous that nobody he knew even paused to consider that the contours of the landscape were formed in places by human remains.

Reese calmly watched as skulls went under the H-K's treads. He could read nothing in the fleshless faces that rolled and spun into the flat metal teeth, until, for a second, the empty sockets of one flashed him a look that seemed to say, *You, too*.

He stopped looking at them after that.

His face did not yet carry the scars it would collect in the coming years. He had just turned sixteen.

The treads were coming fast. Loud. Past deafening. Off the scale. The sound became a solid thing, clawing at his mind, shaking, tearing, and ripping into him.

Reese saw explosions, a rainbow-colored kaleidoscopic ocean of them, strobing the horizon. "Flash to bang" was only a microsecond. They were close. Coming closer. Closing the perimeter with a high-explosive torrent; rolling, pounding, and throwing terrain up into the clouds. Making earth indistinguishable from sky.

Searchlights swept across the shattered landscape. Seeking out the scattered pockets of human pain. Hunting, probing, searching.

Reese was lying on his belly, in the ruins of a blown-out apartment building. The acrid smell of burning flesh and moist dirt filled his nostrils. He fought back the compelling urge to run and tried to sink lower in the fetid ash beneath him.

*If you panic, you'll die*, Reese told himself. *Don't panic*. The CRT screen inside of his helmet was dead. He tried adjusting it. Gone. No visual link with Command. At least the headset and throat mike were working. He could hear the overlapping staccato of urgent battlefield requests and the voices of men and women, some screaming with mortal wounds, calling for more ammo, cover fire, medics, and extraction.

He glanced over his shoulder at the surviving member of his twelve-man squad; Corporal Ferro, a grim, gaunt, female sapper. Fifteen last Tuesday and armed to the fucking teeth. She was staying close to Reese, anchored to her squad leader like a shadow.

He threw a glance up into the blasted spires of the collapsed building and saw a dark shape moving against the night sky; the H-K's turret. Its searchlights swept down through the ruins. Reese checked the "Pulse Remaining" level on his Westinghouse M-25. The rifle had only one plasma pulse left. *Take a shot. Blind the son of a bitch.* Reese aimed up at its eyes, the infrared lenses on the gun mount.

Reese flipped up the rifle's flexy sight—*Oh, shit, faster, faster*—stared into the CRT scope—*Move, goddamit, move*—and squeezed off a burst of high-energy plasma.

The H-K's ultra-high-sensitive lens exploded into a shower of glass and melted microchips.

Then the gleaming black monster fired.

Reese and Ferro dove out of the building as the H-K vaporized what was left of it. But Reese had blinded it on one side. *Good. And now I'm gonna kill you*, he thought.

Reese was moving fast, like a cat in a high-speed killing mode. Images were pouring almost too fast for him to clearly record. His eyes flicked over the body of a child, a boy of about ten, center punched with a smoking hole, clutching a shattered, ancient M-16, face staring into nothing. More bodies. Some in uniforms. Some in rags. Women, old men, children. Dead.

There were more explosions, falling in a traveling dispersal pattern, rolling east from Rexford to Sherborne and taking out everything in between.

Reese tumbled into a dark bunker. A rathole. Filled with humans clutching mud-caked weapons, huddling together against the death outside. Some of them were sobbing. Or screaming. The glare of an explosion lit their faces. Some of them were children.

Soldiers in a nightmare war.

What the hell were they still doing here? The zone was supposed to be cleared for the sapper team. Reese wanted that H-K.

"Where's your team leader?" Reese shouted. The answer was written in their faces—out there somewhere. Fried.

"Let's go!" he bellowed. "You're pulling back." They didn't move. Frozen. Fear had eaten away their ability to think. He pulled them to their feet, dragging them, almost throwing them out of the bunker.

"Now move!" Reese bellowed. "The unit's regrouping at Bunker Twelve." They nodded, sweating fear and blood, and ran off into the night. Some in the right direction.

Reese stood in the shadow of the bunker and did a fast recon. *Where did that fucking H-K go?* Then Ferro dove into the earth.

A burst of H-K incoming plasma hit the bunker. Wood, brick, and tattered canvas mushroomed out, fragmented, and then disappeared. The rush of wind and debris picked Reese up and flung him against a concrete pillar. He came down on his back in a smoking crater. *There it was*.

Reese opened his eyes. His uniform was smoking. His body was shaking from the impact. He screamed. Not out of fear but rage.

Ferro was kneeling over him, shouting something. But Reese couldn't hear.

"What?" he yelled back. "What?" His ears were ringing.

He sat up, stunned. Ferro was pointing to his helmet. It was shattered. He ripped it off—pushing the headset back down onto his matted hair, centering it—and threw the helmet away. *Now get that bastard. Run. Move, move, move!*

Reese and Ferro stopped behind a blasted wall after outflanking the massive H-K. Its flashing blue lights flicked across the walls; its searchlights seared through the debris.

Then it came into full view—a blast-scarred chrome Leviathan on treads. The huge underslung turret guns pivoted in their arc, pounding the surrounding ruins into flat rubble.

Reese unstrapped a satchel from Ferro's back and quickly pulled out one of the cylindrical antitank mines and laid it on his knee. Ferro followed Reese's lead. They could hear the H-K swinging on its axis and coming closer.

*Remove the dust plug.* Reese steadied his breathing. *Test the circuit.* The huge monster was coming into range. *Disengage the safety ball.* Reese's hands were sweating, slipping against the stainless-steel casing. *Grasp the handle and twist, clockwise, from Safe to Armed.* The ring around the top half of the mine lit up. It was hungry.

Reese peered over the edge of the wall. The H-K was only a few yards to the front, the roar of its engines building to a fever pitch. He stared into the treads, locked his eyes on them.

*Now die, mutherfucker!*

He leaped up and straight-armed the mine into the Leviathan's path. One of its treads rolled right over the bomb. The monster paused. Guns and searchlights swiveled. The head turned, ponderously.

As Reese was dropping back behind the wall, he saw Ferro struggling to keep her balance, slipping on the loose concrete fragments in the shadow of the wall. She was still holding the mine, and its timer was running down. "Throw it!" Reese shouted. But she couldn't unless she jumped on the wall, exposing herself, and the H-K was already swinging around.

She had fucked up. Reese and Ferro stared into each other's eyes. Then she jumped and threw. She was halfway back down when the searching power bolt punched into her torso. No scream. She went away in a cloud of pink mist. Some of her landed on Reese. He didn't bother to wipe her off.

Later he'd think about her.

Reese's charge exploded first, directly under the main pivot of the rear tread carrier, one of the few weak points in the machine's armor. The concussion drove pieces of the chassis far up into its torso, shattering one shoulder turret. Sympathetic detonations ripped through the tons of chain-fed ammo coiled within it, until finally the fuel tanks went up and the fifteen-meter-high juggernaut vanished inside an enormous fireball. Ferro's charge detonated ineffectively nearby, having bounced off the titanium carapace, but it added nicely to the inferno.

The whole sky lit up as the H-K disintegrated in a dazzling white nova, spreading itself over the reeking field of death like a universe being born. Reese peered over the edge of the crater and stared at the hot shower of light with intense, passionate satisfaction.

Then he was evac'ing back to the extraction point on Doheny. His lungs were choked with the smell of things on fire. Metal. Concrete. People. Everything burning.

Reese hauled the two other survivors into the APC and jumped behind the wheel. He redlined the engine and threw the Camaro into first. The Aerial was banking over toward them, lining them up in its gunsight matrix, then lost them in the flash-and-then-black-again confusion of the exploding battlefield.

The ruins were a frantic blur of half-seen images as Reese drove like a demon, gunning the APC over, up, and through the blasted-dead terrain. The kid jumped into the gun harness and glued his eyes to the laser sight of the big plasma-pulse gun. He was rapidly searching the sky for the Aerial.

It found them. It came swinging down in a forty-degree banking roll, searchlights glaring, turbos roaring at their top end, and fired a thunderous salvo of plasma.

The charge tore into the side of the Camaro, crumpling it like a beer can. The wheel was torn from Reese's hands. Another bolt punched into the APC and kicked it end over end.

Reese was pinned in the wreck, blood streaming down his forehead, into his eyes. The man who had been sitting next to him was gone from the waist up. Reese didn't want to look at that. He tried to move. Searing pain shot through his left shoulder. He saw flames licking up over the hood, growing steadily until the heat seared his face and hands. Closing his eyes, he clawed desperately to free himself. He smelled burning hair, his own. He heard someone screaming, an inchoate bellow of pain and rage. The voice sounded familiar. It was his. . . .

Reese's eyes popped open. The shotgun that had been on the seat was in his hands, and the wooden slide beneath the barrel was slamming back as a round went into the chamber. He was sweating, breathing fast as that constant, first-upon-waking question gripped his being: *Where am I?*

In an instant he took in the plush interior of the LTD; the magazine, Perrier, and chocolate bars on the seat; and the strange city lying beyond the car's windows. *The mission!* He yanked his coat sleeve back and stared at the red LED numbers on his watch. He'd been asleep for less than three minutes.

Slowly, Reese began to relax, letting the supercharged voltage drain out of him. He glanced over at the innocuous Caterpillar tractor as it lumbered back and forth over the broken field. The construction site held nothing but earthworms and crabgrass. For now. Reese pushed the afterimages of skulls and smoking corpses from his eyes.

## Big Jeff's Family Restaurant
## 5:58 P.M.

Chuck stopped Sarah in the service corridor with a verbal reproach just before she punched her time card. "Where are you going, Connor? You already took a break an hour ago."

Sarah was running out of steam, her shoulders unconciously drooping, her uniform wrinkled and smeary with splattered food. The muscles at the back of her neck had turned to stone, so she couldn't move her head without generating a spiky pain all the way down to her swollen feet and back up to the base of her skull.

She glowered up at the red-eyed camera.

"That's right, Chuck. Very observant."

"So what are you doing?"

"I'm leaving you."

"You're not off until seven."

"That's right, Chuck. On every day except Friday, when Denise relieves me an hour earlier than usual."

Sarah's ragged impatience came through Chuck's speaker despite the 20-percent distortion of the PA system.

"Uh, right, Connor. Where is your relief? You can't leave the floor until your relief—"

Denise, a buxom blonde careening carelessly into her thirties, strolled into the corridor and winked at Sarah.

She faced the camera and spoke soothingly. "What's the matter, Chuck, constipation bothering you again?"

Sarah, suppressing her laughter, clocked out fast. She smiled to herself, happy to have a friend like Denise. It gave the little Sarahs a moment of peace and security.

Then Nancy was clutching her arm excitedly, as if Sarah had been slipping off the edge of the world and at the last moment had been yanked back to safety.

"Come on, it's about you. Well, sort of," she said, her voice made husky by the cigarette dangling from the corner of her mouth. She smacked her gum like a lawnmower as she steered a confused Sarah across the room toward Claudia, who was sitting with her sore feet propped on a scratched teak table in front of the thirteen-inch black-and-white Motorola. She smiled up at Sarah as Nancy pushed her onto a metal folding chair to watch. "Sarah, look. This is weird." Claudia's awe sparked a sense of dread, and Sarah's hesitant smile froze.

Sarah strained to hear the prim newswoman in the smart business suit and lacquered hair, because she suddenly seemed to be talking about her. She was saying, ". . . and a police spokesman at the scene refused to speculate on a motive for the execution-style slaying of the Studio City housewife. He did, however, say that an accurate description of the suspect had been compiled from several witnesses. Once again, Sarah Connor, thirty-five, mother of two, brutally shot to death in her home this afternoon."

The newswoman turned a page and waited for the teleprompter to cue up the next story, something about Teamsters issuing a statement about a strike. But Sarah wasn't listening. *Oh, god, what a horrible thing—that poor woman who has my name. Gee, guess my problems are pretty trivial, but why do people go crazy like that and just destroy a life as if it were an empty bag of potato chips to crumple into a ball and fling out of sight. . . . Her name was Sarah Connor.*

"You're dead, honey," Nancy chortled, patting her shoulder and laughing as if it were the best joke she'd heard all day.

### Hancock Park District
### 6:12 P.M.

Terminator pressed the magazine-release catch on his laser-sighted automatic, dropped the spare clip, and immediately replaced it with a fresh one. He stood over the spasming, crimson-soaked body of Sarah Helene Connor, then chambered a round and aimed the laser dot at the center of her forehead in case another bullet was needed.

It wasn't.

He kneeled down over her in the narrow hall of her cluttered apartment and pulled an X-Acto knife from his coat pocket. Carefully, precisely, and without hesitation, Terminator made an incision at the base of Sarah's ankle and sliced along the muscle surrounding the tibia, stopping at the kneecap. Separating the bifurcated muscle, he probed the gleaming white bone with his fingers.

He did not find what he was looking for. Another kill without confirmed target identification. Ident neg. He put the X-Acto away and got to his feet. Considered the options. Of the three Sarah Connors in the phone book, two had been eliminated. One was left, Sarah Jeanette Connor. Logic dictated that she would be the one.

Terminator selected a strategy. Go back to the base of operations. Rearm. And make the final run.

He purposefully strode into the darkening day.

**Santa Monica
Good Life Health Spa
6:18 P.M.**

Sarah turned into the parking lot of the Good Life Health Spa, hopped off the Honda, and strolled into the big two-story building. It had few windows, like most gyms, and although wood beams and soft yellow stucco framed the entrance, the place still reminded her more of a prison than a health spa.

She waved to the girl at the desk and was gestured through the door to the aerobics studio. As she coursed through a sweaty group of young men, the muffled thuds of Ginger's favorite rock music began to assault her ears. She pushed the door inward, and a blast of air-conditioned but still-stale and body-warmed air greeted her.

The sound of the door slamming shut on defective hydraulics was lost in the endlessly echoing audio jumble of Deniece Williams, who was inspiring a ragtag cluster of puffing females into uneven Prussian calisthenics thinly disguised as "dance." Leotarded cellulite jiggled, bunched, and loosened while Ginger shouted out the count as if recently escaped from an army boot camp.

A few of the women looked as if they might be having fun, watching Ginger's tireless and precise movements and taking energy from them. But most of the others looked as if they had just eaten a Big Jeff's Jiffy Burger and were suffering the inevitable gastric results. Working at the restaurant thirty-four hours a week was all the workout Sarah wanted.

"Two, three, four, streeetch!" Ginger was yelling, utterly in her element. But after three minutes of this, even Deniece Williams became exhausted, and the tape ran out.

The sudden hush as the PA system hissed softly was quickly filled with a chorus of groans. Ginger, barely winded, surveyed her troops with a D.I.'s grimace and asked, "Now, didn't that feel great?"

Extremely enthusiastic mutters of half-verbalized obscenities wafted back at her.

"Let's think positive or next time I'll play the FM version."

Muted laughter rebounded limply off the mirrored walls.

In the locker room Sarah sat alongside Ginger as she finished slipping into her tight-fitting slacks and sweater.

"Same name, huh? Mondo bizarro," she was saying sympathetically.

"Yeah, exactly the same," Sarah said, her eyes defocused on the gray lockers before her, her hands absently twisting the wires leading from Ginger's Walkman to the lightweight headphones.

Ginger faced Sarah with a sort of *Night of the Living Dead* expression, then launched into a fairly good theramin impression, making eerie glissando notes waver from deep in her throat. *Dooooo-weeee-do-waaaaa*.

She whispered urgently into Sarah's ear with clipped precision, "There's a signpost up ahead . . ."

Sarah forced herself not to smile. Ginger was relentless, leering like a looney corpse inches from Sarah's face, saying, "Sarah Connor thought she was going home after a long hard day, but little did she know she was crossing over into the—"

"Okay, okay."

"Always knew you'd make the news, Connor." Ginger retrieved the cassette player and headphones before Sarah knotted the cord.

Sarah caught Ginger's eyes and said, "It made me feel funny, almost as if, you know, as if I were dead."

"How's it feel? I mean, warm enough to wear a bikini?"

"It made me think—"

"Dangerous ground for you."

"Come on, Ginger."

"Sorry. And so . . ."

"Well, I was just wondering, if it had been me who died, would anything I've done up to now really matter? I mean, what difference would it make if I were alive or dead?"

Ginger narrowed her eyes at Sarah. "Serious question?"

Sarah nodded. Ginger pondered.

"Well, you've managed to pay your half of the rent regularly. That's an accomplishment."

Sarah shot back, "You're as sensitive as a fire hydrant." Then Ginger had to give in, putting her arm around Sarah's shoulder, surrendering completely, saying, "You've managed to be my good friend." Ginger beamed at Sarah and quipped, "Come on, let's get the hell out of here. You're breaking my heart."

The girls stopped off in the weight room to say hello to Matt. Ginger walked up to him, openly eyeing a younger man he was instructing on the bench press.

"You're not breathing right, and shift your grip like— Oh, hi, Ginger . . . Let me show you." Matt replaced the barrel-chested youth on the bench and began easily moving the weights up and down, up and down.

Miffed at the abundance of attention he was lavishing on her, Ginger reached around the back of the weights and waited for Matt to let them down in mid-pump, then rapidly moved the selection pin down sixty pounds.

Matt powered up for the next lift and lunged. His eyes nearly bulged out of their sockets, but he got the weights up. Then he let out a deep breath and lowered them back. "Thanks, Ginger."

Ginger wasn't quite finished. She slipped her arm around the young man's waist and gave him a frank once-over. "What's this wimp been teaching you? Sleep therapy? Look at this guy, Matt. You should take lessons from him."

Ginger faced Matt and pounded ineffectually at his stone-hard stomach. "I thought so, soft as spaghetti." Then she pinched, or rather tried to pinch, the pack of muscles on his arm. "Shriveled bi's. Shamefully mushy ab. Disgraceful." She turned back to the beginning-to-get-embarrassed young man whose smaller body was much less defined than Matt's. "This guy works at it—know what I mean?"

That was the end as far as Matt was concerned. He growled and lunged for Ginger. Before she could twist away, he lifted her up over his head as if she were a barbell. "Hello, Ginger. Have a rough day?" he asked blithely.

"Give me a kiss," Ginger said sweetly. Matt promptly lowered her and obediently complied.

Ginger pinched his reddened cheeks and said in a squeaking falsetto, "You're so adorable, Bunky."

A few of the nearby weight lifters guffawed and chorused, "Bunky?"

Sarah stepped up. "Hi, Matt."

Matt nodded. Ginger planted a sloppy, noisy kiss on his neck, leaving a bright red mark there.

As Ginger was occupied with Matt, Sarah went to the water fountain in the corner of the room for a drink. A tall weight lifter with dark, curly hair and the Look raised up from the spigot and nodded to her. "Hi. I've seen you around before. You're cute. Cute I remember. I'm Marco."

Ginger stepped back, shaking her head, watching Sarah go rapidly through confusion, embarrassment, and sudden interest.

"Uh, hi. I'm Sarah."

She stretched her hand out, and Marco leaned down and kissed it. This she wasn't ready for.

She quickly withdrew her hand, self-consciously wiping it on the back of her shorts. Marco wasn't finished. He leaned close and murmured into her ear, "If you're not busy tonight, I'd like to show you a good time."

Before Sarah could summon up a witty rebuke, Ginger stepped up to Marco and casually hooked a finger over the top of his gym shorts, pulling them out. She glanced contemptuously down into the darkness there. Shaking her head with disappointment, she faced Sarah and said, "You're wasting your time. Let's go."

She grabbed Sarah by the arm before she could react and pulled her out the door, giving her a last glimpse, as the door closed, of Marco standing there speechless.

Ginger was grinning in triumph, satisfied with herself for successfully bringing off two mutually exclusive female arts at the same time, the Territorial Claim and the General Taunt.

Sarah turned to Ginger and said, "Gee, thanks. In another ten seconds I might have had to handle him myself."

Missing the semiserious tone in Sarah's voice, Ginger laughed heartily and answered, "I'll bet you would. Save yourself for Mr. Porsche tonight."


**Rampart District**
**LAPD**
**6:31 P.M.**

Edward Theodore Traxler cautiously stepped out of the coffee room into the hectic foot traffic in the main hallway of the LAPD Burglary-Homicide Division.

A big man, black, in his forties, and solid as a monolith, he was carefully balancing a hot Styrofoam cup between two fingers and weaving through the obstacle course like a bear on roller skates. He dodged a snarling handcuffed prisoner and headed for the safety of the right-hand wall. *Made it,* he thought, *without spilling a drop*.

He was doing his famous "compulsive-neurotic" feat of wonder; chewing gum, smoking a cigarette, and sipping coffee all at once.

"Hey, Ed." Traxler heard Sgt. Hal Vukovich calling out to him. He turned and waited for his lean, jaded partner to catch up.

Vukovich was slightly out of breath. He had been hunting all over the station for his boss. He trotted up to

Traxler and slapped a commiserating hand on his shoulder. Traxler winced; burning hot coffee spilled onto his wrist. Vukovich nodded toward the two files in his hand and flicked his eyebrows up, as if to say, "Wait till you see this one. It's so sick it ain't even funny." He handed Traxler one of the folders and opened the door to their office.

Traxler grudgingly set down the now half-empty cup—most of it was on his sleeve—and slipped a pair of bifocals onto the bridge of his nose. Inside the manila folder was a technicolor eight-by-ten Forensic Unit photo showing the upper torso of a woman lying on her apartment floor and wearing all the blood that was supposed to be inside of her.

"What have you got here?" Traxler asked, impatiently tapping the photo. Vukovich perched himself on the edge of Traxler's coffee-stained desk.

"Dead girl," he said, involuntarily smiling—the kind of nervous-reflex smile you get when nothing is funny at all.

"I can see that."

The smile died. Traxler waited and stared at the dead woman in his hand. He'd seen a lot of photos like these. They were always nasty but not particularly unusual.

Vukovich lit an unfiltered Camel and began. "Sarah Helene Connor. Thirty-five. Shot six times at less than ten feet. Large-caliber weapon . . ."

"You know, these do work," Traxler said, pointing to his glasses.

Vukovich silently handed him another manila folder. "What's this?"

"Dead girl two," Vukovich said, as though it explained the whole story, "sent over from the Valley Division this afternoon."

Traxler gazed at the bloody, bullet-riddled corpse of another woman. Well, she was certainly dead. But that didn't seem to explain much.

"I'm sure there's a point to all this," Traxler said, feigning infinite patience.

Vukovich solemnly got up from the desk and pulled the victim-information sheet from beneath the photo. He held it up in front of Traxler's glasses.

"Look at the name, Ed."

Traxler glanced at it impatiently. He paused. *What?* Then he looked back and read it again—slowly.

"Sarah Anne Connor. Is this right?" Traxler asked. Vukovich nodded his head. Traxler still wasn't convinced that this was not some elaborate manifestation of his partner's bizarre sense of humor. He waited for the wink of the eye and smile that would tell him the joke was over.

But Vukovich wasn't smiling.

"You're kidding?" Traxler asked incredulously. His partner quietly shook his head. This wasn't any fun, even for him.

"There's more, Ed," he said soberly.

Vukovich dug deeper into the file and pulled out two other photos. Close-ups of the victim's left legs, the translucent white skin pulled evenly back, like a hideous candy wrapper, revealing the nasty red-and-white secrets inside. There was something supremely disturbing about the incisions. They were precisely straight and even. And perfectly identical on both women. Perfectly. As if they had been turned out on a production line. Traxler felt anger waking up from its room in his brain and coming to view the carnage with him. What kind of shit was this for one person to do to another?

The two detectives stood there, huddled together in the scalloped light from the venetian blind—monks conferring in hushed tones at the grave of sensibility.

"Slit from ankle to knee, both of them. Same incision, left leg only. Same MO," Vukovich said unnecessarily. Then the nervous smile flashed and died again. "Too fucking weird," he added.

Traxler just stared at the photographs, then slipped them back into the manila folders and tossed them on his desk. It was going to be a long night.

Vukovich shook his head in disgust as a new thought occurred to him. "The press is gonna be short strokin' it all over this one," he said.

Traxler nodded, popping a fresh stick of Wrigley's into his mouth. "A one-day pattern killer," he said, seeing the headline floating in the air in front of him. He opened his desk drawer and hunted futilely for the aspirin, trying to beat the headache he knew was coming. It wasn't there. Shit.

Vukovich got to his feet and slowly walked across the room. He grabbed the near-empty bottle of Tylenol from the top of Traxler's file cabinet and tossed it to him.

"I hate the weird ones," he muttered.

**Palms District**
**656 Jasmine St.**
**6:57 P.M.**

They were girding their loins for battle, crammed together in the apartment's one little bathroom after jostling one another in and out of the shower. Ginger, fighting hard for mirror space, was in her hip-length nylon robe, while Sarah wore cotton briefs and a Jetsons T-shirt seven sizes too big. Their images in the mirror were diffuse with deodorant spray and hair set. Their weapons were lined up on the sink top: mascara, blush, eye-shadow pencil, eyebrow brush. Ginger was now spreading hot-gloss pink lipstick across her mouth.

Ginger noticed Sarah's struggle with the eye liner and valiantly came to her aid. The effect was startling. She didn't look all that bad. Not at all.

Her good deed done, Ginger went back to her own ministrations, slipping on the Walkman headphones, inverted under her chin so she could work on her hair. She fingered the volume until there was a 120-decibel rock concert battering her eardrums.

Sarah could hear every beat, even from where she stood, and said, "Ginger, you're going to go deaf."

"What?" Ginger shouted, her legs beginning to pump to the music.

Sarah got the cord from her curling iron tangled in Ginger's headphone wire and accidentally ripped them off her neck. "Sorry," Sarah said. As they were extricating their appliances from the tangle, Ginger asked, "So tell me about this mystery guy."

"His name is Stan Morsky. I met him at work. He studies film at USC and his father's a television producer. And yes, he drives a new black Porsche."

Ginger mock drooled, then wanted to know what he looked like.

"A little strange. Like a cross between Tom Cruise and . . . Pee Wee Herman."

That got a hearty laugh from Ginger. "But the Porsche looks good, eh?" she offered.

"Ginger," Sarah answered, "Hitler had a Porsche, too."

"Yeah? I bet he didn't have a sun roof."

The phone rang again, and Sarah went to answer it. Ginger slipped the headphones back on and drove the volume up to the threshold of pain, undulating to the steady backbeat.

Sarah picked up the receiver and said "Hello."

It was a man. He was wheezing in a low guttural voice as if he were an asthmatic. He said, "First, I'm going to rip the buttons off your blouse, one by one. Then I'm gonna pull it off your shoulders and run my tongue along your neck. . . ."

Sarah was transfixed. Her first lewd phone call. It was kinda neat. She listened as the man went on, his voice straining from keeping it so low. "Then I'm going to lick your bare, gleaming breasts. . . ."

Then Sarah experienced another disappointment to add to all the others she'd had that day. The lewd phone call wasn't intended for her, she began to realize as she recognized the caller's voice. It was for Ginger.

She put her hand over the mouthpiece and shouted for her roommate. "It's Matt!" He was still talking, unaware he was speaking to the wrong girl. She decided she could at least have a little fun with the situation. She listened some more.

"And then, when you're on the floor, I'll slowly pull

your jeans off inch by inch and lick your belly in circles, farther and farther down. Then I'll pull off your panties with my teeth. . . ."

Sarah's throat was bulging with a repressed laugh. She cleared it and tried to sound cross as she spoke into the phone. "Who is this?"

After a satisfying moment of shocked silence, Matt came back on the line, "Sarah? Oh . . . Sorry . . . Christ, I'm—"

Sarah let out the laughter.

". . . sorry. I thought it was—Uh, can I talk to Ginger?"

"Sure, Bunky," Sarah replied blithely.

As Ginger and Matt teased one another about what they planned to do to each other later that night, Sarah held up several blouses for Ginger's approval.

She nodded positively to all of them.

"You're a great help," Sarah groused.

Ginger cupped her hand over the mouthpiece, listening to Matt continue to murmur promises he couldn't possibly keep with one-half her mind while the other focused on Sarah's current mini-crises. "Okay," she finally whispered, "the beige one."

"I hate the beige one."

"Don't wear the beige one."

Sarah gathered up the blouses with exasperation and said, "I don't know why I'm bothering. This guy isn't worth all this hassle. He's just a human being who goes to the bathroom like anybody else. Anyway, we probably don't have a thing in common. He probably likes Barry Manilow or Twisted Sister, or something."

Ginger was doubled over as Sarah stormed out.

A moment later, Sarah stuck her head back in. "So you think the beige one, eh?"

A short time later, the girls sauntered into the living room to wait for their respective dates. Sarah began searching for Pugsly, who had nosed the plastic top off his terrarium and gone exploring for bugs without permission.

Ginger sat on the couch and broke out her nail file while continuing her private concert on the headphones. Her eye was caught, however, by the message light blinking on the answering machine. She had turned it on after she hung up with Matt so she and Sarah could finish getting dressed.

"Probably your mother," Ginger said as she bent over to punch the playback button.

It was.

Sarah half listened as her mother droned on about forgetting to ask her to bring a recipe for sausage lasagna with her when she came up Sunday: evidently Sarah's mother had not heard the news report about the murder of Sarah Anne Connor. She was grateful that she didn't have to call her back and explain. Sarah wanted to get Pugsly back into his terrarium before she left. She finally located him atop the bookcase near the window. As she lifted him into her arms, crooning to him soothingly as if he were a cat or a small dog, Ginger made a pained noise and said, "Disgusting. Reptophilia. Really nauseating."

Then the answering machine clicked onto another message.

"Hi, Sarah," the machine said cheerfully with AM-radio DJ enthusiasm. "This is Stan Morsky. Look, uh, something's come up, and it looks like I won't be able to make it tonight. I just can't get out of it. Look, I'm really sorry. I promise I'll make it up to you. Maybe next week sometime, huh? I'll call you soon. 'Bye."

Sarah just stood there cradling the lizard.

Ginger was infuriated. "That bum. I'll break his kneecaps. So what if he has a Porsche? He can't do this to you. It's Friday night, for Christ's sake."

It occurred to Sarah that she had been secretly expecting this. Not only because the day seemed sculpted by powerful, unseen hands to end on this final little disaster but because Stan had really made the date for tonight in a very casual way. He must have been so enthused about it he simply forgot, and when eight o'clock started coming around, he yanked this pathetic nonexcuse out of his

. . . Porsche. The sinking feeling of rejection still hit her hard. Reflexively, she tried to cover, the way Ginger would. "Well, I'll live," she said. But it came out a sigh rather than sarcastic.

She looked down at Pugsly and his watery, membranous eyes. "At least Pugsly still loves me." She bent down to plant a gentle kiss on the creature's snout. The lizard's only response was to blink in its patient endurance of human affection.

Sarah quickly got out of her skirt and blouse. She was going to take the makeup off when she decided in growing anger and defiance not to waste it. She slipped into jeans, boots, and sweatshirt, then grabbed her jacket. After making a quick check in her purse for finances, she announced to Ginger that she was going to a movie, one she had wanted to see for a long time and had to catch before it went away. She groped in her memory for a title and threw one out, but she could see by the expression on Ginger's face that she wasn't being believed. Sarah certainly didn't want to sit around watching TV, trying to drown out the sounds Matt and Ginger would be making in the next room when they got back from dinner.

"Look, I'll see you later. You and Matt have a good time."

Sarah was looking down, checking her purse for keys, and didn't see the powerfully built figure loom in front of her. He walked right up to her like a slab of shadowed steel and reached out.

Sarah looked up and jerked as he enveloped her in his arm, growling out a wheezy "Come here, little girl!"

She punched his shoulder ineffectually. "Damn it, Matt!"

He grinned down at her in a lecherous but somehow big-brotherly way. She started to walk off, but he grabbed her and slobbered a big wet kiss onto her cheek, letting her go off with a half smile battling its way onto her lips.

The underground parking garage was dark, lit intermittently by cold pools from overhead bare bulbs. The light over her Honda was out. Typical, she thought. Her footsteps echoed ominously. The place was nearly empty. Most of the tenants were out partying already.

She kneeled by the scooter and fumbled with the combination lock. Then she stopped. Had there been a sound? She scanned the interior. Six cars and a motorcycle. She could barely see one of the cars parked in a dark spot near the exit. Must have been an echo of her own actions.

Thoughts of Theresa Saldana and Sal Mineo slithered up her spine and roosted on the back of her neck. She hurriedly stowed the chain and hopped on the Honda. Now that would be a dumb way to die. Murdered in your own parking garage. And considering *this* day . . . She shivered and zipped up her jacket, then got the scooter started. The engine whirred reassuringly.

She relaxed and gripped the handlebars. The newscast that afternoon had started her thinking about her own mortality, about how insignificant her own death would be. "Sarah Jeanette Connor, waitress, dead at age nineteen." Another name on the tube, without impact or meaning for anyone, well forgotten before the college basketball scores came on. She knew the thought had been lurking around her all evening, feeding her usual apprehension about the empty parking structure, heightening it to irrational fear. A sense of being watched, scrutinized by a malevolent presence, welled up.

She rode off the kickstand and putted slowly down toward the cars. As she passed the dusty gray sedan, she looked in and saw that there was no one there. When she reached the apron, she paused, checking for cross traffic. If she had looked back, she would have seen someone sitting up in the front seat, slipping his scarred hands on the wheel.

Kyle Reese.

When she had come out of the security gate at exactly 20:19 hours, his eyes had locked on her and registered the target. Sarah Jeanette Connor. Just like the picture. Right on time. It was she. He knew that. And yet he didn't quite believe it. Conflicting emotions churned in his chest, and he had to force himself to take his eyes off her and duck down before she saw him. He heard the scooter start up and move past and felt certain she could hear the sledgehammer blows of his heart crashing loudly in his ears.

When he sat up, she was about to turn right. He fumbled with the wires to get his own engine started. Letting duty take over, his trembling hands steadied as he focused his thoughts in a spiral down to only what was necessary to complete the mission. Target. Follow. Intercept. When she rode into the street, he was not too far behind.

## LAPD
## Rampart Division
## 7:44 P.M.

As soon as Traxler opened the conference-room door, the crowd of reporters in the hallway descended on him in a storm of video lights and jabbering voices. There were about twenty of them, mostly local newspaper stringers. There was also an Eyewitness News minicam crew aggressively pushing through for the *picture*.

Traxler gazed at them with distaste, then prepared to run through the gauntlet to the safety of his office, eight feet away.

He charged into the mass of reporters, shouting, "No comment," even before he heard the first question. He hated these scenes. They had nothing to do with the work he was trained for except that they usually made it worse. He looked at the bobbing and weaving faces in front of him. No dignity in those faces at all. God, he hated reporters.

The Eyewitness News reporter, no more than a male model with a microphone, stepped in front of Traxler, blocking his path. The minicam was already rolling. Traxler stopped and fixed his eyes on the little bastard. He recognized him from the tube. An asshole. The reporter smiled back for an instant, then jumped into his serious-hero-journalist bit.

"Lieutenant, are you aware that these two killings

occurred in the same order as their listing in the phone book?" he asked in tones that seemed to suggest that Traxler might actually be that one last human being on earth who didn't already know. *Of course I know, you stupid shitbag.*

"No comment," Traxler replied expressionlessly, shoving the reporter to the side and continuing forward.

The barrage of voices went up again, all ignoring each other, each trying to drown the others out. Finally, as always, the babble of the many died away to the momentary victory of one.

"Come on! Play fair, lieutenant. We gotta make a living, too," the voice cried, echoing the sentiments of its brothers.

Such was a moment that Traxler never ignored. He stopped, his hand on the doorknob, and turned to face the crowd. He looked at them and took a breath, as though he were struck by the undeniable logic of what had just been uttered. A hush fell over the gathering. Their eyes were glued to him. Here was the story.

"You see this?" Traxler said, pointing to the door. "This is my office. I live here. Drop by any time."

He was safely inside before the newsmen could make a last futile attempt at his attention.

The voices went away as Traxler slammed the door, shaking his head in disgust. *Good door,* he thought. Almost soundproof.

Vukovich looked from the file spread before him on his desk and smiled sympathetically. They had been camped out there all evening. It made even taking a leak a major drama.

Traxler spit out the used-up piece of gum and unwrapped a new one. He glanced at his partner, who seemed engrossed in the details of the eight-by-ten glossy gore he held in his fingertips. They didn't speak. Like an old married couple, they had become comfortable in each other's presence and didn't feel the need to fill the space between them with words unless there was something of import to be discussed.

Or unless they were bored.

Traxler lit a cigarette and opened his desk drawer. He searched through the confusion until he found the aspirin and dumped a handful of them into his palm. He took a long drag from his Pall Mall and reached for the cup of coffee. He swirled the contents. A greasy film had collected on the surface. Traxler contemplated it for a second. Fresh coffee was down the hall. That would mean going out again. *Screw it,* he thought, and popped the aspirin into his mouth and raised the cup.

He was thinking about the third Sarah Connor. She was an elusive one. They had been trying to reach her all evening. Nowhere. He was afraid that she was lying on a floor somewhere, right now, with her leg zipped open and her brains blown out. He had gotten a copy of her driver's license photo from the DMV and had been staring at it for a couple of hours, trying to read something into it. Or from it. But there was little in her face that suggested anything in particular. Like what kind of places she might hang out in or the kind of company she'd keep. Nothing.

"Did you reach her yet?"

"Connor?"

"Yeah."

"No. I keep getting an answering machine."

Traxler put down the coffee cup and started pacing, going over everything again in his mind. He hated the impotent feeling he was having to endure.

"Send a unit," he said.

Vukovich put down the file and sat up. He knew Traxler well enough to know what was coming. They'd done everything they could for the time being. He wished Ed would take up pot or meditation or masturbation. Anything that would calm him down a bit.

"I sent a unit," he replied. "No answer at the door, and the apartment manager's out."

But Traxler wasn't listening. "Call her," he said.

"I just called."

"Call her again," Traxler ordered.

Wearily, Vukovich picked up the phone and dialed. Traxler unwrapped another stick of Wrigley's, tossed it in with the first, and reached for his pack of cigarettes. *Empty. Shit.*

"Gimme a cigarette."

"You smoking 'em two at a time now?" Vukovich asked, pointing to the lit Pall Mall that Traxler was holding in his other hand. Traxler looked down as if he'd never seen it before in his life. Then he shrugged and took another puff.

"Same shit," Vukovich said, hanging up the phone. The sound of Ginger's chirpy recorded voice was cut off as the receiver slammed down. Vukovich looked over at his boss, who was sitting on the edge of the desk across the room, rubbing his temples, contemplating. He muttered something.

"What?" Vukovich asked.

Traxler raised his tired, bloodshot eyes. "I know what they're going to call it. I can hear it now." In an act of prescience he had seen the morning headline laid out before him. With disgust, Traxler ground the butt of his cigarette into the floor. "It's gonna be the goddam 'Phone Book Killer,'" he said with finality, and was lost in thought again.

Vukovich saw it, too.

"I hate the press cases," he said, "especially the weird press cases." He looked back down at the file, going over it for the umpteenth time. Hoping that he had missed something and knowing that he hadn't.

Suddenly, Traxler got up.

"Where you goin'?"

"To make a statement. Maybe we can make these assholes help us out for a change." Traxler was all focused energy again, straightening his tie and brushing the ashes from his coat. He was even smiling. "If they can get this on the tube by eleven, she may just call up." He took off his bifocals and slipped them into his pocket.

"How do I look?" he asked. Vukovich flicked his eyes over the lieutenant and shrugged. "Like shit, boss."

"Your mama," Traxler replied, smiling. Then he opened the door and stepped into Policeman Hell.

**Palms District**
**656 Jasmine**
**8:05 P.M.**

Upstairs Matt was delighting Ginger with his dexterity on the Walkman volume control. She undulated under him in time to the music pumping through the ever-present headphones into her ears.

All he had to do was support his own weight. Ginger and the music did the rest. This was nice. So nice he wasn't about to get up to answer the door. And as Ginger's movements began to create nuclear explosions all through his body, sending a Niagara of blood pumping past his ears, he could not hear the answering machine in the living room and the terse message from Detective Sergeant Vukovich. It was a serious, if excusable, oversight.

**Midtown Los Angeles**
**Stoker's Pizza Parlor**
**10:08 P.M.**

Sarah was watching a waitress wending her way uncertainly through a heaving mass of loudly laughing humanity toward her table. She knew how that felt. The waitress was small and mousy and doomed to drop the pizza intended for her if the rest of the night was to prove consistent with the day. Surprisingly, however, the nervy girl simply shoved aside a pack of rowdy teens, causing their heavy metal garb to jangle and clink, regained her balance, and lurched up to Sarah with a worn but honest smile.

The pizza parlor was full of people heavily into their own lives and seeming to have a pretty good time of it. Sarah had come here out of habit, hoping that perhaps Ginger and Matt might show up, as well. But they were probably having a rotten time with each other at home in bed.

Sarah returned the waitress's smile knowingly, giving her an "I know how it feels" look.

By the time the pizza she had ordered came into focus, she realized they had given her anchovies. She'd asked for mushrooms. Sarah sighed. She felt a little safer here. The neighborhood was familiar to her, and she had come to Stoker's many times with Matt and Ginger.

Earlier she had strayed into unfamiliar terrain—the Picwood Theatre. She had gone there simply because it was the first cinema she came to. It was a Burt Reynolds film. The kind in which he wore his toupee. The good-old-boy car-chase comedies with nonfunny outtakes at the end. Not the truly warm and funny, romantic kind he made in which he did not wear a hairpiece. She stayed through the whole picture, but she wasn't watching.

She didn't see the scruffy, wild-eyed man sitting two rows behind her. And she didn't notice him follow her to the parking lot and wait until she got on her scooter before starting his car and prowling after.

She'd had enough on her mind.

Suddenly, she heard her name called and looked around to see where it came from, hoping it was Matt. But it was the TV over the back of the bar. A newscaster was saying her name in that self-important, stentorian tone they always use.

*Oh, no,* Sarah thought, *he must be talking about the murdered woman. Sarah Connor. Mother of two.* Then a dark, uncertain dread welled up from the little Sarahs who knew that she better get her ass over there.

She did, forgetting the watery beer and the cold, fishy pizza, pushing through the crowd until she was standing near the set between two men in varsity jackets. They began to watch her appreciatively, missing the fear in her eyes. Fear because the voice on the TV was saying, "Police are refusing to speculate on the apparent similarity between the shooting death of a Studio City woman earlier today and this almost-identical killing two hours ago of a Hancock Park resident with virtually the same name. Sarah

Helene Connor, a twenty-four-year-old legal secretary, was pronounced dead at the scene in her apartment . . ."

Somebody at the bar wanted the station changed. Sarah watched the bartender walk over and put his hand on the dial. "Leave it there!" she shouted, startling the men on either side of her and spilling one of their drinks. The bartender drew his hand back reflexively, then faced her with a puzzled look. Sarah realized she had screamed at the top of her lungs. It got results. And she would scream again if he tried to change the channel, but now the newscaster was smoothly wrapping up. "No connection between the two victims has been established as of yet. On a lighter note, there was cause for celebration today at the LA Zoo as . . ."

By now almost everyone sitting near was looking at her as if she were bananas. Sarah backed away, blinking in shock and listening very intently to those little voices inside her as they cried out warnings.

She found a pay phone and clutched at the directory. Some of the pages were missing, but she found the one with her name. There was Sarah Anne Connor. Then Sarah Helene Connor. Then there was her name.

Then there was none. Isn't that how it went?

Three pretty Sarahs, all in a row. Right, Connor? Right.

The beer in her stomach was boiling. It was doing forward rolls with a double backflip, and she had to get to the restroom fast.

When she got to the stall, it was occupied. She wanted desperately to laugh. Instead, she splashed her face with icy water from the tap and then patted it away with a paper towel.

*I'm next*, she thought. *Yeah. Me.* Because that's the way this kind of day would end, isn't it? There was a maniac with a gun running around the city *looking for her.*

So this was how panic felt.

Sarah had been afraid a lot of times. Of falls. Of fire. Of being rejected. Abandoned. Sucked emotionally dry. Yeah, real scary stuff. Real important and completely puny when you considered that somebody had gotten away with two murders and you were supposed to be the third victim.

A loud clunk sent a shock wave of terror up her back and into her skull like a bolt of lightning, and she whipped around, lungs heaving, to see an old woman fumbling with the lock on the stall door. She walked past Sarah with a cautious look, probably thinking the poor girl was on some kind of bad trip. When the woman went out, the hum of the overhead fluorescent grew loud.

She rushed to the pay phone again and dropped two dimes in. Nothing. Then she noticed the hand-scrawled note taped to the side. "Out of order."

The bartender looked at her as if she might be on PCP when she asked where the hell a working phone was. She couldn't tell him that she was going to be murdered by a maniac who had a personal disdain for anyone with her name. She couldn't ask him for help. She wanted more than one person protecting her. She wanted an army. The police.

"There's a pay phone in Tech Noir a couple doors down."

"Outside?"

Sarah strode through the bustling customers and hesitated at the door. He could be anywhere. Waiting. Oh, god. He has her address. He could have followed her. He could be right on the other side of the—

She stood on the sidewalk, looking for Tech Noir. Whatever it was, she wanted to see it. She eyed the people strolling past. None of them looked lethal. But what does lethal look like?

*Like that.*

*That man over there. In the shadows across the street, wearing a long dark raincoat. Standing in a doorway, watching . . .*

*. . . me.*

He looked dirty and ragged, like a skid-row bum, only even at this distance he looked young. Young but rough, like sandpaper, like a razor strap, like—

No.

Sarah kicked herself into action, walking briskly away.

Would he follow? What would that mean? Coincidence? Paranoia? Or death?

She looked back. He was gone. Where?

She stopped, looking both ways as two tall black teenagers walked by, one bouncing to the rap music on his ghetto blaster, held like a water jug on his shoulder. When the music died down, Sarah realized she was in a peopleless pocket. There was nobody within yards of her, and she felt raw and naked and defenseless.

Then the dirty, wild-eyed man was crossing the street. In no hurry. Straight for her.

Sarah lurched forward again, something insane keeping her from breaking into a full run.

Then the radiation-red glow of a neon sign fell on her, and she looked up at Tech Noir.

It was a dance club. There was strobe light and thunder and chaos in there. Sarah could see and hear through the big vibrating plate-glass window. It was hard, metallic, angular lines and planes, geometry of New Wave, California style. Tech Noir. Dark technology. The place lived up to its name.

Sarah looked back at the man following her and gasped. He was only about ten yards away, looking into a dark storefront as if he wanted to buy what was inside. *Wait a minute, Sarah. Calm down.* Maybe this guy was just walking her way, an innocent victim of her nightmare. Maybe . . .

But then she shuddered with cold terror. He was looking at her now, and she could see the Look, so hard and all consuming that she became suddenly certain that he was the One.

People spilled out of Tech Noir, jostling her, and she spun around and ran in through the door before it closed.

The man walked on by, his stance stiff with what Sarah thought might be frustration.

He kept going down the sidewalk until Sarah couldn't see him anymore.

\* \* \*

Reese was amazed. She was just a girl. Like all these other sleek creatures of the past. She seemed to be walking in a dream of her own making, oblivious to the hundred sharply defined threats in her environment. Could this be Sarah Connor? The picture in his mind said Pos Ident. His instincts said different. But he wasn't here to think. He knew the time was coming when he could execute the primary, and he so badly wanted that.

Nothing was going to stop him.

He had sworn as much to John.

Then he sensed fear in her so strong it carried in the air like an electrical charge between them. She was going to run. He rapidly one eightied the street and crossed. His hand on the shotgun through the coat pocket.

She had scoped him now, and there was nothing to do but close in. When she ran into the building, he hesitated, looking up at the sign over the door and point checking the orders locked in his memory. It was all right. Keep going. So close. But he wanted to go for her now.

Break-off! Keep to the Plan, soldier.

Keep going!

Then . . . double back.

**Palms District
656 Jasmine
10:11 P.M.**

The policemen ordered to stake out the entrance to the apartments were discussing the Lakers game when the dispatcher ended the conversation. There was a two eleven on Venice Boulevard, and they were the nearest unit. They fired up the black-and-white Cruiser and roared away.

The sidewalks were bare of people. Once in a great while a car would pass. And then a man stepped out from the shadows of a eucalyptus tree directly across the street from 656 Jasmine.

He had been evaluating his alternatives and was about to move on the security forces in their vehicle when they suddenly sped away, which radically reduced the possibility of target impedance.

Terminator walked across the street and up to the mailboxes. His eyes rested on the box that read: G. Ventura/S. Connor.

There was a security gate made of half-inch solid wrought-iron bars. Penetrable, but the noise was counter-indicated this close to a possibly wary target.

In the distance he could see Sarah Connor's apartment on the second floor. He moved away, circling the building.

## Tech Noir
## 10:12 P.M.

Sarah was terrified of going back outside. Her Honda was parked several blocks away on the crowded streets. That man was out there. She faced a wire-mesh ticket booth and tried to be heard above the crashing wall of noise and failed. She tried again.

"I need to use your phone!"

The woman inside leaned her ear up to the grille, her spiky blue hair making her bland features punkish and cruel. This time she heard Sarah and indicated the pay phone on a pillar at the rear of the dance floor. Sarah started to move through the turnstile, but the bouncer lumbered up and blocked the way. The ticket woman yelled, "Four-fifty!"

In exasperation, Sarah dug in her purse and then threw the money into the booth.

Sarah stepped onto the serving area fringing the dance floor. The wire-mesh look was carried out there with the tables and chairs. And the long metal bar, with its steely sheen, added to the design motif of industrial chic, as did the open girder work in the ceiling, which created an erector-set ambience.

Massive guitar chords massaged her solar plexus as she pushed her way through the writhing humanity. A sweaty twenty-year-old with a shaved head lunged out of the shadows, hooked her arm, and tried to pull her onto the dance floor. In the strobing flashes of rainbow-colored light, she saw his face twisting and deforming into a hackles-raising imitation of a long-dead and picked-clean skull, the eyes so deep in shadow the sockets looked empty. For a half second she thought a tongue, not unlike Pugsly's, snaked out and jabbed her cheek, then rolled back into his mouth with a leathery snap. She yanked free and staggered back into a table, jarring the half-empty glasses there. She looked back at the twenty-year-old; his face had filled out as he stepped into better light. Swallowing her heart again, Sarah continued on toward the pay phone.

**Palms District
656 Jasmine
10:14 P.M.**

Matt was in a stupor, lolling on the balled-up sheets, his body drying in the cool breeze from the partly opened sliding-glass door at the far end of Ginger's bedroom. The curtains were buffeted by silent breezes. Ginger sat up and gave him a poke. He was out of it.

She slipped onto the carpet and donned her robe, found the headphones and the Walkman, and popped in a new tape.

As it rewound to the beginning, she padded down the hall in bare feet, gasping as her soles hit the cold kitchen tiles. She went up on her strong toes and hopped in a graceful ballet leap to the refrigerator, opening it. In the benign glow from inside she assembled lettuce, tomatoes, pickles, mayonnaise, chicken-spread, and Bermuda onion on the countertop. She was reaching into the cupboard for the bread when she heard the noise. It seemed to come from everywhere—a soft scraping sound not too far away. Ginger looked around in the pale light, seeing nothing. She groped on the bottom shelf and found the Roman Meal bread. Now for the milk . . .

There it was again. Closer now. Sharp scraping. And again, closer.

Ginger had nerves like titanium. Nothing fazed her. She was curious about the noise, that was all. But a loud clunk hit her ears and chased her heart and lungs all the way up her spinal cord to roost on her head. Then she realized the tape had rewound already and shut itself off, tripping a pop on her headphones. Titanium, all right. Now where did she put the mustard. Ahh, up there on top of the—

Something streaked at her in the darkness, and Ginger involuntarily yelled. Spice jars clattered over as Pugsly darted off the refrigerator, more startled than Ginger by their unexpected meeting. The iguana scurried along the countertop and brodied onto the tiled floor, then scratched and slid until it propelled itself onto the carpet in the hall and out into the living room, where it once again could be anywhere in the shadows.

"Yeah, Pugsly, better watch out," she called, "or I'll make a belt out of you." Stupid lizard.

Ginger put a hand to her throat. Wow. *Got the old pulse racing there. Nothing like a good jolt of adrenaline to fire up the appetite.* Exhaling raggedly, Ginger faced the pile of food and realized she had forgotten the Swiss cheese. Bending low to grope for it at the back of the refrigerator behind the coagulated jam and rock-hard peanut butter, Ginger remembered the music and punched it on. Prince and the Revolution thundered in her ears, moving her body with its tight, fast energy.

Light was playing in intermittent patterns on Matt's eyelids. The curtains were billowing out in a sudden increase of wind. He opened his eyes as the sound of faint clinking started from somewhere at the far end of the room. At first he saw nothing but the ceiling; then a human shape leaned into view, the big fist raised to strike. There was something that flashed in the hand. Matt's eyes went wide, and he reached down and yanked himself off the bed just an instant before the fist crashed into the pillow where his head had been. As he staggered back, trying to clear his vision, he saw feathers explode upward as the intruder pulled his hand out of the torn pillow. He had something in that hand. A razor blade or a small knife or—there were too many feathers, coming down in slow motion like dry snow.

He was slightly bigger than Matt and silent as a snake. Only the clink of the chains on his boots gave him away.

*Must have come in through the balcony door,* Matt thought, even as he spun and instinctively snatched a heavy brass lamp off the bedside table. Knocking away the shade and ripping the cord from the wall socket so that it sang through the air like a whip, he brandished the lamp as if it were a war ax, swinging the base in whizzing arcs.

"Don't make me bust you up, man," Matt yelled. Fear laced the bravado in his voice, a bravado formed more from outrage and adrenaline than courage. Matt looked from the glinting knife to the expressionless eyes and back to the knife. When the intruder took a step toward him, Matt put his 230 pounds behind a Reggie Jackson homer with the brass lamp. The base caught the shadowy figure full on the temple, and the concussion nearly tore it from Matt's hand, but the other merely rocked back as if from a playful slap and advanced on him.

Matt swung again, mightily, but Terminator simply shot out his arm and caught Matt's wrist in a grip like a sprung bear trap. Matt's view of the room suddenly spun out of control as Terminator lifted him by his wrist and flung him across the bed to the floor beyond. He rolled like a sack of concrete into a wooden dresser. He came up in a groggy crouch and went for the intruder with a cry of pure rage.

Ginger had located the Swiss cheese and was now nibbling on a piece of celery as she piled the "snack" into a carbohydrate tower of Babel. When Prince hit the third chorus of "Let's Go Crazy," she held the celery up like a microphone and howled along with him.

The man's face was dimly visible. The eyes were dull and lifeless, like a doll's, the jaw unmoving, the mouth a thin, flat line, like the readouts on a medical monitor of a dead man.

Matt had the intruder's forearm gripped in both his hands as he watched the knife descend closer to his throat.

## 102  THE TERMINATOR

It was one of those extendable-blade razor knifes with the points you can break off when they get dull to make a new blade, except it was extended all the way out like a straight razor. Matt's muscles bunched and leaped under his skin as he strained with all his strength against the other, but the arm continued to descend, like some piece of hydraulic equipment. Matt had never encountered such strength. Fear roared and howled through him.

He slammed his opponent sideways, snapping off the knife blade against the wall, only to be grasped around the throat by immensely powerful hands.

*Dead man—gonna be dead man. Got to break this hold. . . .*

Matt brought up his kneecap like a catapult, burying it into the intruder's abdomen. The knee sank in with a satisfying thud but then inexplicably smacked into a wall of muscle so hard it almost shattered Matt's kneecap. Then he was lifted as if he were an infant and tossed through the sliding-glass door. He fell flat on his back and sprawled there as the fragments of glass washed over him in tinkly shards.

Like a sputtering but still turning engine, Matt heaved himself to his feet. His ruined knee caved in, and he shifted weight to the good one, his pummeled body shiny with sweat and warm blood that came from a dozen lacerations.

Terminator was waiting, watching the man step through the broken window so slowly that he considered leaving the room and continuing his track of the target. Before he actually acted on that option, Matt bunched up his will and made his whole body a fist, then drove himself forward.

Terminator adjusted his position by eight centimeters and easily deflected the blow. Matt caromed off Terminator's shoulder into the full-length mirror on the closet door. Glass exploded in his face, and he felt a dozen knives slash his body. He sagged to the floor, fatally wounded, his lungs frozen between breaths, paralyzed by the shock of the blow and the sheer oppressive force of his opponent.

The room was running away from Matt, dwindling into

a colorless void. A massive weight grew like a reverse black hole in his chest. And Matt knew if he could get past that giant knot of pain, it would be okay. He would be dead.

The remembered sound of Ginger's laugh echoed in his fading consciousness like a slowing tape loop, and he barely felt the iron fingers closing out his life.

Ginger grabbed the glass of milk and the triple-decker sandwich and adjusted the headphones before leaving the kitchen. As she walked into the hall, she thought she heard a sharp, sudden crunch, as if something were breaking. Pugsly? That lizard was getting positively psychotic.

But when she peered into the living room, she saw Pugsly playing statue inside the terrarium. Everything looked okay in there. Maybe it was the neighbors having another fight.

There it was again, a loud thump followed by a— Ginger shook her head suddenly, and the headphones slipped onto her shoulders. Now it was quiet. No, someone was . . . groaning? Ginger smiled with growing excitement. Now what was Matt up to? That little adorable devil.

She stood in front of the door to the bedroom, trying to balance the plate on her arm so she could have one free hand to open it, wanting to break in on Matt doing something hopefully lewd. But before she could manage this feat, the door exploded outward and showered her legs with splinters and blood. Matt had just been shoved through as if he were a battering ram. Ginger dropped the plate and the glass, splashing her legs with the chilled milk. Her hands groped in front of her face in a disconnected undulation, her spread-open fingers slicing the air between her eyes and Matt's utterly broken body. Matt was dead. Her Matt was gone.

Something in that room had just killed him.

She dropped her hands and stopped breathing. A figure strode to the door and looked past the body of his defeated opponent to the girl. Terminator paused to sharply etch the details of her features in his brain. She fit target configuration. His hand went to the .45 in his coat. He pushed on the door, but it was weighted with Matt's corpse, which was draped over what was left of it.

Ginger turned and started to run, the soles of her feet shredding over the broken glass as she put all her weight into a desperate pivot. She didn't feel the hot blood geysering out of the cuts as she lifted her right leg and launched herself down the hall.

Terminator wrenched the door open, tearing it off its hinges, and came into the hall.

Ginger sprinted like a champ at full throttle, her lungs pulling in thick clots of air and burning it off for power. She clutched at the living-room doorframe and careened out of the hall just as Terminator was triangulating on her back, lowering the red dot of the laser sight until it crossed her shoulder; then she was in the other room.

There was a volcano of abject terror erupting in Ginger's chest. The door. That was her salvation, she suddenly knew. Not God, not fate, not anything or anyone but that door, that exit from this vile and cruel sickness that was behind her now, grinning and aiming that gun and pulling the trigger, *and fuck you, I'm almost there*! Then Ginger was punched in the back by a rocket ship traveling at the speed of light and vaporizing half of her left lung as it tore through her torso.

As she was falling—it seemed as if she would never hit the floor—she heard the sound of the shot that had hit her. Then another missile struck her, this time in the kidney, the thick flesh capturing the bullet and holding it until the momentum won out and it sped forward in a last vicious lunge to lodge in her lower abdomen. Then she hit the floor, and things got worse.

Terminator moved over her like a monument to death.

Ginger's hands scrabbled on the cold linoleum. It seemed wet under her as she slid forward. Even though her cheek lay pressed against the inane tile design, she felt an intense falling sensation. She heard heavy boots hit the linoleum floor behind her and stop alongside. She couldn't turn, but the figure loomed in her mind, as black and enigmatic as death itself. Fear vanished, replaced by a huge, outraged question mark. Why? Perhaps the answer would be on the Other Side.

Finally, she hoped it wouldn't be Sarah who found her. . . .

Terminator's finger squeezed the trigger. The hammer drove the pin into the primer cap, igniting the powder. Expanding gases drove the copper-and-lead projectile down the barrel, simultaneously jacking the next round into the chamber. The trigger was squeezed again, and the cycle repeated.

And again.

And again. And once more, emptying the pistol.


## Tech Noir
**10:14 P.M.**

Sarah dialed the police emergency line, expecting a reassuring, fatherly voice, full of action and concern, that would immediately dispatch a hundred racing squad cars to her rescue. Or, at the very least, would listen to her story, take charge of the situation, and tell her exactly what to do. What she got instead was a recording.

"You have reached the Los Angeles Police Department emergency number. All our lines are busy. If you need a police car sent out to you, please hold, and the next available . . ."

Sarah held. She didn't know what else to do. Keeping the phone pressed to her ear, she nervously peered around the corner into the crowded room. At least there were a lot of people here, she thought. If someone tried to grab her, one of the fifty guys out there would do something, wouldn't they? Right. Sure they would. Sarah craned her neck. So far there was no sign of the man in the raincoat.

His eyes were so spooky. *Oh, please,* she thought, *please let someone pick up the goddam phone.*

But they didn't. The line went dead. She held the phone away from her ear incredulously, then rapidly redialed the number and got a busy signal. This was not happening.

Ginger. It came up on her horizon like a sun. Call Ginger. And Matt. They'll come get her! Take her to the police.

The phone rang once, and then Ginger's voice came on. That stupid message. She must still be with Matt. All she could do was wait for the message to beep and then hope Ginger had the monitor on and her headphones off.

**Palms District
656 Jasmine
10:15 P.M.**

Terminator dropped the emptied magazine and reloaded. That the target was terminated became immediately clear. So he lowered the weapon and proceeded with the next phase of the operation. He leaned over Ginger's legs and used the knife to make a ruler-straight incision from her ankle to her knee. He didn't find what he was looking for. Ident neg.

Terminator began to consider his options. The phone rang. In one rapid, precise arc, he had brought the laser sight around and centered it on the phone. When Ginger's voice began speaking on the answering machine, he whipped the red dot up and held it rigidly on the new target. Almost instantly he lowered the weapon when he analyzed the source.

"Hi, there," Ginger gushed. "Ha, ha. Fooled you. You're talking to a machine, but don't be shy. Machines need love, too. Talk to it and Ginger, that's me, or Sarah will get back to you. Wait for the beep."

He was almost out the door when Sarah came on the monitor, her voice high and urgent, the fear there like bait for Terminator. He hesitated long enough to hear, "Ginger, this is Sarah. Pick up if you're there."

Terminator came back into the living room.

"I'm at this place on Pico Boulevard called Tech Noir.

I'm really scared. Somebody's following me. Uh, I hope that you play this back soon. I need you and Matt to come and pick me up . . . please!"

Then the machine fell silent.

Terminator considered his options and began to search the place in a rapid and logical sweep.

In thirty-seven seconds he found what he was looking for. A dresser drawer, and in it was a West Los Angeles College student identification card. There was a picture on the face, and below that, a name: Sarah Connor. Terminator focused on the picture, the features locking into his memory. He would know her by sight now.

Sirens began to wail in the distance. Terminator tossed the ID card aside and picked up something that had lain beneath it: a telephone/address book.

The sirens were multiplying now, doppeling in the night, growing louder, converging. . . .

Terminator had no time to study the book. Pocketing it, he strode to the balcony and climbed down into the street to continue his work.

The only things he left alive in the apartment were a potted plant and Pugsly. The iguana was cowering atop the bookcase, peering through a slit in the curtains as the figure of the man disappeared into the shadows outside.

**Tech Noir**
**10:24 P.M.**

Sarah had finally gotten through to a human being. They explained that she needed to contact Lt. Ed Traxler and gave her the division to call. Almost in tears but doggedly hanging on, she fed in more coins and dialed the number. Then, insanely, she was talking to another operator, who punched her into hold again. The moment ballooned into an unending limbo of fruitless existence.

## LAPD
## Rampart Division
## 10:28 P.M.

Eight miles away, Ed Traxler was just coming through the door with his twenty-seventh cup of coffee when Vukovich, slouching in his chair, reached over and picked up the ringing phone. "Homicide," the lean sergeant tonelessly announced. Then he sat up and anxiously spun around to his boss. "It's her, Ed."

Traxler snatched the phone away. "Sarah Connor? This is Lieutenant Traxler."

Sarah was nearly at the point of tears. The fear that had gripped her for the last few minutes and the frustration of being shunted around and ignored by the very people who were supposed to protect her had begun to take its toll. She shouted desperately into the receiver.

"Look . . . Lieutenant, don't put me on hold and don't transfer me to another department."

His voice immediately took on a tone of concern. "Don't worry; I won't," he said. "Now just relax. Can you tell me where you are?"

For the first time all evening, Sarah felt that someone cared about what was happening to her. Traxler's reassuring voice was like a blanket she could pull up around her shoulders against the nightmare she was in.

"Where are you?" he repeated.

"I'm in a club," she said. "It's called uh . . . Tech Noir . . ."

"I know it," Traxler quickly replied. "On Pico."

"Yeah, but I don't want to leave," Sarah blurted out. "I think there's a guy following me."

"All right, listen, Ms. Connor," Traxler said, willing calm into his vocal chords. "And listen carefully. You're in a public place. You'll be safe till we get there."

"When are you coming?" Sarah asked anxiously.

"Now. We're on our way," Traxler rapidly replied. "Stay visible. Don't go outside or even to the restroom. I'll have a car there in a hot minute."

"Okay," Sarah replied. Then Traxler hung up.

**Tech Noir**
**10:31 P.M.**

There was a slight tremble of activity at the front of the club. It caused the heads of a few near the door to turn momentarily toward it. But the heads soon turned away, intimidated into an intense unconcern.

A man had walked through the front door. A big man in a tight gray jacket a size too small and motorcycle boots. He moved smoothly, looking into the faces of those gathered at the door, just flicking his eyes over them for an instant, then going on to the next. The face he wanted was not there.

He rolled past the ticket booth, and the woman inside leaned out and glared at the impassive back moving away.

"Hey!" she shouted to the bouncer. "That guy didn't pay."

"Hey, dude," the bouncer said, slapping a meaty hand on the big guy's shoulder.

Terminator didn't even turn around. He sent his left hand to the section of shoulder where he felt the clamping pressure, grasped the other man's hand, and squeezed. The bones collapsed with a snap. Then he released the mushy lump and kept going. No one heard the bouncer's gurgling scream, and if they did, they pretended not to.

He stepped onto the dance floor, scanning, pushing people away, like a hunter brushing aside branches overhanging a trail. The strobe lights did not affect the big man's vision. He simply ignored them and began a systematic search for one face.

Sarah laid the phone back in its cradle and turned around, already feeling the loss of Traxler's soothing voice. But it would be over soon. "I'll have a car there in a hot minute." The "authorities" were coming. To get her. She would be safe. She clung to that now, like a life preserver, and stepped away from the phone.

She went back to her table next to the dance floor. The menagerie of people floated around her like a dream. Faces distorted in laughter. Bodies flying in an orgasm of dance. A tall blonde in a skin-tight jumpsuit staggered toward a table, drunk, chatting wildly to her girl friends. People having fun. People standing right next to her, in a different world. But the man in the raincoat was not among them. *Maybe he got scared*, she thought. *Maybe he didn't want to be seen by all these people. Maybe he's waiting for me to leave. Maybe.* She tried not to think about it.

*I'll be all right*, Sarah told herself. *Just five minutes. That's all. Just five minutes.* She was starting to believe it. Then she glanced at the bar and didn't believe it anymore. He was sitting there, staring into the mirror in front of him. Right at her.

Reese glanced away as casually as possible, but inside his head the thoughts were racing around at sublight speed. She'd spotted him again. He realized he had really spooked the target now; he could tell by the look in her eyes. He may have blown the ambush. He wanted to go for her now. Break off! Keep to the plan, soldier. He would wait.

When Reese had seen Sarah go into the club, he continued past until he was sure she was well inside. Then he doubled back and scoped out the entrance. The vibrating bass chords of a New Wave band leaked through the front of the building. He had heard about places like this. They were called *nightclubs*. A name came to him from the dim recesses of his memory; Sinatra.

He felt the full blast of the driving, rhythmic music as soon as he opened the door. The sound was thunderous. Colored strobe lights turned the frenzied movement of pink-skinned men and women into a thing more sensed than seen. He started to walk past a bored young woman sitting behind a wire screen in a cage near the door when she reached out and grabbed his coat sleeve. Reese whirled around, eyes alert, hand flashing to the .38 in his pocket.

"Four fifty, space case," she demanded rapidly. Reese stared at her quizzically. Blue hair—this was new. Finally, the woman leaned toward him in an operatic display of condescension.

"Four dollars and fifty cents," she repeated in a slow, patronizing drawl. Reese reached into his pocket, randomly grabbed a large wad of crumpled bills, and shoved them at her. He didn't wait for his change.

Quickly, he reconned the frenzied indoor terrain—*plate-glass entrance, steel exit door at rear, two glass windows left wall, one right*—ignoring the stares he was drawing from the club's fragile inhabitants but checking out their faces. He found Sarah almost at once, huddled over a phone in the back. Reese ducked away as she turned, nervously looking over her shoulder.

The long row of stools before the mirrored bar offered the best vantage point for discreet observation. He took a seat in the center, and facing the mirror, scanned the room behind him. Perfect. Everyone was in the kill zone.

When Sarah sat down at her table, Reese was focused in on her. She was looking around, like a spooked animal that senses something dangerous in the air. Then their eyes locked in the mirror.

For a second, Sarah couldn't move. A frantic alarm was ringing in her brain. It was he. He was *here*. Right now. Watching her. As she stared into his disturbing eyes, she no longer believed that any one of fifty guys in the room would do anything at all to help her. She was suddenly, and completely, alone again. Trapped.

The spooky man in the raincoat coolly looked away. Sarah tried to calm herself. Lieutenant Traxler was coming. Was on his way. Just a few minutes—isn't that what he had said? *Just a few more minutes, honey,* she told herself. *Nothing's going to happen. It'll be all right. Please let him hurry!*

The undulating bodies kept shifting and moving in front of her, blocking her view of the man at the bar. He hadn't moved. He sat there like stone. Sarah glanced nervously at her watch as the music pounded on her fraying nerves.

Terminator was wading slowly, methodically, through

the crowd, moving his head in a continuous scan, first right, then left, adjusting up or down as the object required, cataloging, memory checking every face.

Sarah nervously reached for a Coke on the table before her, not even realizing it had been left by someone else. Her eyes were glued to the back of the raincoat sitting at the bar. Her fingers flicked the top of the can and knocked it off the table. Reflexively, Sarah bent down to retreive it just as the big man in the tight gray jacket approached her table.

Terminator's eyes darted over the empty table and chair. Nothing significant registered. He dismissed both objects and proceeded on.

As he turned away, Sarah sat up in her chair and put the can on the table.

When Terminator reached the far wall, he had not spotted the target. He was in the correct location. The information he had received was, he determined, highly reliable. Logically, she should be here. Perhaps he had missed her. He pivoted around to rescan the room. And there she was.

Reese's mouth had gone as dry as sand. Mechanically, he raised the glass of beer to his lips, allowing himself a sip to moisten them. From the corner of his left eye, he saw a big man move away from the wall in a straight-line path that intersected with Sarah, pushing people out of the way like so much tall grass and reaching with his right hand into the recesses of his jacket. *He* was the one. Reese *knew*. Slowly, he set down the beer and let his hand casually drift to the top button of his overcoat, unsnapping it. His fingers slid over the smooth metal of the Remington 870 and flicked the safety to off.

It was happening. It was now. In that microsecond of preaction, when the muscles tense—eager for the next microsecond—and the surge of adrenaline kicks the heart to a hundred BPMs, supercharging the whole system, Reese put his left hand on the edge of the chrome bar, for momentum, and his right around the handle of the Remington 870. Then he pushed, and the barstool spun around.

Sarah took a sip of her Coke and glanced at her watch. Three minutes had passed since she got off the phone with Lieutenant Traxler. When she looked up, someone was approaching her. A big scary-looking guy in a gray jacket, reaching for his wallet. He stopped right in front of her, towering—a mountain range that had just moved into the neighborhood.

Traxler? Sarah wondered. This wasn't the way she had pictured him at all. Not with eyes like that. This wasn't someone friendly. Then she realized, instinctively, that something bad was going to happen.

Terminator stood there, motionless, for a split second, staring intently down at her, his hand still reaching into the jacket. He checked her face against his memory and got a positive identification. He calculated possible alternatives. Then, in an instant, the .45 was out, cocked, and flashing in an arc that ended with the red dot of the laser sight centered perfectly on her forehead.

Sarah stared up in uncomprehending horror, looking directly into the barrel of the biggest, blackest hole in space that she had ever seen. The entire room seemed to fall away, and everything else with it.

Terminator's free hand pulled back the steel slide of the .45 and let it snap forward, chambering the first round. Despite the pounding din, the clack of the weapon seemed somehow to be the only sound in Sarah's ears.

A thousand thoughts screamed through her in a microsecond. *Oh, my god, this isn't a joke. It's real. I'm going to die right here, right in front of everybody. It wasn't the other guy at all. It was this one. Why is this happening? Why, why, why?*

Reese was still spinning on the barstool, his coat snapping back, the Remington coming up into both hands, when Terminator drew the .45 automatic. He had moved fast. So very fast. Faster than Reese had expected. *Is he a seven hundred or an eight hundred.* Reese hoped he was a seven. He was stepping away from the bar when a man and woman drifted into his path, eyes blossoming like flowers as they registered the barrel of a shotgun in the air before them. There were too many people in the way! *Goddamit!* He didn't think he was going to make it. Reese viciously shoved the man aside and plowed forward, knocking people away, bringing the Remington up and taking aim. The bystanders in front of him were scrambling now, sensing the movement, not understanding but getting the fuck out of the way, clearing a path for whatever it was this man was after. Reese was in midair when a window, framed by diving bodies, opened up before him. He squeezed the trigger, and the Remington roared.

A hundred and thirty-seven separate little universes instantly came to a frozen hush as the patrons reacted to the explosion of sound.

Reese had fired a hundredth of a second before Terminator squeezed the trigger. The shotgun blast would have taken off an ordinary man's arm. But all it did to his opponent was spoil his aim. The Remington's three-inch pattern of .00 buck punched into Terminator's elbow, spinning him around about twenty degrees.

Reese kept coming, stroking the slide back, then viciously slamming it forward, cycling another round into the weapon's chamber. Terminator started to turn toward the threat, adjusting priorities. Reese fired again, this time catching his target full in the chest. Despite his size and strength, Terminator began to stagger back under the impact.

Then everyone started to scream.

And again the whoosh of the slide coming back, then the smack of it slamming forward and another explosion of fire as Reese continued on, intent, a juggernaut, his world reduced to the single, clear, unwavering goal of sending death into the big opponent.

Terminator tried to raise the .45 automatic as he was going back. Reese fired again, knocking him off balance. He saw that Terminator was falling now, the .45 aiming irrelevantly up at the ceiling.

Reese came abreast of Sarah's table. She was screaming and ducking back in her chair, not believing what was happening in front of her. Reese had one shell left in the shotgun and sent it slamming into the tumbling Terminator.

Terminator hit the floor like a building falling into the street. He lay very still on the polished tile. Unmoving. Not even a twitch. The front of his jacket was a shredded field of perfectly tight little patterns of holes, each of them oozing crimson, which rapidly soaked the front of his jacket. He looked very dead.

*He must have been a seven hundred,* Reese thought to himself. He stood there for a heartbeat, the adrenaline still pounding through him, making everything seem slower, feeling the rush, as if he were riding on top of the wave. No one in the room had moved in the six and a half seconds since the first shots went off. Now they were gaping in disbelief at the weird tableau before them. The song ended. The rhythmic rasp of the record going around, amplified moronically, echoed across the room.

Sarah stared in shock at the bloody body sprawled on the floor only six feet away. Then she looked up at the man in the raincoat who had put it there. He turned toward her. She saw only his eyes and the gleaming shotgun in his hands. He took a step toward her when something caught his attention.

And everyone else's, too. Terminator had opened his eyes. A tiny spasm ran down the length of his body. Then he smoothly rolled over onto his feet, crouching defensively, and slipped the UZI submachine gun from its De Santo shoulder rig beneath his jacket. He swung the weapon around, jerking back on the bolt, and took aim at Reese.

Reese rolled like a cat and slid out from the space he had occupied a second before as the first rounds from the UZI impacted against the corrugated stainless-steel bar, throwing chunks of metal into the air behind them.

Tech Noir exploded in an orgy of violence and crashing bodies. Everyone snapped out of the shock that had seized them and desperately ran, tripping, tumbling, toward the windows and doors. A lot of them weren't moving fast enough. A young woman, who'd been having a particularly bad night to begin with, passed in front of Reese just as he crossed behind her, going the other way. The UZI's 9-mm shell punched effortlessly through her rib cage.

Sarah leaped from her chair and jumped into the stream of racing arms and legs that hurtled toward the front of the club. She was just reacting now, like an animal, instinctively taking herself away from death.

Terminator was standing calmly in the center of the room. He saw Sarah running for the front of the club, surrounded by other patrons. He started to squeeze off another burst from the UZI when Reese caught his attention, moving toward the bar.

Reese dove over the top of the bar just as the UZI raked the polished metal barricade, starting low and traveling up, to the top and over, missing Reese's flying calves by inches, disintegrating the mirror behind. Glass shards expanded in a thousand different directions, showering the room and raining down on Reese's back as he hunched into a ball behind the bar.

Sarah was halfway to the front door when Terminator dismissed Reese from his mind and turned back to the primary target. He saw the top of her head bobbing in the stampeding crowd of terrified people.

He raised the UZI, extending it out in one hand, and sighted down the barrel as though it were a pistol. He waited until her head came up, then pulled the trigger.

The 9-mm rounds were screaming toward a point in the center of Sarah's wavy hair when the girl behind her selfishly tried to push her out of the way. She caught the bullets instead. They tore into the girl's back and pitched her forward, tripping Sarah and bringing them both down.

Behind the bar, Reese reached into his pocket, slamming shells into the Remington as fast as he could. *Faster, faster!* His hands were flying.

Sarah was pinned under the heavy dead-weight body. She looked back in horror as the huge murderous hulk advanced, steadily, calmly, almost casually, toward her. Sarah tried to pull herself free. The girl was too heavy. Sarah was frantic. She pushed and tugged with all her strength, but it was too late.

Terminator was moving in for the kill, dropping the spent magazine from the UZI, reaching for another one with his bloody hand and slamming it in—an island of slow, precise movement amid the confusion and panic. Then he was standing right over Sarah and taking aim at point-blank range.

Sarah stared up helplessly into his cold flat eyes. They held nothing but death. And it was all focused on her.

Suddenly the Remington exploded again. It caught Terminator in the shoulder and spun him completely around. Reese had fired in midair as he leaped from the back of one vinyl-covered booth to the next. He landed agilely and came up firing. He fired again—*Die, fucker!*—and stroked up another shell. The Remington kept exploding, one blast after another, brutally, savagely, unrelentingly, pushing Terminator backward, toward the plate-glass window. The fifth shot picked him up and threw him through it. It exploded outward in a cascade of tempered glass fragments.

Sarah rolled over in time to see the window open like a shimmering gate to accept the blasted body passing through it.

Terminator hit the sidewalk like a crashing jet, sliding along the pavement before coming to rest. Blood ran over every visible inch of his tattered clothing.

Reese picked up the UZI from the floor and examined it. No good. One of his shells had torn into the upper receiver. He tossed it away and looked down at Sarah. She might be going into shock, he thought. It was time to go.

He pulled the dead girl off and took Sarah's hand. She shrank away from him like a terrified animal. Then Reese glanced out the front window and realized things were worse than bad—it wasn't a seven hundred. Quickly, he kneeled down beside Sarah and took hold of her arm. His voice was full of urgency. "Come with me if you want to live," he said.

Sarah shook her head, resisting. Then she saw what Reese already knew. Outside the window, Terminator was rising, unsteadily, to his feet. Shards of glass ran off of him like water. She had never seen a dead man before. But Sarah knew they weren't supposed to stand up.

A lightning bolt of terror, greater than anything she could ever have imagined, pulsed through her. She stared, dumbfounded for a moment, at the smoking, bleeding tower of death rising up in front of her and fixing its cold eyes on her like a sentence.

"Oh, my god," she whispered.

"Come on!" Reese yanked Sarah to her feet, grabbed her hand, and clamped onto it, hard. She wasn't resisting him anymore. No matter that he was probably a murderous lunatic or that five minutes ago she had been cringing in fear at the thought of being in the same room with him. Now he was someone who wanted to take her away from the thing in the window, and when Reese pulled Sarah's hand, she was ready to go.

With Reese leading the way, they ran like hell toward the rear of the club, stumbling over the sprawled bodies of the two dancers who hadn't moved fast enough. The unmistakable rhythmic crash of the big man's feet thudded behind them.

Reese hit the kitchen door at full throttle, throwing it open with a crash and dragging Sarah through without slowing. The door at the far end of the cluttered kitchen was wide open, left that way by the Korean chef who had used it when he first heard the gunfire. Reese hauled Sarah through, then spun around and slammed it shut, throwing its bolt into place, then facing Sarah again and brutally pulling her on.

An instant later Terminator hit the door. The sheet metal buckled, and the hinges half jumped out of the frame, but the bolt held. The huge man took a step back and slammed into it again. This time the half-inch steel bolt bent as easily as a bobby pin, and Terminator followed into the corridor.

Reese and Sarah were already at the far end, racing toward the alley door. Sarah slipped, but Reese viciously yanked her back to her feet and kept moving.

The alley door flew open before them, and they spun out onto the dank asphalt. Sarah started to slow, running out of breath. Reese brutally slammed his open palm into her back and shoved her forward. "Keep moving!" he shouted.

They heard the pounding of Terminator's feet following over the glass-strewn ground.

They reached the first intersection of alleys at a dead run; Sarah was out of breath, clutching desperately to Reese. They turned the corner by careening off the far wall.

Running full out, Reese grabbed a shell from his pocket, letting go of Sarah's hand, and tried jamming it into the Remington. Sarah started to fall back. Reese roughly shoved her ahead. "Move, goddamit!" He slammed another shell into the magazine.

Behind them, Terminator spun around the corner and charged after, gaining ground. Sarah heard him coming up; somewhere inside her she found a few reserve ounces of energy and poured them into her legs. Shotgun shells clattered to the asphalt as Reese gave up reloading on the run. As Sarah came abreast of a gray LTD, the last car in the row, Reese smacked her on the back, pitching her face first into the rough gravel. Then, spinning around, he flung the LTD's door open and hunched down behind it, aiming the shotgun at the gas tank of a '67 Impala farther back. Just as Terminator was about to reach the Chevy, Reese fired.

The shot hit beside the gas tank beneath the rear of the car, striking sparks off a rear spring shackle. *Shit! One shell left. Steady down.* Terminator was abreast of the car, eating up distance in long, powerful strides. The angle was bad. Reese shifted the shotgun, lowering the buttstock almost to the ground. If this didn't work, Terminator would be sticking the empty rifle down his throat in about two seconds. He pulled the trigger. Red-hot pellets of .00 buck tore into the cold tank. It erupted in a tremendous explosion of expanding gas. The ball of flame instantly filled the space between the alley walls and then climbed up toward the night sky. Terminator slid to a stop before the living wall of heat and light. He knew his prey was safely on the other side and that he must act fast. For a microsecond he considered his options.

Reese didn't waste any time. He stuffed Sarah into the front seat of the gray LTD, then climbed over her to the driver's side and slammed the door shut. The fireball was still blocking the alley when Reese reached for the ignition wires and sparked the sedan's engine into life.

Suddenly, a silhouetted figure erupted from the flames and rocketed over the roof of the burning car. Terminator, his hair and clothes engulfed in flames, impacted onto the hood of Reese's LTD with a thunderous crash. Reese slammed the car into reverse and nailed the pedal to the floor. The tires smoked and screamed as the LTD began barreling backward down the alley. Sarah sat in open-mouthed shock; the man on the hood was staring directly into her eyes through the windshield and drawing back his fist.

Reese fought the wheel of the slewing car as Terminator brutally punched through the windshield. Exploding glass shot through the interior of the car. Sarah opened her eyes and saw the bloody hand emerging through the window, inching its way toward her throat. She screamed as Terminator's fingers grasped the front of her blouse and pulled her toward him. That hand was about to drag her over the dash and right through the window when the LTD cleared the alley and charged, tail first, onto Pico Boulevard.

Reese cranked the wheel hard, and the big sedan slewed sideways, all four tires smoking, then plowed across the street toward the far curb.

Officer Nick Delaney, who had just passed Crescent Heights, heading east on Pico, when he got the call to respond to a shooting at Tech Noir, was reaching for the patrol car's mike when he saw the LTD come barreling out of the alley. Some asshole was crouched on the hood, using it for a surfboard, which was weird enough, but the asshole was also on fire. He watched, amazed, as the sedan plowed broadside into a parked car and the smoking surfer sailed over the roof and smacked hard onto the sidewalk. DOA, Delaney knew instinctively. He locked brakes on his black-and-white cruiser and skidded to a nose-first halt at the curb. The LTD gunned its engine and one eightied in the street, then screamed down Pico, heading for the ocean.

Delaney was out of the car in a flash, shouting into the radio mike as he stared at the unmoving body on the sidewalk.

"This is one-L-nineteen. I've got a hit-and-run felony!" Trying to get a description of the rapidly disappearing sedan, he looked away from the inert smoking body. He didn't see it shudder, then slowly get to its feet and look around. When he finished calling in a description of Reese's car and finally did turn back, the vision he saw took a few years off his life. The big man was moving toward him. Delaney dropped the mike and reached for his service revolver. It never even left its holster. Terminator brutally slammed the door that Delaney was standing behind. The officer heard his right arm snap, and he knew something real bad was about to happen to him. *DOA*, he said to himself instinctively. In the next second, Terminator slammed the officer's head into the window and casually flung the lifeless body into the street. Then he slipped behind the wheel and pulled out into the street.

Ahead, on Pico, shooting past La Cienega, Sarah sat paralyzed in the LTD. Her face was bloodless. She began to shiver, ceasing to comprehend the events of the past few minutes or the roaring blur of the world just outside her window. The sedan was moving like a night demon now, without the headlights, and Reese pushed the accelerator till they were hurtling through the shadows at ninety miles an hour.

His eyes flicked to the mirror, then back to the road, then over his shoulder, then back again. Without glancing at Sarah, Reese shouted, "Hold on!" and threw the sedan into an expertly controlled slide around the corner of Oakhurst Avenue. He sprinted up to Whitworth and made a left, squirreling the LTD between a slow-moving Toyota and an oncoming pickup, then dove onto Rexford and power slid around the corner. The street was full of sluglike traffic, so without hesitation or the slightest concern, Reese vaulted the curb and raced along the sidewalk doing sixty.

Fortunately, there were no pedestrians.

In a single graceful, breathtaking, and utterly horrifying move, he shot directly from the sidewalk to the fast lane of Olympic Boulevard before anyone could react.

No one seemed to be following now. Probably no one could if they tried. He glanced at Sarah and realized she was slipping into shock.

"Are you injured?" he shouted in clipped military tones. "Are you shot?" No response. She stared blankly ahead. Reese reached over and ran his hand across her arms, legs, torso. He was direct, impersonal, like a medic in the field. He methodically searched for wounds. She seemed to be undamaged.

Sarah flinched. The vague sensation of being touched became clearer. She realized Reese's hand was all over her, and the resentment of this gross male violation energized her. She shoved Reese's hand away and reached for the door handle in a blind panic. It opened on a roaring blur.

Reese slammed her back into the seat and yanked the door shut. Then, without taking his eyes off the road, he slapped her face with the back of his hand. Hard. She sat completely still as her mind jolted back to rational consciousness. Then Reese spoke.

"Do exactly what I say. Exactly. Don't move unless I say. Don't make a sound unless I say," he ordered. "Do you understand?" With the speedometer registering 85 mph, he calmly reached over and locked her door, then fastened her seat belt, cinching it very tightly, with the same methodical movements as his body search. Sarah didn't answer, didn't nod, didn't move at all.

"Do you understand?" he repeated, shouting.

"Yes," Sarah replied, her voice cracking. "Please don't hurt me."

"I'm here to help you," he informed her. His voice was less menacing but still just as clipped and purposeful. "I'm Reese. Sergeant/Tech Com DN38416." There was a moment of clumsy silence. Then Reese did the only thing he could think of that second. Sarah stared numbly at his outstretched hand. With zero enthusiasm she automatically shook it.

"I'm assigned to protect you," Reese said. "You've been targeted for termination."

Fourteen blocks behind them, cruising smoothly through the late-night traffic was LAPD unit 1-L-19. Terminator scanned the street in an unbroken series of perfectly symmetrical sweeps. He listened to the babble of radio traffic, filtering out the irrelevant broadcasts, listening for anything about the stolen gray sedan. Finally, he heard what he'd been waiting for. "Suspect vehicle sighted on Motor at Pico, southbound," the dispatcher said. "Units one-A-twenty and one-A-seven, attempt to intercept. Unit one-L-nineteen, come in."

Having logged the unit number as it was spoken by the car's ex-owner, Terminator understood that the call would have to be answered. He replayed the few syllables he had recorded and stored at the time and digitally synthesized a reply. In a voice Officer Delaney's mother would not suspect, Terminator calmly said, "This is one-L-nineteen. Westbound on Olympic approaching Overland." He wasn't, really. He was now racing down Pico back toward Motor. And Sarah.

"This isn't happening," Sarah said, trying to make it real by saying it. "It's a mistake. I haven't done anything."

"No. Not yet," Reese replied, "but you will." He fixed his eyes on hers. "It's very important that you live." Sarah looked away and did everything she could to shut it all out, but every time she opened her eyes, she was still in the LTD.

"It isn't true. That man. He was dead. How could he get back up after you—"

"Not a man," Reese cut in. "A machine. A Terminator. Cyberdyne Systems. Eight hundred series. Model one zero one."

"A machine?" Sarah repeated incredulously. "Like a robot?"

"Not a robot. A cyborg." Reese craned his neck around at two tiny pairs of headlights far back down the street behind them. "*Cyb*ernetic *org*anism."

"No!" Sarah shouted. "He was bleeding."

"Just a second," Reese said. "Keep your head down."

The pairs of headlights had jumped up the street and were now closing in on them. The first LAPD cruiser pulled alongside and flicked on its searchlight, illuminating the battered sedan, checking it out, searing into the faces of Reese and Sarah.

Reese caved in the cruiser's door panel. The officer tried to swerve away, but at sixty miles an hour a car just doesn't behave itself. The cruiser skidded sideways, then swapped ends and flew through a newsstand into a parked cab. End of story.

Sarah stared at the dead LAPD cruiser, then hunched down in the seat and tried to make herself disappear.

Reese jumped into a tiny alley near Glendon. The other police cruiser piled in after, inches from the LTD's bumper, and together the two cars raced down the narrow dark corridor. Sparks flew like fireworks as they scraped the walls and slalomed around protruding dumpsters. As Reese pulled his foot from the accelerator and stood on the brake, the officer jumped on the cruiser's brake, but in doing so, he flinched and turned the wheel. Just a fraction of an inch. Enough to catch the cruiser's front fender in the brick wall. Instantly, the car went sideways and jammed itself in the narrow alley.

Reese squealed to a halt, threw the LTD into reverse, and gunned the motor, hurling the battered sedan backward toward the black-and-white cruiser. He slammed into the cruiser at forty miles an hour, making it a permanent part of the alley. Then Reese raced back onto Pico.

Sarah sat up and glanced around, then over at Reese, still digesting the last piece of information he had given her. They were running from a cyborg, huh?

Sarah took a good look at him. He was unshaved and filthy. He had an intense, dangerous look—more than likely insane.

Reese glided the sedan off of the street and into the driveway of a four-story parking complex on Colby. The LTD's grille sliced through the painted wooden bar blocking the entrance, and the sedan climbed onto the first level.

It was quiet now. Sarah looked away from Reese, afraid of the new calmness around them and what he might do in it. The image of that big man, the man who *had* to be dead, getting up and running after them had burned itself forever onto the back of her eyelids. No matter how crazy the guy sitting next to her was, at least he wasn't *that man*.

Reese was still ultra-alert, cruising through the aisles of parked cars very cautiously. In the distance he could hear the blare of sirens as dozens of police cars raced around hunting for him.

He had to get her out of the city. Somewhere safe. It would be better if she helped him. If she understood. He could protect her against her will if necessary. But it would be better the other way.

Reese looked over at Sarah. Just being this close to her made all the machinery inside of him churn to a crashing halt. For a second, he couldn't speak. He was amazed that her presence, right there on the seat next to him, was such a casual fact. There she was. And so normal. And scared. Somehow it hadn't occurred to him that she would be scared.

He turned down another aisle, staying on the lower level, and continued prowling the lot, looking for signs of trouble and finding none.

"All right, listen," he said calmly, still scanning from right to left. "Terminator's an infiltration unit. Part man. Part machine." His intensity suggested he was telling her, unfortunately, the absolute truth. Sarah turned to him and listened.

"Underneath," he went on, "it's a hyperalloy combat chassis. Microprocessor controlled. Fully armored. Very tough. But outside it's living, human tissue. Flesh, skin, hair . . . blood. All grown for the cyborgs . . ." He was talking faster now. She heard the words, but they didn't make sense. His explanation was only making things worse.

"Look, Reese. I know you want to help, but—" Sarah said, trying to make her voice sound soothing so he wouldn't get angry. It didn't work.

"Pay attention!" he shouted, snapping his head around toward her.

"The six hundred series had rubber skin. We nailed them easy. But the eight hundreds are new. They look human. Sweat, bad breath, everything. Touch it, you'd feel warmth. But by then you'd already be dead. Very hard to spot. All those people back there—" Reese hesitated, caught up in a sidebar emotion. "I had to wait till he moved on you before I zeroed him. I didn't know what he looked like."

Sarah realized he was referring to the people who were injured or killed at Tech Noir. His manner had gone uncertain when he spoke of them. Then he hardened at a thought he spoke aloud. "They would have died in the war, anyway."

He wasn't making any sense now, and she thought he might be spinning into utter madness right before her eyes. *War? What war? And sweating cyborgs?*

Sarah was shaking her head. "I'm not stupid, you know. They can't make things like that yet."

Reese nodded. "No," he said, "not yet. Not for about forty years."

*Don't scream,* said one of the little Sarahs in her abused mind.

"I've got to ditch this car," Reese said in a distracted voice. He nosed the LTD into an empty parking space.

Something really bad was undeniably happening. A horror story on two feet was stomping around the city, obsessed with killing her. Even if Reese didn't have both oars in the water, he had saved her life. She wanted to believe him. She really did. But this was too much.

"You're saying it's from the future?" Sarah finally asked, almost unable to form the word.

"One possible future from your point of view," Reese said haltingly, as if groping with a concept even he didn't have the words for. "I don't know tech stuff," he added a little defensively.

"And you're from the future, too?"

"That's right."

"Right," Sarah answered. She decided that not only were his oars out of the water; he didn't even have a boat. A second later she had unlocked the passenger door, flipped up the handle, and was halfway out before Reese could react. He lunged and caught her arm, squeezing until the skin turned white, and pulled her, kicking and struggling, back into the LTD.

In a panic, Sarah reverted to her animal instincts. With all her strength, she sunk her teeth into his wrist. She bit down hard, as hard as she could, but Reese's grip didn't slacken.

Slowly, he reached across her and pulled the passenger door shut. Sarah glanced up, her teeth still clamped on, and looked into Reese's face. There was no reaction there. No pain. No anger. Nothing. Quietly, she drew back. There was blood on her tongue. She looked down at his wrist. A little rivulet of it ran from the crescent-shaped puncture marks she had left there.

"Cyborgs don't feel pain," Reese said coldly. "I do. Don't . . . do that . . . again."

"Please," Sarah quietly implored, "just let me go."

Reese shook his head. It was not going well. Not well at all.

"Listen," he said, trying again, his voice slow, determined, intense. "Understand. That Terminator is out there. It can't be reasoned with. It can't be bargained with. It doesn't feel pity or remorse or fear." He leaned very close to her face. She could feel his warm breath on her skin. His words hammered themselves into Sarah's head.

"And it absolutely will not stop. Ever. Until you are dead."

Sarah knew that all he had just said was four-star bullshit. But what about the technicolor bloodbath she'd just been whisked away from? What about the man who had leaped through the fire, his demon-dead eyes fixed on her as he reached down, hair flaming, punched through the window, and tried to pluck her out of the car? *Her.* Little Sarah Connor. And what about those other Sarah Connors someone had been offing all day? There had to be a rational, wonderfully reasonable explanation for all this madness. But logic and rationalism were out the window and far down the block, abandoning her. Because . . .

*. . . It was dead and calmly got to its feet . . .*

Think, Sarah; come up with an answer.

*. . . oozing blood from bullet holes . . .*

Because if you can't,

*. . . it came after . . .*

you'll go insane yourself—

*. . . after you, Sarah.*

How could it do that unless—unless . . . Maybe Reese wasn't as crazy as he looked.

Sarah slumped back into the seat. There was a moment of silence; then she spoke very softly.

"Can you stop it?"

"Maybe," Reese said. "With these weapons, I don't know."

**Westwood
11:03 P.M.**

Unit 1-L-19 slowly cruised up Sepulveda and turned right onto Massachusetts. Terminator sat impassively behind the wheel, focusing its twin infrared eye cameras into the darkened shadows of the near-empty street. The cyborg quickly scrutinized the interiors of the cars parked along the curb, flicking its vision into each one, methodically probing for the target.

Suddenly, the abstract pattern of static coming from the unit's radio was broken by the calm female voice of the police dispatcher.

"All units, all units. Suspect vehicle located at parking garage at Colby and La Grange . . ."

Instantly, Terminator slewed the police cruiser around in the middle of the street, narrowly missing a red Volkswagen bug loaded with five very stoned teenagers on their way home from a Van Halen concert.

The VW jumped the curb and smacked headfirst into an old oak, crumpling the front of the VW like tinfoil.

"Shit!" the bug's young driver shouted. He saw the police cruiser tearing away and shouted again, pounding the dash in a fury of frustration. Cops were always fucking you up, and now they had fucked up his beloved bug.

### West LA
### 11:06 P.M.

Reese raised the butt of his Remington 870 and slammed it against the ignition assembly on the Eldorado's steering column. When the lock cylinder broke free on the third impact, he slid the mechanism out between two fingers and examined it. Simple. He'd done this kind of thing many times. Reese dropped the key-actuated cylinder onto the floor and reinserted the starter switch into the hole. Giving it a half twist clockwise brought the rewarding sound of the starter. When it caught, Reese revved the big engine of the Cadillac Eldorado and let it idle, then shut it off. He turned to Sarah. She sat scrunched below the dash level, seemingly dwarfed by the large front seat. They'd left the LTD and skulked together among the parked cars until Reese found this one.

Below them, on the first level, half a dozen LAPD cruisers swarmed like bees around the abandoned gray LTD. Two black-and-white cruisers went up the ramp to the second level, prowling slowly, flashing their searchlights around, methodically checking every vehicle, moving steadily toward the top of the parking structure.

No one noticed when unit 1-L-19, driven by someone who was obviously not a cop, glided into the structure and joined with the other cruisers in the search.

Reese motioned for Sarah to stay down below the dash as a pair of headlights swept across the row of cars near them.

A searchlight stabbed through the windshield of the Eldorado. As Reese and Sarah ducked lower, their positions brought them closer together in a forced intimacy neither one addressed. She felt the warmth of his cheek and the uncomfortable scratch of his beard. The low rumble of the cruiser's engine sounded close, as if it were in the back seat. They huddled together, very still. Then the searchlight flicked away, and the sound of the engine faded.

"Why me?" Sarah asked quietly. "Why does it want me?"

Reese's lips were almost pressed into her ear. When he spoke, his voice was a hoarse whisper. Where to start was the problem. Forty years of history that hadn't happened yet.

"There's so much," he said.

"Tell me."

Reese retreated a few inches—the smell of her hair was distracting him. "There was a war a few years from now. Nuclear." He gestured with his hand to include the car, the city, the world. "All this is gone. Everything—just gone."

Sarah knew by the intensity of his eyes that it was true. It had happened. Or it would. The sheer finality of the word "gone," combined with Reese's resigned shrug, hit her like a cinder block in the gut.

Sarah didn't move. Reese went on, his voice clipped, tinged with a sharp military edge. "There were survivors. Here. There. Nobody knew who started it." Reese looked over at her. "It was the machines," he said.

"I don't understand."

"Defense Network computer. New. Powerful. Hooked into everything—missiles, defense industry, weapons design, the works—trusted to run it all. They say it got smart; a new order of intelligence. Then it saw all people as a threat, not just the ones on the other side. Decided our fate in a microsecond. Extermination."

Reese paused again. He glanced back over at Sarah. Into her eyes. When he spoke again, his voice had lost its edge. A subtle shift had taken place, from dispassionate briefing to personal memory.

"I didn't see the war. I was born after. In the ruins. Grew up there. Starving. Hiding from H-Ks."

"The what?" Sarah asked in a hushed whisper.

"Hunter-Killers. Patrol machines. Built in automated factories. Most of us were rounded up by the machines or machine collaborators and put in camps for orderly disposal."

Reese pushed back the sleeve of his jacket all the way to the elbow and held his forearm up to Sarah's eyes. She stared in amazement at what she saw there—a ten-digit number etched on the skin. Beneath the digits was a pattern of lines, like the supermarket-package bar codes. She tentatively reached out and touched it with her finger.

"Burned in by laser scan," Reese said flatly. This man, huddled beside her, had lived and walked in some unimaginable purgatory. A nightmare place where machines marked you for easy identification like a can of chili as part of the Final Solution for homo sapiens.

"Some of us were kept alive . . . to work. Loading bodies. The disposal units ran night and day. We were that close to going out forever." He held up thumb and forefinger, with only the tiniest space between them.

Reese rolled down his sleeve and began feeding shells into the Remington.

"There came a man . . . a great man," he added reverently, "who kept us alive. Ragged and half starving but alive. We got stronger, and he taught us to fight. To storm the wire of the camps. To smash those metal motherfuckers into junk. He turned it around and brought us back from the brink."

His voice became a hoarse whisper cracking with emotion. She watched him trying to form the words.

"His name is Connor. John Connor. Your *son*, Sarah. Your unborn son."

Sarah's mind slammed the gates shut, and his last sentence was echoing around in her brain like an explosion. It wasn't true. It couldn't be true. She realized that his hands had wandered to her shoulders and had been holding on to them very tightly for some time. When she opened her eyes, he was still gazing at her. There was so much pain etched in his face, the emotion in his eyes so real, that

Sarah felt drawn inexorably toward believing him. But this! It had no meaning or substance for her. Being suddenly the mother of a son who existed in another time and place had no reality. Even the tide of apocalyptic images, civilization shattered, cities crumbling into rivers of molten concrete, even that seemed more reasonable somehow by comparison.

Her brain just stalled out, nosed over and dropped. She could only stare at him, mouth open.

"No," Sarah said finally. "It's not true. It can't be . . ."

The rear window of the Eldorado went nova white.

Reese spun around and stared into the searchlight for a microsecond. It was coming from a police cruiser. But the thing behind the wheel was not a member of the LAPD. Reese shoved Sarah flat, cramming her into the tiny space under the dash as the rear window exploded inward from the horrendous blast of Terminator's SPAS-12.

Frantically, Reese started the Cadillac and at the same instant throttled the huge engine to life as another shotgun blast tore through the rear window, shearing away the remaining shards. Stray pellets whizzed around the inside of the car, bouncing off the windshield.

Sarah threw her arms over her head, closed her eyes, and screamed. Reese slammed the Eldorado into gear, and the car lurched out of its parking space.

Terminator anticipated the target's movements almost as fast as Reese could think them up. The black-and-white cruiser roared forward, racing along the next aisle parallel to Reese's machine.

They were charging toward the exit, almost side-by-side, on opposite lanes, separated by a row of parked cars. Reese was driving blind, keeping his head below the level of the window. He was up to forty-five miles an hour and gaining speed. The ramp loomed closer and closer. The sound of eight screaming tires and the redline roar of two engines echoed wildly around the concrete walls.

Reese knew the ramp was only seconds away. He threw a quick scan over the top of the door and saw that

Terminator had pulled ahead, cleared the row of cars, and was now moving in a diagonal course toward him.

The barrel of Terminator's shotgun glided out of the police cruiser's open window, and Reese saw it pointing right at him. Instantly, he dropped back down, and the glass above his head disintegrated. Reese popped up and slammed the 870 barrel across the top of the windowsill next to Sarah, holding it like a pistol. The twelve-gauge went off three inches from her ear. The shot center punched Terminator's rear door, and Reese saw that the cyborg was stroking another round. He jerked the wheel, and the big car swerved with an echoing scream toward the cruiser.

Reese slammed the heavy Eldorado into Terminator's car; and both cars locked together, still hurtling toward the exit ramp.

The police cruiser, clipping the rear fender of a Chevy pickup truck, was yanked away from the Cadillac and sent spinning in place.

Every cop in the building heard the gunshots. Some even caught a glimpse of Reese as he flashed down the exit ramp and jumped onto Colby Avenue. They felt a slight sense of relief and pride when they saw, in the next second, one of their own boys, unit 1-L-19, right on his tail.

All sixteen squad cars quickly converged at the exit.

When the Eldorado hit the street, Reese was doing forty plus. One block later he was pushing eighty.

Sarah climbed out from under the dash and peered through the empty hole that used to be the rear window. She saw Terminator fishtailing out of the building, shooting back a comet's tail of sparks, and behind the cyborg, the real police—sirens blasting.

Soon Terminator was gaining speed, coming up alongside Sarah. Civilian cars around the charging pair lurched and slewed, trying to get the hell out of the way as the twin juggernauts weaved across all four lanes.

Another shotgun blast from Terminator's cruiser tore into the side of the Eldorado. Reese was doing his best E and E, escape and evade, but Terminator kept blowing holes in the armorlike door and body panels.

Finally, Reese just tired of being shot at. He grabbed the Remington from the floor.

"Drive!" he shouted at Sarah, then took his hands off the wheel and turned away. He stuck the shotgun out the open window, slammed it onto the roof of the Cadillac and dragged his body out the opening. Sarah stared at the wheel for a microsecond as the car roared along at eighty plus and then reflexively seized it in both hands. Reese had set the cruise control, and she couldn't find the switch, so she had no choice but to steer and hope for the best.

Reese, halfway out the window, was aiming the shotgun back across the roof of the car at their pursuer. Terminator swerved, staying tightly to the Eldorado as Sarah fought to control the hurtling machine.

The wind buffeted him as Reese lined up and fired. His first shot blew a hole in the police cruiser's windshield.

The second tore into the hood. Terminator didn't even slow down. The next shot went right into the driver's window, and the cyborg ducked its head, throwing the cruiser up against a cement freeway buttress, gliding along it like an electric train, tossing a wave of hot metal sparks into his wake.

Sarah realized with horror that they were not on a main street any longer. They were on a city utility road that ended in an enormous concrete wall. She shouted to Reese, but all she could see of him was from the waist down, and the wind tore her words away long before they reached his ears. The wall roared toward them.

Later she wouldn't even remember doing it, but she grabbed the shift lever and slammed it hard up into reverse with such force that she almost broke her wrist. Reese fired simultaneously as the transmission tore itself into junk and the car's drive wheels locked in a shrieking cloud of smoke.

Reese's shot shattered the windshield and drove Terminator back in the seat, blasted in the shoulder. Stunned for a split second, he shot past the Eldorado, his vision clearing in time to see the wall.

Sarah pulled Reese back inside and cranked the wheel right, sending them into a radical tire-smoking slide. The Eldorado ground to a halt a foot from the wall.

Terminator hit it head-on at eighty-two miles per hour. The police cruiser folded around the cyborg like a cheap accordion. Terminator's vision dropped out first. Then all the systems in its microprocessor went off line due to the horrific impact to its hardened chassis.

Sarah peered up over the doorframe and saw close to twenty LAPD cruisers pulled up in a semicircle. The officers were squatting down behind the shields of their open car doors, aiming an arsenal of pistols and shotguns at them.

Reese lunged for his Remington, but Sarah pushed him back, grabbing his arm.

"No, Reese! No! Don't," she shouted urgently, "they'll kill you."

He stared past her into the barrels of more weapons than he could hope to silence. Every instinct told him to move. To fight. Now. The last thing Reese wanted to do was give up Sarah to the authorities. He wondered if Terminator was dead—he couldn't see the wreck from where he was.

He looked back at Sarah. Her eyes were full of fear and concern. He was surprised when he realized the concern was for him.

"Please," she implored.

Slowly, Reese let go of his grip on the shotgun. Sarah quickly tossed it out the window. It clattered to the ground and lay still.

"All right, you in the Cadillac," an officer shouted, "I want to see your hands. *Now!*"

With resignation, Sgt. Kyle Reese raised his hands. A moment later they were roughly pulled from the car. As they were being handcuffed and led away, two officers approached what was left of unit 1-L-19.

"I don't believe it," one of them said. "It's empty."

*What does that mean*, Sarah wondered. She saw Reese whip around, suddenly resisting his captors, trying to get a look at the wreckage—to see for himself.

In his face was the answer Sarah needed—a grim tightening of the lips that told her it still wasn't over.

# DAY TWO

**LAPD**
**Rampart Division**
**1:06 A.M.**

Sarah gazed intently at the fabric covering the arm of the couch she was sitting on in Traxler's office. Dimly, she heard the foot traffic and chatter of telephones coming from the rest of the station. Objects in the room seemed to shimmer momentarily as another round of tears welled up and spilled over her lashes.

She did not want to think about what Lieutenant Traxler had told her an hour ago. But secretly she knew she would be thinking about it for the rest of her life.

Traxler walked in, precariously holding two cups of coffee. Behind him was another man. A fat man, balding and pink, whose eyes glittered with an unsettling, dispassionate scrutiny.

Traxler advanced slowly toward Sarah. He could see, even from across the room, her red-rimmed eyes and the look of shock that still hung about her.

"How are you doing, Sarah?"

Sarah made a small nod, trying not to look at anyone.

"Here, drink some of this," Traxler said.

She dutifully took a sip of coffee, then stared off into the middle distance.

"Lieutenant," she asked, her voice empty, "are you sure it's them?"

Now it was Traxler's turn to nod his head silently. Sarah looked into his eyes, searching for some sign that would tell her he had doubts.

"Maybe I should see the—the bodies. You know . . . maybe it's not—"

"They've already been identified." Traxler didn't like this part. Not at all. "There's no doubt," he added, as he always did.

Behind her eyes, in the CinemaScope window of her imagination, Sarah saw the brutalized bodies of Ginger and Matt, her only friends, "her family," lying in an ocean of blood on the living-room floor. They were gone. Horribly snatched away from her, forever. The full impact of that was finally settling over her, and now she felt a physical pain.

"Oh, God . . . Ginger . . . kiddo." Her voice sounded far away to her. "I'm so sorry."

Traxler grabbed the coffee cup from Sarah's hand as her arm sagged, threatening to dump the steaming contents over her knees.

"Sarah," he said gently, indicating the corpulent bald man near the door, "this is Dr. Silberman."

"Hi, Sarah," Silberman said in a friendly lilt that rang as hollow as a cheap bell. Sarah gazed at him through bleary eyes.

"I'd like you to tell him everything Reese said to you," Traxler went on. "Will you do that for me?"

"I guess so." Her voice was almost inaudible. "Are you a doctor?"

"Criminal psychologist," he answered. Sarah watched him bobbing there at the door and decided that she didn't like him at all. But he might know what he's talking about, she thought, and what she needed most right now was answers. She needed to know why her normal, quiet life had been blasted off its hinges. Why Ginger and Matt were lying dead on the living-room floor. Why someone was trying to kill her. She needed to know if Reese could possibly be right, if it wasn't the random intrusion of insanity but really because of her.

"Is Reese crazy?" Sarah asked, her eyes intently searching Silberman's innocuous face.

"Well," he drawled in a detached voice, "that's what we're going to find out, isn't it?"

Reese's arms were drawn back tightly and handcuffed to the chair's rear legs. Before him was a simple wooden table on which sat a black plastic ashtray; beyond it, a large two-way mirror stared back at him from the wall.

The pain had been building up between Reese's shoulder blades for quite some time now. He didn't mind. In fact, he welcomed it. The pain was not excruciating, and it helped him focus his thoughts away from the questions he was being asked by the tall, lanky man who paced the floor.

Vukovich stopped directly behind the prisoner. He stared at the back of Reese's head, knowing he must be hurting now but seeing no strain in the neck muscles that would give the pain away. One tough son of a bitch, Vukovich thought. He slowly continued around the table until he was facing the sullen young man. There was no expression on his prisoner's face. None. Zip. That was a little weird. God, I really hate the weird ones, Vukovich thought.

"Okay, kid," he said, "let's take it from the top. How long have you known Sarah Jeanette Connor?" Reese stared at the wall behind Vukovich's head, counting the little holes in one of the tiles. There were 138 so far.

"Reese, Kyle A.," he repeated in a staccato monotone, "Sergeant Tech/Com DN38 . . ."

". . . 416," Vukovich said, finishing in unison.

"Okay, man. I know the fuckin' number already." He dropped into the chair opposite Reese and leaned across the table until he was inches from the young man's face.

"Let's cut the gung-ho shit. We know you're not military—there's no record of you with any branch of the service. There's no record of you anywhere . . . So far."

Vukovich lit a Camel. "I don't like that. Not at all. It

means we're going to have to spend a lot of time in this room, and when that happens, I get cranky."

Reese had been only half listening to Vukovich's rant. His mind was elsewhere. On the mission. On Sarah. He could see that these guys were going to fuck around until all they could do was bury her. That was not acceptable.

"Where's Sarah Connor?" Reese asked suddenly. It was the first time he'd said anything except to identify himself.

"Don't worry about her. Worry about you," Vukovich said in his best tough-guy voice. But it was obvious to both of them that the toughest guy in the room was handcuffed to a chair.

"Where . . . is . . . she?" Reese growled.

"She's safe."

"She's dead," Reese said flatly, and turned back to the tile behind Vukovich's head. Vukovich could sense that he'd just lost something, but he wasn't sure what it was. Anger took over his emotions.

"Listen, asshole—" he began. But he stopped abruptly as the door opened.

It was Silberman. The psychologist glanced at the two men in the room, feeling the hostility, and rubbed a smile onto his face.

"Are we having a nice time, gentlemen?" he asked, then glanced at Vukovich. "I'll take it from here, sergeant."

"He's all yours," Vukovich said in disgust, and sauntered out of the room.

Traxler was waiting for him in the hall.

"How did it go?" Traxler asked.

"Fuckin' hard case."

"Yeah?" Traxler replied, unsurprised. He popped another stick of gum in his mouth and lit a Pall Mall. "Let's see what happens."

They stepped into an adjoining room, which was dark and tiny as a closet. In the corner was an old videocassette recorder on a cart, hooked up to a camera aimed through the two-way mirror at Reese and Silberman. It was used to record confessions and statements, although with this Reese guy it would probably be a waste of tape. The two detectives stood before the mirror and began to watch the show.

Outwardly, Reese paid little attention to the fat man. *He must be in charge,* Reese thought, knowing that you never see the most important man in the chain of command first.

Silberman lumbered into the other chair. He took out a pack of Marlboro's and tamped the box loudly against the table three times, which was the signal to roll tape. Vukovich started the VCR.

"Reese, Kyle A.," he pondered aloud. "May I call you Kyle?"

Reese said nothing.

"I'm Dr. Peter Silberman." He paused, then smiled commiseratingly. "You've had a busy night. Can I get you anything?"

He offered Reese a cigarette, holding it up in front of his eyes. Nothing. Not even a blink. Interesting, Silberman thought. He shifted his gaze back to the report.

"I see you're a military man. Sergeant Tech/Com. Serial number DN38416 . . ."

"Don't patronize me, asshole!" Reese barked.

Silberman looked up quickly. There was a lot of anger in the kid's eyes. That may be the way.

"Okay. Let's start again. Everyone around here seems to think you're out of your fuckin' mind."

"That's their problem."

"No, stupid. That's your problem."

Reese tossed a little ball of hate at Silberman. *Good,* Silberman thought. "What do you expect?" he said. "Put yourself in their situation."

"I'm not in their situation," Reese replied evenly. "I'm in mine."

"All right," Silberman said reasonably, "convince me that they're wrong."

Reese turned away and began counting the holes in the tile again.

Silberman tried again. He'd try to work with some of the story the Connor girl had given him, maybe draw him out that way.

"Okay," he said, "let's talk about your mission. I'd say you blew it. In a few minutes she'll walk out of here. But not you. You're staying. You're out of the game." He paused and looked up at the sullen face staring past him. "You'd better give that some thought."

"What's the point?" Reese asked coldly.

"The point is, my friend, that you can't help her while you're tied to a chair."

Silberman could tell he was making progress. Working within the context of the kid's delusion was the key. He flashed a look of paternal concern across his face and leaned toward Reese.

"Talk to me," he said. "Maybe I can make them take the right precautions. If you help me, I can help you."

"You can't protect her," Reese announced flatly.

"And you can?"

Reese's face flushed red as he shifted his gaze back to the fat psychologist. Slowly the anger subsided into guilt. Reese realized that what the man had said was true—he had really fucked up. Silberman continued to pursue his quarry like a trained hawk.

"Hold back one fact and you may be risking her only chance. Help us."

Reese slowly nodded. Logically, he had to agree; if he could convince them, perhaps they would help him stop Terminator.

"I'll tell you what I can," he said, resigned.

"So. You're a soldier," Silberman said with a smile of victory. "Fighting for whom?"

"With the one thirty-second under Perry. From '21 to '27."

Silberman interrupted. He was getting excited. This was better than he had hoped for. "The *year* 2027?" he asked.

In the observation room, on the other side of the mirror, Traxler was deep in thought, trying to put all the pieces of the puzzle into some kind of order. Vukovich was just having a good time; this was like peeking into the girl's shower. "The *year* 2027?" they heard the psychologist ask over the monitor.

Traxler stopped chewing on his gum and leaned toward the glass. "This is fucking great!" Vukovich snorted.

Reese glanced into the mirror, where he knew he was being observed, then back at Silberman.

"Yes," he replied. "Up to the end of the Oregon and New Mexico offensives. Then assigned Recon/Security, last two years, under John Connor."

"And who was the enemy?" Silberman asked.

"Skynet. A computer defense system. Built for Sac-Norad by Cyberdyne Systems."

"I see." Silberman nodded gravely, scribbling notes. This was better than good, he was thinking. This was gold.

"It sent back an infiltration unit, a Terminator, to stop John Connor," Reese explained.

"From what?" Silberman asked.

"From being born."

Silberman scratched his cheek thoughtfully. He glanced down at the report and reviewed the fragmented pieces of the story that Sarah had given him.

"And this . . . computer, thinks it can win by killing the mother of its enemy. Killing *him*, in effect, before he is even conceived. A sort of retroactive abortion?"

"Yes."

Behind the mirror, Vukovich quietly laughed.

"That Silberman just cracks me up." Shaking his head in wonder, he turned to his pensive boss.

"He had this guy in here last week—set his Afghan on fire. Screwed it first, then set it on—"

"Shut up," Traxler grunted, unwrapping a new stick of gum. In the other room, Reese continued his story.

"It had no choice," he was saying. "The defense grid was smashed. We'd blown the main frames—we'd won. Taking out Connor then would have made no difference. Skynet had to wipe out his entire existence."

Reese paused. Silberman looked up from his notes, alarmed. *Don't stop*, he pleaded silently. But outwardly he smiled and gently said, "Go on."

"We captured the lab complex," Reese continued in a

tired voice, remembering the fleeting seconds of victory, "found the—whatever it's called—the time-displacement equipment.

"Terminator had already gone through. They sent me to intercept, then zeroed the whole complex."

"Then how are you supposed to get back?"

"I can't," Reese replied with quiet intensity. "Nobody goes home. Nobody else comes through. It's just him and me."

## Panama Hotel
## 1:09 A.M.

A shadow among shadows, Terminator climbed with slow, patient steps up the fire escape to his second-story window. It avoided using its disfunctioning right wrist until it could determine the full extent of damage it had sustained in the initial combat.

It had taken the cyborg nearly an hour to get from the site of the crash back to its hotel room.

It had moved on foot for the first couple of miles, allowing the systems to come fully on line in order to assess their condition. Aside from the wrist, there was almost total visual occlusion of the left eye. The eye itself seemed to be functioning properly. It was the surrounding tissue that was hindering performance.

Now Terminator pushed open the hotel-room window and slipped inside.

It quickly scanned the near-black interior. Nothing had been touched. No intruders. In one stride it was across the tiny cell and flicking on the single bare bulb above the grimy sink. In the full light it took a look at itself.

The eyebrows were gone, completely singed off. What remained of the hair was little more than charred stubble. The socket surrounding its left eye was a pulpy red mass of randomly attached shreds of flesh. Glass fragments were imbedded all around it. Seven gunshot wounds and lacerations covered the shoulders, chest, and arms, pulpy craters filled with congealed blood and 12-gauge pellets. Internal status readouts indicated that damage to the armored chasis beneath was superficial.

The only real problem was the wrist. A shotgun blast had torn through the exterior layer of skin and punched into the servo-actuated control system beneath.

Carefully, it laid out its tools on a folding table near the sink. The charred remains of the jacket were quickly stripped off and flung into the corner. Terminator took a seat and gingerly laid the damaged arm on the tabletop.

The arm looked bad. Much worse than it actually was. Blood flowed over and around the swiss-cheese remains of skin covering the wound.

Terminator was not disturbed. The term pain was irrelevant. Only functional impairment of combat effectiveness was of concern here. With an expression of mild concentration, it selected an X-Acto knife and nervelessly made a six-inch incision along the inside of the forearm. Tying the flaps of skin back with locking hemostats, it peered into the exposed cavity.

By wriggling its fingers, it could clearly see the problem. One of the control cables in the complex trunk of sheathed machinery and hydraulics had been severed.

The cyborg wiped away the blood, and using its good eye, began to patiently disassemble the damaged part with a jeweler's screwdriver. If Terminator had been programmed to hum, the picture would have been complete.

In a few moments, the cable was bypassed, function assigned to a redundant hydraulic system, and the incision sewn shut to keep the forearm skin from crudely shifting around. This would have led to premature tissue necrosis, gangrene, and an unacceptable social-attention index.

Standing above the fouled sink, Terminator examined the lacerated eye. The lens was fine. Vision impairment was due to the shredded flesh around it. Clearing it would not take long.

The X-Acto blade sunk into the gory socket and in a few smooth cuts scooped out the ruined sclera and cornea.

With a faint plop, it fell into the sink basin and slowly drifted through the water to the bottom, leaving an expanding pink trail.

Terminator dabbed at the socket, soaking up the excess blood. Now the chromelike alloy sphere was clearly visible, suspended within the metal socket by tiny servos, its high-resolution video tube glowing behind the concussion-proof lens. They were functioning acceptably. However, there was no way to easily explain away its radical appearance. But anyway, Terminator was not much of a talker.

It fished a pair of sunglasses from the small horde of clothes and equipment it had gathered and put them on. Its eye was barely visible beneath the dark shades, which were a wraparound design that even hid the damage from the side.

Terminator went to work on the chest and abdominal wounds, pulling the ventilated tissue closed over the dented carapace of its hyperalloy torso-chassis, then suturing it crudely with household thread. It had to dig around a bit in the interstices of the shoulder assembly, between the axial drive-motor housing and the clavicular trailing link. It got most of the shotgun pellets that were impeding the movement there. The muscle tissue was shredded and detached, but since it was merely a superficial camouflage and not actually responsible for locomotion, Terminator packed it back into the wound and sewed it shut with little regard for surgical deftness.

With a new T-shirt, a pair of leather gloves, and the collar of the black leather jacket turned up, the cyborg looked almost normal, if a little pale and gaunt.

Starting with the A's, Terminator rapidly dialed every police station in Los Angeles until it reached Rampart Division.

Now it was time to move out. The target was waiting. Terminator flipped the stained mattress to the floor and collected the required tools to complete the mission profile—the SPAS-12 auto-shotgun, a 5.56-mm AR-180 assault rifle, its sear pin filed for full auto, and a .38 special. Just the essentials.

With the grace of servomotor precision, Terminator hefted the weapons and disappeared out the window into the Los Angeles night.


**LAPD
Rampart Division
2:10 A.M.**

Sarah leaned forward, perched on the edge of a swiveling desk chair, and gazed at the image on the video monitor before her.

Traxler stood next to her. He was continually gauging her reaction. He wanted her to see this. It might trigger something she had forgotten to tell him.

Silberman reached over and turned up the volume on the black-and-white monitor.

"It's just him and me," Reese said from the video monitor.

"Why didn't you bring any weapons?" Silberman's recorded image asked, "something more advanced. Don't you have ray guns?"

"Ray guns," Vukovich repeated, chuckling. On the screen, Reese was not amused at all. He glared back defiantly. Silberman paused. "Come on," he said, "show me one *single* piece of future technology and we can settle this whole thing."

"You go naked . . . something to do with the field generated by a living organism. Nothing dead will go."

"Why?"

"I didn't build the fucking thing," Reese retorted. He was starting to lose it.

"Okay, okay. But this uh"—Silberman glanced down at his notes—"this cyborg . . . If it's metal, how—"

"Surrounded by living tissue."

"Of course," Silberman nodded understandingly on the video screen. The real Silberman got up from Traxler's desk and punched the pause button on the monitor. When he turned to Sarah and Traxler, his voice was self-congratulatory.

"This is great stuff," he babbled. "I could make a career out of this guy. You see how clever this part is? It doesn't require a shred of proof."

Sarah looked up at him, still unsure. Puzzled.

"Most paranoid delusions are intricate," he continued, "but this is brilliant." *And so am I,* he thought to himself as he restarted the tape.

"Why were the two other women killed?" the black-and-white Silberman asked.

"Most records were damaged or lost in the war," Reese said. "Skynet knew almost nothing about Connor's mother, because her file was incomplete. It knew her name and where she lived—just the city, not the address. Terminator was being systematic."

"What about the incisions in their legs?"

"It was the only physical identification left in her records. Sarah had a metal pin surgically implanted in her leg. What Skynet didn't know, what Terminator doesn't know, is that she doesn't have it yet. That's supposed to happen later."

"How do you know?"

"John told me."

"John Connor?" Silberman asked.

"Yes."

Silberman tapped his pencil on the pad, thinking, a tiny smile unconsciously on his lips. "You realize there's no physical proof of this, either."

"You've heard enough," Reese said, his voice with anger. "Decide. Now. Are you going to release me?"

"I'm afraid that's not up to me," Silberman answered, keeping his voice friendly and reasonable.

"Then why am I talking to you?" Reese started to stand, still handcuffed to the chair. "Who is in authority here?"

"I can help you." Silberman was trying to stay in control of the situation, and losing.

Reese was on his feet now, staring straight into the camera, right at Sarah, and shouting, "You still don't get it, do you? He'll find her. That's what he does. All he does . . ."

Sarah's eyes went wide. Traxler gestured to Silberman, who was closer to the monitor, to shut it off. But Silberman was watching the screen, fascinated by the performance there.

"You can't stop him. He'll wade through you, reach down her throat and pull her fucking heart out!"

Reese was trying to climb right through the monitor when Silberman snapped out of his reverie and hit the pause button, stopping him.

Sarah was transfixed by the desperate will etched in Reese's electronically frozen face. She was pale. So many questions were racing through her mind that she couldn't keep them straight.

"I don't have a pin in my leg," she said.

"Of course not," Traxler replied. "Reese is a very disturbed man."

Sarah wanted to believe that. She turned to the psychologist for a more professional opinion, one she could believe. "Is Reese crazy?" she asked.

"In technical terminology," Silberman answered, smiling, "he's a loon."

"But—" Sarah started to protest when Traxler cut her off. He handed her something that looked like an unpire's protective padding.

"Sarah, this is body armor. Our SWAT guys wear it. It'll stop a twelve-gauge round. This other individual must have had one under his coat."

She wanted to believe that was the explanation, but somehow it wasn't enough. "What about him punching through the windshield?"

Vukovich shrugged. "Probably on PCP. Broke every bone in his hand and won't feel it for hours. There was this guy once—"

Traxler cut him off by dumping the bulletproof vest into his hands. Dutifully, Vukovich shut up and sauntered away.

PCP? Sarah had read about people on drugs doing

incredible things in a berserk rage. *Maybe*, she thought. *That must be it*. It wasn't so much that she believed it but that she needed to believe it. And these guys seemed so certain. She felt suddenly gullible, with a hot flush of embarrassment at her own stupidity—to have been drawn into belief in that demented story of Reese's. But he had seemed so compelling and his account of the future so detailed. Even down to the tattoo on his arm. Self-inflicted, no doubt. *There are some five-star whackos out there*, she thought, *and I just found myself two of them*. Still, though she refused to address it, there remained a nagging background chatter of unvoiced doubts.

Traxler put a hand on Sarah's shoulder. "You're gonna be okay," he said, and despite his world-weary gruffness, Sarah sensed true concern.

"I called your mother and told her the situation. This hasn't hit the news yet, so she hasn't heard a thing about it."

"How did she sound?"

"Pretty good. She just said, 'I'm on my way,' and hung up."

*That's my mother*, Sarah thought. *The crisis-management expert. Seventeen years as a registered nurse will do that to you*. Sarah wished she had a bit more of that pragmatic toughness. Find out your daughter has been abducted by a mad gunman and involved in a running gun battle and that her best friend was killed by mistake in her place? No problem. Just grab the car keys.

"It'll take her at least an hour and a half to get here from San Bernadino. Why don't you just stretch out in this office and get some sleep."

He gestured through the door to a small adjoining office and a swaybacked couch against the wall.

"I can't sleep," she said.

Though wracked to the limit with physical and emotional exhaustion, Sarah knew that sleep was far off. Her brain whirled with half-formed images of destruction that would take years to fade and memories made bright and bitter by the loss of Ginger and Matt.

She shuffled like a sleepwalker, then sat down on the couch, Traxler kneeling beside her.

"It may not look like it, but this couch is pretty comfortable. I've spent a few nights here myself. Now just stretch out and don't worry."

Sarah did lie down, but her eyes stayed open, unwilling to shut out the bright safety of the office.

"You'll be perfectly safe," Traxler said soothingly. "There's thirty cops in this building. How much safer can you get."

He smiled and patted her arm, then rose to his feet. She heard his shoulder holster creak as he stood and saw the blue steel of his service revolver. His hands were delicate, but his arms were thick and his shoulders broad. She took comfort in the images: the .357 under his arm, the badge clipped to his belt, the thick-soled cop shoes she'd always thought looked so outdated and silly. They didn't seem silly now.

She let her breath out slowly, and her strength seemed to go with it. Her eyes closed.

Traxler backed out the door and shut it quietly, leaving the light on.

He stood outside the door, pulling on his chin. His eyes, focused on nothing, looked big and vacant in his bifocals. Vukovich knew that look.

"What?" he said.

"There's something going on here."

"Bullshit," Vukovich said. "Coupla' whackos, that's all."

"Right. Sharing the same delusion. How often does that happen?"

Vukovich sighed in frustration. "Man, you're losin' it. Have another cup of coffee. Have another Juicy Fruit, pal. The kid's a whacko, Ed."

"He'd better be," Traxler said, gaze still distant. The kid was smart and tough, as if he'd been drop forged and come out tempered like no street punk he'd seen. Some of the 'Nam special-forces guys had that look, but this one was too young for 'Nam. Nineteen. Twenty. He would have been four during the Tet offensive. It wasn't adding up, and something was setting off his radar.

"Whacko," Vukovich said, handing him a smoke. Traxler caught his eye.

"Think about something for a second. Just play the hand and think it through," Traxler said.

"What's that?"

Traxler lit the cigarette.

"What if he's not?"

## Homocide Division
## 2:33 A.M.

Sarah drifted fitfully around the edges of sleep. She would coast down to the warm promise of unconsciousness, then back away, too wired awake to surrender to exhaustion.

So much death surrounded her. Ginger and Matt. All the innocent people who had been walking and breathing this morning, and who now no longer were, seemed to stretch ahead into her future like an accusation. It all belonged in someone else's life, not hers.

Why were two women with her name killed in her place? Why was a madman stalking her through the city and another, now in jail, protecting her? And the question that outshouted all the others—why me? Why Sarah Connor? Why not Mertyle Cornwaithe? Or John Smith?

She thought about Reese's strange story. Computers starting World War III. Mankind on the outs. A revolution by humans scurrying between the legs of colossal machines. And a man leading them to desperate victory. Her son.

A shudder went through her body, and she grew solemn. Her baby. A baby she would raise to lead a battle to save the world. No. Ridiculous. A few hours ago she had been thinking about her own mortality and how insignificant her death would be. Then an insane man tells her that on her life and death hangs the life or death of humanity. Too much . . . too much. But why would an insane man seek *her* out and concoct this bizarre nativity?

Fragmented images of an infant came to her then, a

round-and-pink bundle cooing in her arms. Its eyes really *were* mahogany, and the wisps of new hair on the nearly bald scalp were chestnut colored. She could almost smell the baby's skin. A strange feeling passed through her, something like yearning but too far away to feel directly, only a dissipated echo of it as it faded; but she was aware that the hot tears coming now were not just for her murdered friends. They were in part inspired by an inexplicable emotion she could not define—yet.

She could not even get close to an answer. She needed not to think for a while. Not about Reese and his psychotic visions. Not Ginger and Matt. Or what being a mother might be like.

The last thought she was aware of was a kind of half-formed prayer that Reese really *was* insane.

It was a prayer that would go unanswered.

Silberman tapped on the Plexiglas partition next to the bulletproof glass booth enclosing the night desk sergeant. The sergeant, Eddie Rothman, glanced over at the psychologist, then pressed the little red button below the top of the counter. There was an annoying buzz-clack as the electric bolts on the stainless-steel security door slammed back. Silberman stepped into the lobby, mumbling a distracted good night to the sergeant. He was nearly out the door when his reverie was disturbed by the staccato beep-beep-beep-beep of his pager. He noted the number on the digital readout. His home number. That would be Douglas calling to see when he'd be home. Silberman, wide awake and feeling aggressive, hoped that Douglas would still be up when he got there.

If he hadn't looked down and flicked off the beeper, he might have seen the big man who came through the door. Then he might have noticed that he was wearing sunglasses at two o'clock in the morning. He might have noticed that there was a lot of damage to the man's eye behind them. And that there was the faintest red glow in the pupils, like something you might expect from a cyborg from the future. Silberman might have saved a lot of lives if he had looked up before stepping out of the station.

But he didn't. He went out the door.

Terminator walked purposefully to the desk sergeant and patiently waited until the man glanced up from the pile of paperwork before him.

"Can I help you?" Sergeant Rothman asked in a very bored voice. He noticed the big man's nasty palor. Rothman was sure that behind those sunglasses were very dilated eyes. *Another junkie*, he thought to himself cynically.

"I'm a friend of Sarah Connor," Terminator said flatly. "I was told she is here. Can I see her, please."

"No, she's making a statement."

"Where is she?" Terminator asked slowly, in case the man on the other side of the glass was having trouble understanding the request.

Sergeant Rothman tossed down his pencil and glared laconically at the big man. *Why do they always wander in on my shift?* he pondered.

"Look, pal," Rothman began like an impatient schoolteacher, "it's gonna be a while. You wanna wait, there's a bench."

He adjusted the thick glasses on his nose and returned to his paperwork.

Terminator took a step back, not in the least perturbed at the sergeant's rebuff. Not at all.

It scanned the booth, noting the thick, probably bulletproof glass. To the side was a heavy steel door—the entryway. Beyond were various rooms and offices. And somewhere inside was Sarah Connor.

Terminator politely stepped back up to the booth and rapped on the glass.

"I'll be back," it said.

With that, it turned around and unhurriedly strolled out the front door.

Behind the lobby, deep in the maze of hallways and offices, Reese was being escorted by Vukovich and another plainclothes detective to a holding room where he would await transfer to the psycho ward at County General for further evaluation.

His worst fears were coming true. He had given away

everything and received nothing in return. Tactically stupid. The price was going to be Sarah's life and the lives of millions yet unborn.

John had been right—trust no one; depend on nothing. It was time to get her out.

For the next few moments, Sergeant Rothman absorbed himself in the meticulous task of filling out duty reports. If he had been more alert, he would have noticed a pair of headlights swiftly approaching the front of the station. Like Silberman, he allowed his petty concerns to distract him from life's essential data. Unlike Silberman, he would not live to regret it.

As the headlights of Terminator's stolen Chevy Impala charged toward the glass entrance, Rothman squinted into the blasting glare. He chose as his final act to say the words, "Oh, shit." Statistically, the most popular last words in violent deaths.

Six hundred pounds of plate glass exploded in an opaque white storm as the four-wheeled juggernaut tore into the lobby, tossing broken beams and other debris like a wave before it.

The car charged up to Rothman's booth and punched through it at fifty miles an hour. Both the booth and the sergeant were crushed together into an indistinguishable mass and driven through the wall behind.

At the other end of the building, on the couch in Traxler's office, Sarah was jerked awake by the distant crash. She blinked her bleary eyes and tried to place the sound.

Terminator's Chevy, dragging half of the lobby behind it, slid to a halt about twenty feet inside the main station area.

In a flash, the cyborg kicked out the shattered windshield and leaped onto the Impala's hood. In one hand was the AR-180, in the other, the SPAS-12. Brandishing both like pistols, Terminator dropped to the corridor floor and began hunting.

The first casualties were a pair of six-year veterans who stepped into the hall to see what the hell was happening; one of them still held the cup of coffee he'd been sipping.

Terminator nonchalantly squeezed off a couple of rounds from the AR assault rifle and ended their lives in a shower of plaster and blood.

Sarah now heard the faint but unmistakable sound of gunfire echoing back to her. The seed of apprehension she had felt upon waking was now blossoming into full alarm.

Terminator stepped over the two very dead officers and continued forward without breaking stride. It glanced into the room they had run out of—empty.

Rolling up to the next door, the cyborg tried the handle. Locked. The big machine took one step back and kicked it in.

When his office door flew open, the man behind the desk was desperately reaching for his revolver and jumping out of the chair.

Three feet away was another door. An open door. *If I can just reach it,* the officer thought. He saw Terminator raise the AR-180 as he ducked through the door.

*Safe . . .* he thought.

Terminator's computer-enhanced vision tracked the cop as he dashed around the wall. Behind its infrared eyes, Terminator's microprocessor still saw the target in animated outline—a probablistic extrapolation of the officer's movement based on his trajectory and speed.

Terminator lined up the barrel of the AR-180 with a point on the wall about six feet from the door and fired. The 5.56-mm slugs passed through the drywall and tore large holes in the cop's chest and lungs. He died a very surprised young man.

The shots were still echoing when Traxler flung open his office door, startling the hell out of Sarah. She instinctively jumped back before recognizing the lieutenant.

Traxler and Sarah stared at each other for a second. He gave her an expression as if to say, *I know what you're thinking, but you're wrong.* However, he could tell from Sarah's expression that she was in no mood to believe him.

All he said was "Stay here."

He locked the door from the inside and slammed it shut, leaving Sarah alone.

All over the building cops were running, guns drawn, passing frightened glances to each other and shouting questions.

Controlled panic had seized them. The sound of automatic-weapons fire in a police station brought out the worst nightmares in any officer. And now they were all having the same bad dream at once.

Terminator rolled like a death harvester up to the end of the hall and turned left. It was flinging open doors and blasting cops out of existence in a steady, regular rhythm.

Halfway down the corridor the cyborg encountered the station's main electrical panel, and ripped the cover panel off the hinges.

Quickly scanning the interior, Terminator spotted the hoselike 440-volt incoming line and viciously ripped it loose. A mini-explosion of sparks and live current enveloped the cyborg, arcing back into the hall.

It casually smashed open a small junction box and fed all 440 volts directly into the lighting circuit. Every light in the building, 134 overhead flourescent tubes, exploded simultaneously, throwing the already-chaotic station into darkness.

Sarah happened to be standing directly beneath one in Traxler's office when it disintegrated with a nerve-shattering *bang*. The room fell into darkness that did nothing to steady Sarah's attempts to remain calm. The gunshots had increased in number and volume. She could plot the movement of battle with complete accuracy; it was coming for her.

In the holding room, Reese was still handcuffed when the first shots went off. His soldier's mind instantly took in the situation. He was not surprised. He knew who had come.

Vukovich jumped to his feet and ran for the door, drawing his pistol. He turned to the other plainclothes detective and spoke urgently. "Watch him," he said, then disappeared into the hall.

The other detective nodded and rose to lock the door. In doing so, he turned his back on Reese. That was stupid.

He heard the rush of air and was just beginning to pivot around when Reese crashed into him. The detective's head slammed into the door, and he felt Reese's kneecap drive into his chest once, twice, battering him against the wall. He sagged, gasping, to the floor as Reese scrambled to his feet, searched for the key, removed his handcuffs, and grabbed the officer's revolver.

Traxler was already inside the armory when Vukovich reached it. He and his partner exchanged grim glances. Secretly, they were both thinking the same thing: Reese's playmate is here. But neither of them were ready to admit that one man could be causing all this havoc.

Traxler silently grabbed an M-16 assault rifle and tossed another to his partner. Without a word, they ran into the hall toward the sound of gunfire and screams.

Terminator's room-to-room search led down another corridor. The SPAS-12 blasted the first open door. Rapidly, the man/machine scanned the interior, failed to locate the target, and moved on.

Next door. Blast the lock. Scan. Nothing. Move on. The pattern was fixed but fluid enough to react to any unforeseen obstacle or threat.

A group of uniformed officers stumbled into the hall and took aim at the target lumbering steadily toward them. Six pistols erupted at once, punching holes into Terminator's chest, arms, and legs. It glanced over at them, then casually raised the AR-180 and blew them away with precise, discrete bursts.

The shots seemed to be just outside the door to Sarah's untrained ears. She wasn't wrong by much.

Her eyes darted around the tiny room, looking for a place to hide. *Don't panic*, she ordered herself. *Do something*. A memory from her childhood shot into her conscious mind. Whenever she had wanted to hide from her father's angry voice, she would run to her room and crouch beneath her little white—

Desk! Behind the desk. Sarah ran to the big metal desk and stuffed herself into the cramped space where the chair had been.

Terminator rapidly reloaded the AR-180. The cyborg had taped banana-clip magazines together, butt to butt, jungle style, and merely turned the thing over and reinserted it. Flames danced up the walls; the corridor was ablaze with jumping fingers of yellow light.

In the adjoining office, Traxler heard the unmistakable metal click of a rifle being reloaded. He froze, listening for footsteps. A heavy man was clomping past, his boot heels echoing in the long corridor. Traxler flung the office door open and aimed his M-16 at the back of the wide leather jacket. He carefully lined up the barrel's sights with a point exactly between the man's shoulder blades and squeezed the trigger.

The M-16 barked loudly as half its clip sailed out the barrel. Traxler saw the leather jacket being chewed to pieces, saw the bullets slam home, and he was amazed.

He was amazed because the man simply turned, didn't even flinch, just casually turned and leveled the heavy AR-180 like kid's plastic. It wasn't a toy.

The slugs caught Traxler in the shoulder, stomach, and chest, slamming him into the doorjamb. He saw his own blood splatter against the opposite wall.

Slowly, he slid to the floor. The explosions in his chest began to diminish in intensity. There was a loud buzzing in his ears.

The last thing that Traxler realized was that Reese wasn't crazy at all.

Vukovich leaned down and stared in disbelief at the shattered remains of his boss. Outrage boiled up, making him jump, foolishly, into the corridor and aim his rifle at the retreating figure of Traxler's assailant.

"Hey, you!" he shouted angrily.

The man spun around and stood there, accepting Vukovich's fire like thank yous.

Much to Vukovich's amazement, the big man hefted a shotgun in one hand and blasted him into the next world.

Terminator moved on.

Sarah jumped as a loud rattle broke the new silence. It was the doorknob. Someone was trying to get in.

Her teeth were chattering with fear as she peered over

the top of the desk. A large silhouette was visible just beyond the opaque glass door. It was him. She knew it.

Sarah ducked back under the desk. Raw terror was creeping over her. These were to be the last moments of her life.

There was a loud crash of glass. Someone punched through the door's window and reached inside for the lock.

The door flew open, and a single pair of footsteps ran in. Sarah closed her eyes. Nothing happened.

"Sarah?" a voice cried out.

It was Reese.

Without a second of hesitation, Sarah scrambled out from beneath the desk and ran to him.

Reese was even more relieved than Sarah. She was alive; the mission was still alive. He grabbed her hand, and they raced into the hall.

The fire that had begun in a single room at the front of the building had spread, threatening to engulf the entire station.

In the hallway that Reese and Sarah raced through, smoke was billowing all around, accompanied by the screams of dying men.

Reese had an iron grip on Sarah's hand as he flashed through the bullet-shattered rooms. He was keeping out of the open hallways—that's where all the bodies were.

And that's where Terminator was prowling.

Reese was used to fighting room to room and in small rat-warren tunnels. This was his territory.

The fire was raging now, eating the station whole. Reese knew that in a few seconds the heat alone would kill anyone still inside.

He plowed through a padlocked door into a supply room and saw the parking lot through its window. Reese smashed it open, grabbed Sarah, barely conscious from all the smoke, and stuffed her through.

Terminator felt the temperature rising. Very soon its skin would start to blister and die, though with its cover abandoned, that didn't matter much.

The gunfire had abated. There were no more things to kill, and still it had failed to locate the primary target.

The cyborg began to consider the various scenarios of her possible escape when the faint sound of an automobile starter motor whining came through the roar of flames.

Instantly, Terminator realized where the target was. Dropping the empty shotgun, it ran to the rear-exit door.

When Terminator reached the parking lot, Reese had already hot wired the red Pinto and was racing toward the driveway. He saw Terminator standing, backlit by fire, in the open doorway. "Get down!" he shouted to Sarah.

Terminator carefully aimed the AR assault rifle, taking into account the car's speed and tangential course. It fired three quick shots before the gun emptied and the target passed from view around the building's corner.

Reese and Sarah were lucky. The first bullet hit the left fender, just behind the headlight. The second passed over the top of the engine; an inch lower and the Pinto would have been dead. The third slug punched into the driver's door and sliced through something soft before embedding itself, harmlessly, in the floor mat.

For the next hour Reese drove with total concentration, pausing in his vigil of the road only briefly to observe Sarah's condition.

She had been near hysterics when they left the parking lot and charged down Alameda toward Interstate 10.

He wanted to get out of the city. To buy a little time. To get back on top of the situation.

They headed east on the 10, away from the coast. Away from the smoking bodies and the nightmare on legs that Reese knew would be coming after them.

Reese was traveling blind, merely putting distance between them and the carnage at the police station. But after the first few minutes, he slowed down, turned on the headlights, and began doing a fair imitation of the few other drivers on the road. Sarah, who had been white knuckling the dashboard, anticipating another sidewalk-driving demolition derby, allowed herself to relax a little. But she was still too numb to speak and rode in silence while Reese concentrated on escape and evade.

"I'm glad you're alive," Reese said without turning. His tone was so earnest. It reached her, and she silently agreed, relaxing more as the shock and adrenaline wore off.

"Where we going?" she managed to mumble.

Reese realized he had no destination, so he glanced in the rearview mirror, checking for any suspicious-looking activity, then pulled the car to the curb and flipped open the glove box. Behind the spare fuses, the Pepto Bismol, and the dozen fast-food packets of ketchup and mustard, he found a Thomas Brothers map. It was old and faded, more than likely out-of-date, but better than nothing. He searched for open country. Found it. "South is the best bet. Maybe Mexico."

They rode in silence, each locked in their own separate thoughts. Sarah was trying to put Matt and Ginger to rest. It was going to take a long time.

They veered southeast onto the Pomona Freeway, and twenty minutes later they turned due south onto the 57.

The gas was running low. At that time of morning nothing stayed open; every gas station they could see from the freeway was dark.

Heading through the hills north of Brea, where the freeway cut through the green slopes like a silver ribbon, the Pinto's engine began to sputter.

Reese coasted to the first off ramp he spotted, Brea Canyon Road, and drifted down it until they rolled onto the soft ridge of the unlighted canyon highway.

He and Sarah wearily climbed out, Sarah under mild protest. She saw no reason to sleep in the open when they had the perfectly good car in their hands.

But Reese knew better. And Sarah knew at least enough not to argue with him.

He removed a first-aid kit and flashlight from the trunk of the car; then she helped him push the vehicle to the edge of a stand of trees dotting a gentle slope. With a heave, they launched the Pinto down the slope into the darkness, where it could not be seen from the road.

## Brea Canyon Road
## 3:31 A.M.

Sarah was watching Reese closely. The way he hunkered down ahead of her, a ragged, hypercombat dancer, balancing his body as he weaved through the brush. His eyes scanned almost like a security camera, unblinking, darting in quick jerks, looking at the edges of objects rather than right at them, drinking in the chaotic terrain.

He was a cat on the prowl, grace in action, his battered body hard and yet flexible, the bruised muscles gliding under the skin.

He *was* a soldier. She could see that now. He had done this kind of thing so often that it was second nature. It was an anticlimactic revelation, but now she fully believed his story. Everything that had happened up to now—the slaughter at the police station, the maniacal maelstrom of the streets, the utterly incomprehensible explosion of reality at Tech Noir—were superreal. Somehow, in the police station, her mind had disconnected from her body, and now it was a calm, simple observation of Reese's professionalism in the field that caused her to reconnect and accept the truth.

A robot from the future was trying to kill her. *Sorry, cyborg*, Sarah corrected mentally, as if it mattered. A killing machine in the shape of a man had cut through thirty armed policeman like one of the harvesting combines that thrashed through fields of wheat. It had been hit by numerous bullets and kept on coming. And all that seemed to stand between her and the monstrosity was this soldier, who looked very young, and even though he moved with practised precision, seemed as afraid as she felt.

They came to a concrete drainage culvert under the 57 Freeway, forming a dark, smooth-surfaced cave for them to huddle in.

Reese aimed the flashlight he had taken from the car into the interior. The floor was wet with brackish green-skinned water. Sarah wrinkled her nose at the dank smell but slid down the wall opposite Reese, anyway, exhausted. Reese squatted on his haunches, eyes following the beam of the flashlight, still examining their impromptu haven, slowly winding down from the night's frenzy. He looked at her finally, his eyes now surprisingly soft. His voice was a raspy whisper that cut through the thick silence with a militaristic efficiency, but there seemed to be real concern there, as well.

"You damaged?"

Sarah laughed abruptly and then sobered as she realized she could have easily been shot. She looked down. No blood. No pain in any particular spot.

"I'm okay," she replied, and then felt compelled to add, "Reese . . . it's real. I mean, the war . . . everything you said." It was an acceptance, not a question, so Reese did not answer. He was looking at her with the same intensity he had previously devoted to the landscape. *Is he watching for me to crack?* Sarah wondered. *Break down into hysterics?* She wasn't going to do that. She was amazed she wasn't, but no, she wouldn't, though the hysteria still hovered in the wings, not far away. There was only one problem facing her, and it was a real puzzler. She couldn't cry now. It seemed to Sarah that she should, considering that in the near future the world would go so insane, that millions would die in agony under the grinding heel of some hideous descendant of an Apple computer. Like Chuck's little "Organizer." But she couldn't cry, because none of it had happened yet. But then, where did this man opposite her come from? And that . . . thing, so intent on destroying her, it had killed dozens of innocents. As the chill of the cold cement seeped into her back, a deeper chill flowed from within to meet it. If Reese hadn't made it through time displacement to protect her, she'd be dead. And no one would have known why. She was alone in this thing, without even the luxury of feeling secure about police protection. Alone and shivering in a damp hole in the middle of the night, with a stranger, an insane-looking street tough in torn rags, a scarred teenager wise beyond his years in dealing death. *He* had saved her.

Sarah caught his eye and tried a trembling smile. "Reese . . . uh, what's your first name?"

"Kyle."

"Kyle," she went on, her voice wavering, "I wouldn't be alive now unless you came along. I . . . want to . . . thank you."

Reese allowed himself to look into her eyes. *Just a girl,* he kept mentally repeating to himself. *A target that needs cover,* he added. And then, to help him maintain, he said aloud, "Just doing my job."

Sarah nodded, satisfied with that for the time being. Reese went back to listening. A car was coming. Maybe a thousand meters out. Hostile? Unlikely. He waited, poised between tense and relaxed, and let another sound in; the wind blew so soft and huge out here that it seemed as if he could hear the whole world breathing. It humbled him. He could sense the smell of animals on the wind—maybe dogs; he wasn't sure.

The car rushed by overhead in a rumbling *whoosh*. Reese's hand had tensed on the police service revolver at his waist, then relaxed as the car sped on without hesitation.

Sarah was holding herself and shivering uncontrollably now, a combination of aftershock and keen air. He came across the tunnel in an efficient, fluid movement and slipped his arm around her shoulder. At first, Sarah recoiled. His clothes were rank with ancient sweat. But his body was blazing with heat. Even through the raincoat she could feel it and was instantly warmer. She looked up gratefully, but now he was staring out at the night, his expression gone intense and focused, yet somehow far away. There was no emotion in his action except duty. Despite that and the rank odor, she slid her arms around his torso and clung to him. She felt his body contracting with measured breaths. His muscles felt like heated metal bands beneath his skin. Maybe he was a cyborg, too.

A cyborg from an unimaginable future of pain and horror.

"Kyle, what's it like going through time?"

For a moment he stopped breathing, thinking about it as if for the first time. "White light. Pain. A kind of pushing through . . . something. I don't know. Like being born, maybe."

Then she felt something like thick hot coffee trickling down her arm and pulled back. She grabbed the flashlight from him and aimed it at her hand. Blood.

"Oh, my god!"

Reese looked down at the blood oozing from his arm as if he were remembering an unpleasant dream. "I caught one back there."

Sarah didn't get it for a second. "Caught one? You mean you got shot?"

He nodded. "It's not bad. Don't worry."

She put the beam on his arm. There was a tiny hole in the raincoat, like a cigarette burn, but the whole upper arm was slick with blood.

"Are you crazy? We gotta get you to a doctor!"

"Forget it."

Sarah gingerly opened his raincoat and pulled it off his shoulders. "Here, take this off."

Reese carefully removed the coat and looked at the wound with suppressed relief. He had thought it was bad, really, and just didn't want to look. "See," he said. "Passed right through the meat."

Sarah stared at the tiny hole neatly punched into his tricep, still oozing blood around a clump of navy blue fabric that had been driven into the wound from the raincoat. Reese gently turned the muscle in the wavering flashlight beam, and Sarah saw the larger and more ragged exit hole. Despite all the violence of the past few hours, this was her first real look at what a bullet did to human flesh. It was both appalling and fascinating, mostly appalling.

The wound needed dressing, and she was elected. That was why Reese had handed her the first-aid kit. *Get to work*, she thought. *Try not to think about it*. She would have to clean it first. That would mean touching it. Jesus, this was getting too real.

Sarah opened the first-aid kit. Bandages. Ointment. Pills. Gauze. Peroxide. Swabs. This stuff was for scraped knees, not bullet holes. She grabbed the cotton swab and edged closer to him. He watched her, fascinated and amused.

"Jesus . . . this is gonna make me puke. Talk about something, would you? Anything, I don't care."

"What?"

Sarah almost laughed. She had a billion questions she wanted answers to. Like . . . her son. She had a child, he had said. Or would have. Will have. Will have had. They didn't make tenses for this situation.

"Tell me about my son. Is he tall?"

"About my height. He has your eyes."

She started soaking the blood out of the wound, and he winced, then motioned for her to continue. As gently as she could, Sarah went back to work, biting her lip and concentrating on his words so she wouldn't upchuck all over his arm.

"It's hard to explain him. He—you trust him. He's got that strength of will. You know he could do anything once he decided that was what had to be done. My father—I don't remember him. I always picture him like John. He knows how to lead men. They'll follow him anywhere. I'd die for John Connor." He spoke the last in a low, passionate voice, and she believed he meant it, and Sarah now knew he *was* capable of emotion. The pure, hard, undistilled fanaticism of the young, a passion she had never been able to feel for anything or anyone. "At least now I know what to name him." She chuckled. It was a joke, right? Reese didn't smile, and she realized it really wasn't. There was too much pain behind his eyes.

She tried again. "Do you know who the father is, so I won't tell him to get lost when I meet him?"

Reese shrugged. "No, John never said much about him. I know he died before the war, and—"

"Wait," Sarah interrupted. "I don't want to know."

She went back to the impromptu bandage. He was quiet, watching her fingers becoming more sure as she worked. Then Sarah asked, "Did John send you?"

Reese turned away, going grim and tight again. "I volunteered."

"Volunteered?"

He faced her again. "Of course. A chance to meet John Connor's mother. You're a legend. The hero behind the hero."

He winced as she tied off the gauze.

"Go on, make it tight," he said, then continued. "You taught him how to fight, hide, organize . . . from when he was a kid, when you were in hiding before the war."

Sarah held up her hand, a confused look coming into her eyes. "You're talking about things I haven't done yet in the past tense. It's driving me crazy." She yanked the gauze ends into a knot, forgetting herself for a moment, and Reese muffled a groan. More gently, she finished tying off the bandage. "I'm sorry, but are you sure you have the right person?"

He locked eyes with her. Sarah saw that look again. And it had nothing to do with his duty. It was he looking directly into her, the Sarah inside the body. The little Sarahs cringed back under his naked stare.

"I'm sure," he said. And he was . . . physically certain at least. His doubts were in other areas.

Sarah got to her feet, exasperated. "Come on, do I look like the mother of the future? Am I tough? Organized? I can't even balance my checkbook!"

Reese heard the tone of her voice more than the words. It was the same whining, defeated tone many of the scavs had voiced when John asked them to risk danger for the cause. It was a tone of voice he despised, because it was the same attitude that had prevented men from defeating the machines years earlier. The blind, bleating acceptance of whatever the "fates" had in store for them. Whole religions and elaborate philosophies had been developed to give weight to this sickeningly weak tone of voice. Until John had stepped out of the ashes with a pincer grenade and blown the tracks off an H-K. Until John risked death, standing in the flaming wreckage, siphoning off the unburned fuel to power his armored car.

Because of his example, John's call was answered. Men rallied to him and kept rallying. And when Reese was old enough, he cut himself loose from the street pack and joined, as well, glad to be away from that pathetic "Why me?" bleating that he despised so much.

Reese had been reeling back and forth from awe to disgust ever since he had first seen Sarah earlier that day.

He remembered his briefing. Sarah Connor was simply a twenty-year-old part-time waitress who was still in school and who so far had exhibited no unusual abilities or talents. She was the equivalent of a gangly female scav, rooting around blindly in the rubble, unaware of her own power to resist and change her fate. He had known many scavs like that. And once they had been shown the way, they had become good soldiers. So it might be with Sarah. But he was no recruiter. All he knew was survival. He had volunteered for this mission fully expecting to be passed over in favor of an older, more tempered fighter. When John had personally summoned him, he was flattered by the sudden realization of the enormous responsibility he was taking on. His performance would profoundly affect all human history. John had told him that.

Before volunteering, all Reese had thought about was the chance of carrying out the most important order John had ever issued and the glorious honor of meeting John's beautiful mother in the flesh. Most of the mission's impact had escaped him. It had all happened so fast . . . so fast. Once John's forces had captured the time-displacement lab, he had been notified of the special mission and immediately put his name into the hat. Minutes later he had reported to John's command bunker and was rapidly briefed. He recalled now what John had stressed—the awesome importance that he succeed in the mission and the wondrous certainty that Reese *would* succeed. That look of confidence, more than the uppers the meds were hypoing into Reese's veins, had jumped him into combat ready. And then, as Reese saluted, John had embraced him. That caught Reese completely by surprise. John Connor was a hard man to get close to. After his mother had died, he became a brooding loner who opened up to no one. He was adored by his followers because he never asked them to do anything he wasn't about to do and because he knew what to do. He was never really intimate with anyone. But John said that Reese was the pivot of fate and then threw his arms around him as if they were old friends. As John turned away to see to other technical matters, there was an expression of deep sadness that Reese knew he was not meant to see. Perhaps John's confidence had been faked to give Reese courage. That other look troubled him. Now, as he thought of what he and Sarah would have to do to survive, he remembered both of John's expressions and how little the briefing had actually told him before they shunted him through that endless instant of time travel. As far as Reese knew, he was the first living man to be temporally displaced. Skynet had developed the hardware as part of its voracious research and development, a geometrically expanding computor-generated repertoire of new technologies.

The human raiders had seized the place intact, and the techs had scurried to download the system files and analyze them. When they realized what Skynet had done in its coldly rational desperation, John had opted to use its own technology as counterforce. But when Reese had stepped into the biaxial node of the field generator, no one really knew if the time displacement was survivable. He might have arrived in 1984, an already-cooling bag of meat, his heart stopped by unfathomable energies.

"Look, Reese," Sarah was saying, "I didn't ask for this. And I don't want any part of it." She was going to cry. Her hair was matted with drying sweat. Her clothes were filthy and torn. She wasn't a legend. She was a whining little scav about to weep uncontrollably at his feet, and now, in addition to keeping her alive, he had to keep her sane and strong. Something he hardly knew how to do for himself.

Then he remembered the last thing John had told him he must do. He made his voice loud and calm. "Sarah."

She stopped pacing like a cornered animal and faced him.

"Your son gave me a message to give to you. Made me memorize it."

She froze in position, blinking, not knowing what to expect. Reese went on, his voice softer, a hint of the original speaker's love behind the rote repetition.

"'I never got a chance to thank you properly for your love and courage through all the dark years. I can't help you with what you must soon face except to say that the future is not set in stone. I have seen humanity rise up from defeat, and I have been privileged to lead the way. You must preserve our victory. You must be stronger than you imagine you can be. You must survive, or I will never exist.'"

Reese could see her calming down. The words were washing over her. He hadn't meant to let so much of his own feelings spill through, but it was all right, because she seemed to be responding.

Reese flexed his hand. There wasn't much pain now. Nothing he couldn't handle, anyway, and his hand still retained over 75 percent mobility.

Maybe, just maybe, they had a chance of making it. If they could stay in the clear, leaving no traceable data, they could lie low indefinitely. To encourage her, Reese said, "Good field dressing."

Sarah smiled wearily. "You like it? It's my first."

She felt the irony of her words. She still rejected the mantle of responsibility thrust on her; at least she did emotionally. But some very logical component deep inside her had accepted that she would one day do these things, just as she now accepted the impending incineration of civilization some years hence and all the horrors of the world thereafter.

There would be many wounds, many bandages. Tragedies and losses unimaginable. Sarah shivered as the endless dark landscape seemed to spread out before her. A word came to her. Destiny.

It was like being in a play. You could change the performance, but you could not change the ending. She remembered a play she had been in back in junior high.

She had liked one of the other characters, but he kept dying in act three, night after night. And she remembered how naively bitter she had been. Just once she wanted the character's illness not to have been fatal. She didn't like acting that much after that, and she didn't like destiny as a concept much, either.

Another vehicle rumbled past overhead. A long-bed truck, diesel engine hammering out a thunderous rhythm. Reese could see she was dead on her feet. "Get some sleep. It'll be light soon."

She sat next to him, back against the cold concrete. The tension between them still hung in the air, and he put his arm around her.

For a moment he thought he might be suffering from time-displacement aftershock, for it seemed as if huddling there had always been his life and she had always been with him.

Sarah was exhausted. She had to sleep and was halfway there when Reese stiffened as the sound of the crickets began. It made her feel more secure. She realized that even though Kyle must be bone tired, he would come awake should anyone, or anything, approach. He was a strange, haunted boy. She realized that Reese might never have heard a cricket before. Being next to him in this necessary intimacy made her feel serene despite the psychotic nightmare she had just come through. When he made his voice soft, she felt soothed and protected. She wanted to hear more.

"Tell me more about where you're from. Just anything you want. It'll help me sleep."

"All right," he said. "You stay down by day, but at night you can move around. The H-Ks use infrared, so you still have to watch out. Especially for the Aerials. They're not too bright. John taught us ways to dust them. It got tough when the infiltrators began to appear. The Terminators were the newest. The worst."

She felt herself drifting, melting into him, as he talked about a place of noise and flame, of white ash and fire-gutted ruins, moonlit patrol craft sending harsh beams and plasma bursts into the rag-wrapped scavengers—rooting through the collapsed cities for unburned cans of food—blackened bones, and gleaming human-hunting machines grinding their blood-streaked chrome bodies through a pack of scavs like sharks in feeding frenzy.

Reese was still talking when Sarah's eyelids fluttered closed. Her head sagged against his shoulder. He could see only the top of it and could not tell if she was asleep. He went on with his account, which had no narrative structure whatever and consisted of stark images unplaced in his personal chronology—bits of combat lore and survival tips, anecdotes and slices of life in the twenty-first century.

Sarah's last conscious thought was a curious one, and she would only recall it later. She thought he sounded poetic, like a street poet who can convey images clearly with coarse and unstructured juxtapositions of words. Born into another life and time, he might have been an artist or songwriter, but those countersurvival impulses were virtually eradicated, and their faint vestiges manifested themselves now only in the vivid starkness of his description.

Her thought that Reese was a soldier with the heart of a poet would resurface later, only then to be tinged with desperate sadness.

Reese's words still reached her as she slipped into REM sleep, and they triggered images both stunning and surreal in the dark catacomb of her dreams.

There was a light. A bright light, searing, like the sun. It split the night landscape and licked over the shattered concrete shapes, etching razor-sharp shadows. There was wind, too, blasting straight down, and a screaming sound, like metal dying, that she realized was a jet engine or engines.

The downblast whipped the ash drifts, exposing a jackstraw heap of bones. Ash was blasted from the sockets of skulls, and shadows from the searchlights tracked across the empty orbits in a parody of life. The machine was like an enormous chrome wasp except that where the wings would be, at the center of the thorax, there were two turbojet housings aimed straight down. The thing hovered and dipped, scanning on visual and infrared frequencies. Then it banked, nosing down and picking up airspeed like an Aircobra helicopter. Its underslung gun fired once into a burned-out building and then retracted into the belly nacelle as the craft continued its patrol.

A kilometer away, across the blasted landscape, another of the machines was settling to earth on insectile hydraulic legs in what looked like a depot or staging area. There were several of the tanklike ground H-Ks parked under the reflective-infrared floodlights. On tapered concrete pylons, twenty-meter-long automated cannons stood guard, with tiny antipersonnel machine guns swiveling beneath them. Searchlights swept the darkness.

When the flying H-K had passed, it was safe to emerge. In their mottled two-tone gray cammies, the troopers blended perfectly with the environment. Gray on gray. Black on black.

The leader lay prone under an angled slab of concrete, and he was looking through a scope attached to his rifle, an image-intensified video screen on which the landscape glowed bright as day. The green glow lit his face. It was Reese. Sweat trickled down, leaving clear streaks in the layer of ash on his face. He was dirty and hadn't shaved lately, and none of the other troopers looked much better. They all wore headsets, and there was a constant low murmur of communication from other units in the area.

"LRRP team Yankee one three to fire base Echo niner."

"Come in Yankee one three. What's your stat?"

"Concluded sweep to the three-thousand-meter line. Didn't see much. Ran into some scavs out at the shopping mall. They're unregistered, but they got some stuff to trade."

"What sort of stuff?"

"Canned food, some tools and gasoline. They need shelter and some two two three ammo."

"Roger one three, send them on down."

"We're comin' in. Our spotter's got a bad paw, so I'm cutting the patrol short."

"Roger one three."

The voices murmured incessantly. Reports of patrols in all nearby sectors, sapper teams looking for H-Ks to disable and salvage components from, a long-range recon team on the run from a new Mark Eight Aerial—it was zigging when they zigged, and it didn't look good. A unit up in the hills, near bunker twenty-three on old Mulholland Drive, was requesting a mech team to help unship the cannon from a salvagable H-K. Someone out by the beach had gotten into it with a couple of series 600 terminators dressed in trooper cammies. The result was one deader, three for the medevac, and two burning terminator chassis. Their spotter, a beagle, had bought it, as well, and the team leader was disconsolate.

And so on.

Reese signaled a move, and the unit descended through a manhole hidden by debris into a stairwell that led downward. Sarah's mind's eye moved with them as they trooped wearily into the earth, down level after level, guided by a flashlight beam. Four levels below the surface, Reese pounded on a crudely welded steel door with the butt of his rifle. Once. Twice more. Then once again. A steel plate grated as it slid aside, and a sentry's eyes appeared at the slotlike opening.

"Reese. Kyle. DN . . ."

The door clanged and rolled open before he finished. Reese entered. Warmth, fire smoke, and cloying human body smells assailed him. Three armed sentries stood inside, weapons raised. Reese held his hand out to be sniffed by the two sentry dogs, a shepherd and a doberman. Probably the most well fed creatures at the fire base. Their tails wagged, and Reese was passed. Still human.

The sentries stepped back, relaxing the grips on their Westinghouse M-25s. Reese's squad entered, signed in at the duty station set up on an old card table, and then separated into the labyrinth.

Firebase E-9. It had once been D level of the parking

structure under the ABC Entertainment Center in Century City. Now it was shattered, partially collapsed, and the home of soldiers, children, scavengers, the sick and dying, and lots of rats.

Sarah seemed to be moving with Reese, as if he were her guide. They passed emaciated, haunted faces whose eyes flicked, barely registering their passing. They were dressed in scavenged rags, layers of mismatched clothing, sizes too large or too small, cloaks or vests made of long-shag carpet, canvas, black plastic held together with multicolored bits of wire. Their faces were pale and pinched, eyes hollow. Only the children seemed to have any life as they scurried in the shadows, catching rats for the stewpot.

The catacomb flickered with small cook fires, and everywhere faces peered from the shadows like ghosts, men and women whose souls had fled. They were living in the hulks of cars, steel trash dumpsters turned on their sides, or maybe just behind a ragged blanket hung on a wire. Some of the older faces showed scarring from flash burns received during the war, their flesh melted and bubbled like burned cheese. A thin wail drifted from somewhere in the darkness, and from a niche nearby a mindlessly repeated dry sobbing droned on and on. It was a walk through hell, and Sarah was torn between an overwhelming urge to flee and the intense desire to help in any way she could to ease the desperate suffering. As she walked among them, she reached out, as if she could crush them to her breast and make them well. All the poor nuclear children. But it was as if she were the ghost, because they looked right through her. She wasn't there. Not yet.

Reese and Sarah approached a group of men huddled around a transmitter base station, under a bright fluorescent light. Reese saluted as he passed. There was a lot of brass. Some he knew, and some he didn't. Several captains, two majors, and a figure seated with his back to them, flanked by guards. He wore a black beret with a general's star pinned to the side. Only one man in the motley guerrilla army that spanned the globe wore a black beret like that.

John had come to this fire base the previous night to organize a raid on the nearby automated factories. It was known that Skynet produced the chain-fed plasma cannons used in the Mark Sevens and Eights. A big raid, scheduled three days hence. Reese was looking forward to it. One of the lieutenants had mentioned that Reese might be up for a transfer to Connor's personal unit, and John himself had actually spoken to him shortly after arriving. It had been a curious meeting, with Reese feeling self-conscious as Conner gave him a slow, careful scrutiny. It was as if Connor had been sizing him up in some way beyond the ordinary evaluation of an officer. Whether Reese was wanting was not revealed in Connor's eyes. "Carry on, sergeant," the general had said, and turned away.

It was always that way with John, and although Reese had served in action with him several times, the man remained an enigma.

Now, surrounded by his staff, John was coordinating a dozen major offensives throughout the world via his mobile telecommunications unit.

Reese had been told that they actually pirated channels off Skynet's own satellites, knowing the enemy would destroy anything men could put up there but that it couldn't afford to destroy its own global relay system. Reese didn't have a clue how that stuff worked, but that wasn't his job, anyway.

Sarah saw the men crowded together in a pool of light. She saw the figure in the black beret as two of his aides stepped aside. His back was to her. His broad shoulders drooped wearily, but his hands moved with sure strokes, indicating actions on a battle map. She could hear his voice but not the words, and she wished he would turn. But the aides moved together, and he was blocked from view again. She wanted to go to him but found it impossible. It was something she wasn't to see. Reese moved on and found a place to bunk down for a few hours; a half-burned leather couch. He unbuckled his web belt, then unslung his rifle and laid it across his knees, keeping his hand on it. "My lover and my best friend," he said to her, patting the buttstock of the M-25. "We always sleep together."

Sarah sat beside him on the couch. He leaned back, his body leadened. Opening a zippered pouch, he removed a small, flat, plastic rectangle. It was a crumpled Polaroid photo, but she couldn't see the picture. As Reese studied it, his gaze grew soft and distant. He held it motionless for a long time.

Reese glanced up as he heard the security door being unlocked and opened. Another patrol was coming through, visible in the distance under the dim portable fluorescents. Two scouts. The dogs were smelling their hands. Then another man pushed through before the sentries could close the door. He was a head taller than the others and carried something bulky under his torn gray poncho.

The dogs began barking furiously at the last man. The sentries were already going for their weapons. One was yelling, "Terminator! Terminator!"

Reese hung frozen for a half second as the terminator threw back its poncho and lifted the General Dynamics' RBS-80 to fire. The weapon cracked, and the bunker was seared with light.

Reese gripped the precious photograph in his teeth to free his hands and leaped up with his rifle, sprinting toward the action.

A terrifying series of blinding pulses lit the bunker as Terminator sprayed the interior with lethal fire. Screams punctuated the concussive blasts, and a siren began its maniacal hooting. In the middle of the smoke and pandemonium, the terminator was moving with frightening precision toward the command center. Connor was barking orders, return fire was zapping all around the terminator. Some ammo exploded. The scene became obscured by a fireball rolling across the low ceiling.

Reese had been flung to the floor, beneath a rain of flaming debris. He rolled, stunned by pain, groping for his rifle. The photo had fallen nearby and lay burning amid some other debris. Sarah watched Reese looking at the

Polaroid, his eyes glazing with shock as it shriveled in the flames.

Now it was only impressions. Screams. Running feet. Power bolts lighting up the smoke like flashbulbs. A six-year-old girl crying amid the chaos. The dogs whining and howling. One of them, the shepherd, snarling and biting at its own back, where the fur was ablaze.

And in the middle of it, a relentlessly moving silhouette with glowing red eyes, its gun speaking death. The RBS-80 wheeled around, its massive barrel aimed right toward her. Sarah felt her stomach drop as she knew she couldn't dodge fast enough. She stared, paralyzed, for the microsecond before it fired, which dilated into a century. The red eyes fixed on her. Then white light blasted her being into mist. The dream had no place to go from there, so it stopped abruptly, like the end of a film flapping through a projector.

Sarah moaned, coming half awake, and clutched at Reese, turning toward the warmth of his body. Then she subsided back into full sleep. This time without dreams.

Reese felt Sarah stir, and it jerked him awake. He realized he'd almost drowsed off and went through a couple of quick mental exercises he used on long patrols to stay awake. The sky outside the culvert was beginning to lighten. He must have talked for a long time. He realized he'd probably said more words in an hour than in the previous two years of his life. Why he'd gone into such detail about that attack on the bunker he couldn't immediately say. It was certainly a common enough occurrence, unremarkable from a military standpoint. He had been trying to give her an overview of his world, so it served as a bit of everyday life in A.D. 2029. Maybe the picture had something to do with it. The combination of the picture and Terminator and John's being there—somehow these elements made the whole thing vivid.

John had given him the picture originally a year before, when they were hunkered down in a storm drain much like this one and the ground shook from plasma bombs that poured artificial daylight in on them intermittently. John had taken a leather case out of his fatigue pocket, an old prewar billfold, and from it he produced the Polaroid. What it meant or why Reese should carry it was never mentioned, and it still remained a mystery. Reese had recognized the face immediately, of course, for there were lots of pictures of Sarah Connor available, and some soldiers even carried them in battle for luck. But to have an original Polaroid meant a great deal more.

He had carried it with him everywhere after that, even on bad missions where he was bound to get soaked to the bone or worse.

The picture was seared into his memory as a result, though the image itself was enigmatic. She seemed to be sitting in some sort of vehicle; there wasn't enough of it in frame to identify. Her hair was different than now, though she seemed about the same age, maybe a little older; it was shorter and bound by a headband. Her features were slightly drawn, but there was a set to her jaw that radiated strength, and her eyes gave the impression of inner calmness. Her lips were curved in the faintest vestige of a smile. Perhaps a smile of remembrance. But the overall effect was almost somber. The overcast sky added to that. There was something behind her out of focus. It was a long time before Reese had recognized it as the shoulder and flank of a dog. Probably a German shepherd, judging by the size and coloration.

When he got to the part about Terminator entering the bunker while he was gazing at the photo, he had skipped over mentioning that it was a likeness of her. He had felt a rush of embarrassment, as if it would be an admission of some strange voyeurism to tell her. Even his pragmatic honesty couldn't overcome that.

He thought of the explosion that had stunned him and how his first image, as his eyes refocused, had been of her picture burning nearby. When a Polaroid burns, it shrinks, shrivels, and distorts, although the image is still visible, melting and mutating.

He glanced down at the real Sarah, lying now in his lap, lost in a troubled sleep. He felt that strange dislocation and double image as he gazed at her features: déjà vu. Like when a terrain map is memorized before a mission, and then later, crawling through the actual area, there is a sense of the abstract overlaid on the real. The preparation for an event becoming the event.

He sucked in cold morning air. Sunlight washed the gray cement of the drainage culvert a harsh white.

Sarah stirred and murmured. Her face was turned up to him, opened in innocent sleep. He followed the simple lines of Sarah's geometry. Despite a face puffy with sleep, mouth slack, one cheek crushed against his soiled shirt, and although her expression now was far from noble, she was beautiful. He traced her nose with the tip of his finger, and ran it lightly across her full lips. They yielded to his touch. There had been nothing as soft in his whole miserable life. A feeling like a miniature copter blade churning in his chest caused his breath to quicken and his hand to tremble.

Reese's whole body was a mass of aches, but he didn't care. A nasty cramp was forming in his left calf. He ignored it. The feeling had gone out of the arm supporting Sarah. He hated that. She was in his arms, but he could only half feel her.

He gingerly moved a strand of hair off her cheek. Sarah wrinkled her nose and sighed. He could feel the warm exhalation, smell the sweetness . . . Reese clamped down. Willed his head to clear.

Sarah opened her eyes and focused on Reese. "I was dreaming . . . about dogs," she said, sounding puzzled. The dream was a churning blur of terrifying shadows.

"I told you about them last night," he explained. "We use them to spot terminators."

At the mention of terminators, Sarah rose completely to the now-placid surface of consciousness and in memory looked back at the distant, choppy maelstrom she had passed through last night. "Oh, god," she said. But it wasn't a prayer.

## Brea Canyon Road
## 9:02 A.M.

Reese and Sarah climbed the embankment to the two-lane road. Birds flew overhead, then dove into the bushes at the bottom of the wash behind them.

A gauzelike fog glided in ghostly sheets across the field opposite the embankment. The air was heavy with the morning musk of moist leaves and plant sap.

Reese took Sarah's hand and began walking south along the dirt shoulder. The scrub-dotted hills that rose only a few meters back from the road made them feel protected. The opposite side saw the embankment rising into the 57 Freeway running parallel with the highway. The subsonic whoosh of cars and trucks intermittently reached their ears. They were in an uninhabited pocket of chaparral between Diamond Bar and Brea. Up ahead they could see another line of hills pockmarked with derricks and slowly revolving oil pumps. Reese stopped at the foot of an on ramp.

"We need a car," Reese said. "We've got to keep moving." He pointed to the freeway above them. "Where does that go?"

Sarah consulted the map. After going from page to page so she could see the interchanges, she answered, "We can get on the 5 Freeway and continue south."

Reese had no idea where they were and didn't care. He just wanted to be going away from the 800. When a dark blue Toyota sedan began rounding a curve in the road ahead, he pulled out the police revolver. Before he could step onto the highway, Sarah hissed, "Put that away." She pulled his arm down, using both her hands, then turned and raised her arm straight out, the thumb extended upward.

The car slowed as it neared, then turned onto the ramp and sped up. The passengers, two teenaged boys, yelled obscenities as the driver, a rough-looking man wearing a hard hat, honked the horn.

Reese wanted to raise the pistol again, but Sarah assured him, "This works, really." He didn't understand the ceremony with the thumb but decided to give her the benefit of the doubt. After all, she was Sarah Connor.

Three minutes later a large, primer gray Chevy pickup rounded the curve. The driver slowed to a stop at the bottom of the on ramp. Sarah and Reese approached the idling truck. "Can we get a ride?" she asked in her sweetest voice. Long, matted hair and a full beard, eyes and grinning mouth, protruded from the window. "Yeah, sure, but I'm just going to Irvine, ya know."

"That'll be fine," Sarah said gratefully. Reese helped her climb into the back, among two bald spares, a bag of dirty clothes, and a battered wooden box of tools. He was glad her approach had worked, because the next one would have been his way.

## Panama Hotel
## 9:22 A.M.

Terminator was running a systems stat check on the internal display. The long column of readouts was sensed over the infrared image that came through the microlenses in its eye sockets. Internal damage was nominal. The chassis seals were intact, the interior hydraulics functioning at capacity. Only the outer skin of organic flesh was subnominal.

A patch of scalp had been blown away, revealing chromed metal crusted over with a thin coating of dried blood. Skin dangled from the cheek, and the drive cables underneath, which moved the jaw, glistened in the tepid light.

All over the cyborg's body there were bruises and abrasions, some of the latter putrid with gangrene. The circulatory system had been shut down when the tiny pneumatic pump that maintained pressure had been obliterated by a twelve-gauge projectile. Terminator had already sewed up or Krazy Glued the most severe of the ragged tears and gaping bullet holes that pockmarked its body. But the flesh was not healing. The room was filled

## 184  THE TERMINATOR

with the cloying odor of decay. Several flies had spiraled up from the open garbage dumpsters in the alley below and had come through the open window.

Terminator was only vaguely aware of the insistent aerial assault. It only brushed a fly away if one crawled or flew into the eye socket and obscured the machine's vision. The rest feasted freely on the lacerations Terminator had not bothered to clean or repair.

The internal stat check concluded on a readout of Terminator's power supply. Consumption rate was low, under .013, less than one thousandth of the total energy available.

Where a man's heart would be, shielded in a case-hardened subassembly inside the hyperalloy torso, was the nuclear-energy cell. It supplied power to run the most sophisticated system of hydraulic actuators and servo-motors ever constructed, enough power to run the lights of a small city for a day. It was designed to last Terminator considerably longer, especially if intense activity was varied with conservation procedures.

When Terminator dropped off line into economy mode, compact energy sinks collected and stored the excess. If the torso was breached and these vital power supplies disturbed, Terminator could be stopped. But the torso was triple armored with the densest alloy ever smelted.

Terminator could keep operating at full power for twenty-four hours a day for 1,095 days. During that time it would certainly have opportunities, like now, for economy mode, where power was cut to 40 percent of nominal function. The optical system switched to infrared only. The motivation units lost 40 percent of hydraulic pressure as the pumps slowed. Power was shunted into sinks and stored. With conditions like those so far encountered on this mission, Terminator could operate indefinitely, plow through all opposition, and complete the target elimination, then stagger programless through the nuclear devastation caused by Skynet and walk up to its machine masters to be programmed anew.

Terminator would be around for a long, long time.

The flies, already bloating on the cyborg's decaying flesh, would have been happy to hear that.


## 5 Freeway South
### 9:57 A.M.

The truck had veered onto the 5 Interchange and was slowing in the thickening morning traffic. The mechanical thunder of semis rumbled Reese into alertness. They were surrounded by cars, vans, and trucks for as far as the eye could see.

They were coming into Tustin, and the opposing sides of the eight-lane freeway were now bordered by recently constructed three- and six-story glass-and-concrete buildings, most of them banks or savings and loans. Orange County was a prosperous, entrepreneurial, and doggedly conservative metropolis. Although cities had flavorful names like Villa Park, Orange, Placentia, and Yorba Linda, they were basically alike.

Reese could make nothing of any of this. There was just too much . . . too much.

Traffic began to lighten, and the truck sped out of Tustin. Buildings began to give way to the few remaining orange groves left in Orange County. Sarah looked into the wind and saw they were approaching a wall of eucalyptus trees. She suddenly remembered that El Toro Marine base was on the far side of those trees. If she ever needed a battalion of marines—but then she remembered the police station.

She stole a glance at Reese. He was just one man, really not any older than she, although his eyes seemed ancient. He alone had snatched her from certain death. Again and again. A tough kid with one hell of a sense of duty.

And yet now, huddled as he was in the back of the pickup, he seemed diminished, insubstantial, a cowed and vulnerable phantom.

## 186 THE TERMINATOR

The truck was slowing, drifting into the outside lane. Sarah craned around and saw that they were getting off the freeway at Sand Canyon Road.

The truck turned into a gas station at the foot of the off ramp.

"End of the line," the driver cheerfully told them.

### Panama Hotel
### 10:05 A.M.

Rodney pushed the squeaky cart out of the bathroom at the end of the hall and grunted when his voluminous stomach folded like an unwilling accordion as he bent low to retrieve the Out of Order sign that had fallen off the door. He tossed it onto the cart where it slid between bottles of disinfectant and cleanser. Rodney relit a half-smoked cigar, then puffed on it savagely, blowing smoke around his bald head to drown the acrid odor of the cleaning fluids.

Rodney knocked perfunctorily and opened the door on 102. Jasmine smiled when he came in, looking up from the red-lacquered nails that hadn't dried yet. "Jasmine's" real name was Bob Hertel, but Rodney could never get over the shape of "his" legs as he strolled the sidewalk in front of the Panama. The high heels really sculpted his calves. Rodney didn't care how they paid the rent as long as they paid. Jasmine, wearing a long slip, sat amid his life's possessions in the eight-by-eleven room and crooned to Rodney, taunting him as always.

Rodney was inured; he swept up quietly, then left.

When he got to 103, he was met by bad news. The odor was faint but unmistakable, and all he could think was "Oh, shit, not another dead wino. This'll be two this month, with fuckin' cops everywhere, and all the girls'll be bitching and throwing their eyebrow tweezers at me."

Figuring he'd better get it over with, Rodney knocked on the door. He heard brittle floorboards creak, but no one answered. He knocked again, then said, "Hey, buddy, what you got in there, a dead cat?" hoping that was all it was.

Terminator had been arranging the things he had taken from Sarah's apartment on the bug-infested bed when the rap on the door caused the cyborg to kick back on line into alert status. Within 1.7 seconds the .375 magnum auto was in its hand, cocked and aimed at the person on the other side of the door.

A faint infrared heat trace outlined the figure of a man standing there. Since it determined from the subject's tone of voice, physical condition, and passive behavior—no attempt at entry—that the man was not a threat, Terminator did not fire through the door. This action could threaten the security of the base of operations and was therefore not a viable option. A list of alternative verbal responses came up on the internal display.

> NO
> YES
> I DON'T KNOW
> PLEASE COME BACK LATER
> GO AWAY
> FUCK YOU
> FUCK YOU, ASSHOLE

The last flickered prominently, and Terminator vocalized loudly enough to be heard through the door.

"Fuck you, asshole."

"Fuck you, too, pal," Rodney answered, then pushed the cart to the end of the dingy hall. A live son-of-a-bitch wino beats a dead one any day.

Inside the fetid room, Terminator brushed at the flies that were laying eggs in the open eye socket. Clearing the lens with a rag, the machine picked up Sarah's address book and began to scan methodically the rapidly flipped pages.

Preliminary probability analysis indicated that the clue to track down its quarry would be in here. It might take time, but time was meaningless to it.

**Sand Canyon Road**
**10:48 A.M.**

After gassing up, the battered pickup had rumbled off down Sand Canyon Road, leaving Sarah and Reese in a cloud of exhaust. Sarah looked around. A Mobil station. Across the way a recreational trailer park. Alongside that a picnic area where two families and their children romped in the brown grass.

Sarah saw Reese studying a damp field of strawberries that abutted the picnic area. He seemed so strange standing there, a man torn out of one time and never able to fit this one. Reese sensed she was watching and faced her with a weary, sober expression. His face was dirty, and his hair looked as if rats had been nesting there. Sarah gave him a small encouraging smile and indicated the restrooms around the corner of the service station.

"We'd better get cleaned up while we can." Reese nodded and simply followed her quietly. When they reached the doors, he continued to follow her into the women's room.

She stopped him with one hand and chuckled when she saw the confusion in his eyes. Pointing at the other door, she said, "That one's yours. I'm afraid you're on your own." Reese looked from the door marked Women to the one that said Men. Realizing his mistake, he shrugged, bemused, and went in the right one.

Sarah took care of business with great relief and then examined the battered facade she presented to the mirror. The watery soap from the encrusted dispenser couldn't get all the makeup off, but it did take care of the obvious dirt. Her hair was another matter. She didn't even have a brush. Wrinkling her lips, she ran her fingers through the tangle and frowned at the results. Beyond windblown. Hopefully, people would think it was a new style. Then she laughed softly to herself about that for a moment. What the hell did it matter what anyone thought now?

When she emerged from the bathroom, she could not see Reese. Sarah knocked on the men's room door—nothing.

A club of fear slammed down. She rounded the building and saw a pack of children tossing a small green nerf football over the head of a big, panting Irish setter. It barked and loped in lazy circles as the green missile soared from one youngster to the other. A Lincoln Continental was guzzling gas at one of the pump islands. Reese was gone.

She blinked with rising depair, suddenly realizing how powerful her need for his protection was. All the other roots of her life had been yanked out. Except for her mother. Realizing in a painful crush all at once that her mother might think she was dead, Sarah rushed to a pay phone at the corner of the lot.

She had no money, but she remembered her calling-card code and dialed the little house in San Bernardino. Almost before the first ring was finished, the anxious voice of her mother came on the line.

It took over a minute to assure her that her daughter was still alive and well. The police at the Rampart Division were looking for her and what they assumed was a suspect in the slaughter there. Sarah was about to explain the situation and ask for her mother to come and get her when she saw Reese standing in the strawberry field.

Relief washed away the fear in a sudden gush. Sarah gripped the phone and closed her eyes, her lower lip quivering. Her mother was demanding that Sarah tell her where she was so she could pick her up. Sarah realized she was better off with Reese for the time being. No one else could really help, because no one else would believe and take whatever precautions Reese knew to take.

Sarah ducked around the edge of the wall-mounted phone booth, pulling the receiver with her. Reese had made it clear that she was to have no contact with anyone, and she was afraid of what his reaction might be if he caught her on the phone.

She cupped her hand around her mouth to keep her

voice from carrying. She spoke rapidly and with a commanding urgency that would have surprised her had it been recorded and played back later.

"Mom, listen carefully. I don't have much time to talk—"

"What is it, dear? What's happening?"

"Just listen! I want you to pack some things; pack quickly and go to the cabin. Don't tell anyone where you're going, not even your friends. Not even Louise. Just go; do it right away. I can't explain now; you'll have to trust me."

"I have to know what's—"

"Just do it. If you don't, I won't be able to contact you again."

"God, Sarah . . . all right. All right."

Sarah glanced at Reese, standing strangely immobile, facing away from her. If he started to turn, she would have to drop the phone and start walking. Wouldn't that just freak her mother out.

"Okay, Mom. I'll call you up there later. Don't worry about me. I'll be okay."

"Sarah, listen to me. You have to get word to the police somehow."

"You don't understand. They can't help me. Nobody can. I've got to get going—"

"Sarah!"

"'Bye, Mom." She hung up, cutting off the tiny voice. Reese was kneeling now, his back to her, picking a strawberry. He brushed it off and bit into it. She couldn't read his expression from this distance, but somehow his former rigid and precisely controlled body language had now seemed to completely melt away.

He got slowly to his feet, licking his fingers, deep in thought. Then the green nerf ball was spiraling through the air right at his back. Just before it struck, Reese's body snapped into a crouch as he whirled around and batted the ball to the ground.

The children froze, then huddled for a moment before sending the youngest of them, a little girl not older than six, out to retrieve the ball.

Sarah felt some alarm at the tense stance Reese was maintaining, as if he thought the kids had tried to strike him deliberately. She hurried her steps across the street toward the field, but the girl was already standing at Reese's feet, staring up and squinting in that sidelong and sage way kids do when they suddenly get a fix on an adult.

As Sarah came up behind Reese, she slowed. The little girl was saying, "We didn't mean to scare you. Can we have our ball back now?"

Reese slowly unwound, like a metal band, and dropped his eyes to the ball. He swallowed the tension in his throat and bent to pick it up. With the same gentleness he had shown Sarah early that morning, the soldier offered the nerf ball. The girl hesitated, looking into those wild eyes from another time, perhaps sensing the horror and despair there, but then she sensed something else, something stronger and much more benevolent. She began to smile as she grabbed the ball out of Reese's hands. Immediately, she wheeled around and held up the object of her mission and screamed triumphantly, "I got it. I got it!"

Just then the setter completed its high arc, initially aimed at the ball in the child's hand, a bit lower than desired, smacking the girl against Reese's legs. The dog scrambled after the fallen prize. A moment later, it lumbered into the knot of youngsters and dropped the now-slobbery ball in their midst.

Reese helped the stunned girl back on her feet. He was wearing something a little like a smile, but it was too new an expression for him to get quite right. The girl primly pulled down her dress and sniffled with solemn distaste. "You smell icky," she announced, then pranced off to rejoin her friends.

"Kyle? Are you okay?"

Furrows like the ones on the ground began to form on his forehead. He wanted to speak, but some powerful inner force resisted it. Finally, his mouth began to move, forming words that were all but inaudible.

"I wasn't meant to see this," he said simply. When he reopened his eyes, Sarah was amazed at the lost expression there, almost as if he were about to cry.

"They briefed me. I've seen pictures, maps. I'd heard the stories. But I didn't expect—"

He was having trouble speaking again. Sarah moved closer. "I'm all wrong here. I can't . . . stop wanting to be a part of this . . ." He had no vocabulary to encompass her world.

Sarah made an attempt to touch his shoulder. He was locked on her face, oblivious to her touch. She tried to soothe him with words of her own.

"Kyle, you *are* a part of this. This is your world now."

He shook his head with such violence that Sarah recoiled. "No, no, no," he was muttering, "don't you see, Sarah. I can't stop for anything. I can't be anything but a soldier with a—" And here he stumbled again, but more from emotion than lack of words.

"Kyle, I—"

"Duty!" he interrupted. Reese realized he wasn't making much sense. He grabbed her shoulders and tried to shake the reality of the situation into her. "Sarah, don't you realize, all this is gone! Where I come from, this is a wasteland, littered with the bones of people like that!" He pointed toward the families at the picnic tables.

Sarah looked around, trying to see it as he did. The children, the dog, the fields, they were all so familiar. She was no more aware of them than a fish is of water. But to him it must be some idyllic dream, the paradise lost, of which only bitter half memories survived into his time. Now that she had glimpsed his world, she could begin to fathom the pain and disorientation he must be feeling just walking down the street.

And then he stopped, because he realized that the children were staring at him with a mixture of curiosity and fear.

The parents were craning back toward him and Sarah. He was making them conspicuous, failing his primary duty. Failing John. Failing himself. Threatening Sarah's precious life with his lack of emotional control. He clamped down, slamming all the doors shut on his feelings, and grabbed her arm. "We gotta move," he said, and pulled her toward the freeway on ramp.

## Panama Hotel
**11:52 A.M.**

A knife slit of hot sun fell across Terminator's back as it sat on the bed, considering options. Automatic heat diffusers shunted off the excess thermal energy as the machine's brain electronically communed with itself. The probability of locating the target at the address the cyborg analyzed as the mother of Sarah Connor was high enough to initiate an attack run.

Methodically, Terminator gathered up the tools required. There weren't many left. At the conclusion of this run, if it was negative, the cyborg would have to relocate the base of operations.

## Oceanside
**1:23 P.M.**

Sarah and Reese stepped down from the semi's cab after thanking the burly driver. As the truck thundered away, Sarah tugged Reese toward the Tikki Motel, across the street. It looked paperboard sleazy, the flat roof bordered in broken neon tubing, the entire structure leaning to one side, but it had beds. And showers. As they approached the place, Reese gazed at the uniformed marines strolling down the street in groups, out for a cruise away from Camp Pendleton, just north of town. He was struck with envy at the pristine uniforms but amazed at the softness in the young faces. Their warriors were like civilians, he thought, careless and unconcerned as they sauntered in the clear and open daylight. It still seemed incredible to him.

"Come on, Kyle," Sarah urged.

The motel office had been boarded up and converted into a cinema-style box office for security reasons. Oceanside had a lovely view of the Pacific, plenty of sun, and a high crime rate. The bedraggled pair stepped up to a grille with a slitlike opening. Reese dug in his pockets and pulled out a knotted wad of dirty paper money. "Is this enough?" he asked her.

"Yes," Sarah exclaimed. "And I don't want to know where you got it." She extracted the required amount to cover the overnight rate and spoke into the grille. "We need a room."

"With a kitchen," Reese added.

While Sarah dealt with the bored manager, Reese turned his attention to a large, dusty German shepherd tethered by a chain to a weathered doghouse alongside the office. It had just finished slurping water from its bowl. Reese caught its eyes. The animal was old, maybe ten years. But Reese could still detect a muted spark of fight behind the now-limpid brown eyes. Reese slowly approached, extending his hand. The dog hesitated only briefly, then got up and met Reese halfway. It licked his hand affectionately. He had cleared canine check again. Old habits. He relaxed a bit, subconsciously feeling more secure with a dog around.

A few moments later they entered the spartan room they had been assigned. There was a bed, a dresser, a tiny kitchen alcove, and a bathroom. Sarah could see the rust-stained tiles of the shower through the door. It wasn't the Waldorf. It was just heaven.

Reese prowled fussily, checking the place out with practiced efficiency. To him, the comfort factor was less important than the placement of the windows, which affected line of sight and line of fire, or the thickness of the walls. Concrete block. Good. Low penetration. The back door, which sported a deadbolt and an iron slide bar, also met with his approval.

The sign on the door, which read Do Not Use This Exit, meant nothing to the soldier. Even though the last one to paint the room had sloshed a coat all across the threshold, Reese would loosen it.

Sarah collapsed on the bed and said, "I'm dying for a shower." Reese glanced down at her as if that were the least of his priorities.

"I've got to go out for supplies," he announced, and started for the door.

"Kyle, wait." She had sat upright, not liking the idea of being left alone one bit. "Uh, we should change your bandage."

"When I get back." Then he saw the look in her face and realized what was troubling her. He walked over and tossed the .38 on the bed beside her. "I won't be long." He pivoted and got to the door fast. The sooner he took care of business, the faster he could return.

Sarah watched him leave and sat in the slatted light from the blinds listening to muffled traffic. She looked down at the snub-nosed weapon. It looked brutal and threatening, although she knew from her experiences with the cyborg that the gun could not stop it. Perhaps Reese left the weapon so that if the machine found her while he was gone, she could use it on herself. But no, Reese would never want that. His whole being was canted in the direction of her survival. He would want her to go on living until that right was forcibly removed. Then why leave it? It certainly didn't make her feel better. She nudged it tentatively, then picked it up. There was a sharp, snarly kind of oiled-metal smell to the weapon that made Sarah feel small and weak. But somehow, it felt right in her hand. Of course, the thing was designed to feel right in a human hand. But no, there was something else, Sarah realized. And then she developed another theory about why Reese had given her the gun.

He wanted her to get used to it. With a sinking feeling, she began to grasp the outer edges of something so large it completely overwhelmed any normal scale of thinking. She might have to use guns like this for the rest of her life.

Reese was losing forward momentum fast. All his reserves were hitting empty. But he had to maintain maximum alertness for just a little while longer. He was walking toward a large supermarket, crossing the parking lot jammed with people and new, shiny vehicles. His mouth watered to see the magnificent interiors with the complex-looking dashes and the—

*The mission, soldier. Mission, mission . . . Have to balance the scale . . . upgrade defense . . . build a wall of firepower even the 800 couldn't break through.* Reese shook his head wearily and sauntered on bruised and battered feet into the Fort Knox of food. *Yeah, no sweat,* Reese thought. *Just one more impossible job.*

The shower almost washed away the residue of blood and thunder Sarah had been carrying with her for the last dozen hours. She scrubbed herself raw with the plain white soap bar and scalded her body with steamy water. Later, sitting on the bed in a towel, her now-greaseless hair still dripping globules of moisture down her back, she almost felt clean. Almost.

She stretched out on the bed for a moment just to remain still, to reduce temporarily the insistent pull of gravity, and immediately fell into a deep, black sleep.

Sarah was cornered. The hulking figure of Terminator burst through the door with a lurid, eager grin, almost lascivious in its desire, and aimed the gun at her chest. Sarah saw the miniature red sun of the aiming laser roll across her body and freeze position over her right breast. Before she could thrust herself off the bed, there was an explosion like the world erupting, and the ball of lead whistled toward her, cutting the air like a surgical knife. When it struck her body, she felt the dull snap of rib bones and was lifted up and back as if punched by a giant. She could feel the hot life pumping out of her and thought serenely that the pain was too far away to hurt her very much, and then Terminator was standing over her and pumping bullet after bullet into her once-pretty body, each one a tiny battering ram punching holes in her meat and making her flop and bounce. Then she screamed, because it was not just death happening here but mindless, insane, and unfair mutilation, and she sat up and sucked in air to scream again and realized it was very quiet, so she couldn't have just screamed, and that meant she hadn't screamed, and that meant—

She had been dreaming.

When she was completely conscious, she realized two things simultaneously. It had become dark, and Reese had not yet returned. The grimy electric clock on the bed stand read 6:03. She sat up and immediately regretted it. Her muscles felt like tenderized steak, brutally abused by the hammerblows of the last twelve hours. She hadn't had nearly enough sleep to feel good.

The gun was on the dresser, pointed toward the wall, drawing her eyes like a summons from the Supreme Court. *Don't like the way I look?* it seemed to say. *Tough. You and I are now partners in life. Sleep without me if you dare.* Sarah shuddered and picked up the phone. A few seconds later she was talking to her mom.

"Believe me, Mom," she was saying, "there's nothing you can do to help. Just stay up there where it's safe. I can't tell you where I am. It's too dangerous."

But her mother was very persistent this time. She wanted at least a number she could call in case she had to leave. Sarah wouldn't be able to get in contact with her. That was certainly true enough.

"Mom, if I give you a number, you have to promise not to tell the police or anyone. I mean it. We'll probably only be here for a little while, anyway. Okay, okay, here it is."

She gave her mom the number written on the motel phone, then told her that she loved her. There was a brief hesitation, then the expected and warming answer. After Sarah hung up, she stared at the phone. All this mystery must be tearing her mother to pieces.

But she had to be protected. An errant thought skipped across her mind like a stone over a pond. It didn't touch down long enough anywhere for Sarah to consider it in any way significant. But that characteristic waver in her mom's voice was gone.

## Big Bear
### 6:04 P.M.

It wasn't a big place as far as resort cabins go. Basically, there were three rooms: a loft bedroom connected by steep stairs to a large downstairs area split into a kitchen area and a living room.

The door hung loose on its hinge like a torn ligament. On the floor underneath an overturned chair lay the body of Sarah's mother. The ambient temperature inside had come down in the last ten minutes to something close to the thirty-four degrees outside. The blood on Mrs. Connor's head had thickened. Her sightless eyes were staring blankly up at the thing in the desk chair that had murdered her. It was holding the phone to its ear, listening.

"I love you, Mom," said the voice on the other end.

Terminator hesitated for the briefest of moments, considering its options. Several verbal replies were passed over until the cyborg selected one that had the lowest factor of error that could alert the target to the digital synthesis of the voice of the battered woman at its feet. "I love you, too," it said, and hung up.

It did not smile as it dialed another number. Nor did it look down at its recent kill. It waited with the patience of the dead until someone picked up on the other end of the line. "Tikki Motel," the voice said.

Then it spoke again, this time in its own voice, precise, clean, conscienceless, and somehow devoid of any human perspective. "Give me your address there," it requested blandly.

## Tikki Motel
**6:27 P.M.**

When the man came to the door, Sarah's heart froze. He knocked once. Twice more. Then once again. Sarah gasped with relief and unlocked the door.

She wanted to throw her arms around Reese and kiss him, but he was pushing past her toward the kitchenette before the thought fully blossomed.

She locked the door again, her body rush taking its time slowing down, and faced Reese. She wanted to tell him she was glad he was back. Very glad. But he was putting two grocery bags on the counter and tearing them open perfunctorily. Several bottles rolled onto the stained tiles. Sarah glanced at them in confusion, reading the labels. "What have we got here? Corn syrup, ammonia, mothballs. Umm. What's for dinner?"

Reese didn't rise to the limp attempt at humor. He was unpacking another sack filled with ammunition for the .38, road flares, tape, scissors, a small pan with a strainer, and matches. "Plastique," he answered, distracted.

"Plastique? What is it?"

"Nitroglycerin, basically. Bit more stable. I learned how to make it when I was a kid." Sarah stared down at the smelly bottles and sighed.


## San Bernadino
**8:12 P.M.**

It was coming down the mountain like the grim reaper on a Kawasaki 900-cc motorcycle. All the way it maxed the cycle to a friction-breaking point, many times narrowly missing a nasty slide off the steep and winding roads into the ravine far below.

All this effort to intercept such a fragile biological process as the life of one young human girl. These soft, warm, wet machines were so easy to destroy, their systems so weak. A tiny bit of tissue removed here and there—or a single heartbeat missed—was all it took. Had it been designed for emotions or even value judgments, Terminator might have felt some professional shame that the process was taking so long. But of course it didn't. It felt nothing and would simply grind on indefinitely until it succeeded in its mission or its nuclear power cell was depleted, whichever came first. And at this rate of power consumption, the cell was good for at least twenty more years.

Terminator opened the cycle throttle all the way and weaved through the light traffic on the southbound 215. Fortunately for the highway patrol, none of its officers noticed the cyborg traveling at ninety-eight miles an hour. It was navigating a line from one death to another, crossing a sleepy desert city to the final death, the only one that mattered, the one that it had been created for.

## Tikki Motel
8:42 P.M.

If you squinted your eyes and didn't pick out the details, Kyle and Sarah could have been a couple preparing dinner side by side, a heartwarming domestic image. Instead, they were making the old guerrilla mainstay recipe—pipe bombs.

They were in the kitchen, beside each other at the small plywood table, which was now covered with utensils and containers.

Reese was holding up one of eight ten-inch sections of plumber's pipe. He was pressing the last of the high-explosive putty they had just made into the pipe with a plastic spoon. "Leave a little space, like this. Make sure there's none on the threads."

Sarah watched him gently scrape off the excess and then thread the end cap on.

"Screw this on—very gently."

He helped her get started; then, when certain that she could complete the pipe bombs without his assistance, Reese went to work on the back door.

Sometime later, when Reese had it operational, he came back to the kitchen to help Sarah make the fuses.

Streetlit patterns cast by the thin drapes waved gently on the walls. Sarah watched the shadows in the dark room, hoping that the swaying would put her to sleep. But she couldn't sleep, only stare at the ceiling.

Reese was an unmoving silhouette at the window, squatting where he could see out the slit between drape and wall. He might have been a statue entitled "Vigil." Stripped to the waist, his body looked lean and hard in the stark streetlight, the raised scars like insignia.

Sarah shifted her gaze to the table; the completed bombs lay neatly in a row next to a nylon bag, which had already been stuffed with a lighter, some packages of food, and various other incidentals for survival on the road. Across the way, sitting in a chair by the window, was Reese.

She got up and walked over to him. He looked at her only briefly as she sat beside him on the arm of the chair, then went back to peering out the window, watching, his .38 in his lap.

At Sarah's unwavering insistence, Reese had bathed. His face stubble was gone, showing smooth pink skin, his hair clean and damp. He was wearing the new jeans he had purchased earlier and tennis shoes. Across his naked back ragged scars marred the flat expanse of tensed muscle. It was like a road map of agony, and Sarah was filled with a sense of futile doom. Flesh was no match for machine.

"Do you think he'll find us?" she asked.

"Probably," Reese said.

"Look at me; I'm shaking. Some legend, huh? You must be pretty disappointed."

Reese let the shade go and faced her.

She was wearing no makeup. Her hair was tangled. Her lower lip quivered. "I'm not disappointed," he said in as neutral a voice as he could.

Sarah looked at his eyes. Looked away. She knew how she must compare to the image of her he had brought with him. She was sure that even the lowliest female scavengers in his world were better suited to survival than she was.

"Kyle, the women in your time—what were they like?"

Reese shrugged. "Good fighters."

"Kyle . . ." she began, then hesitated, realizing that she was looking at a sweet young face, handsome, really, despite his scar. He was her protector, but somehow she sensed Reese needed her. What she was about to ask was something new; it had nothing to do with his duty or her fear or their shared nightmare. "In your time, was there someone—"

"Someone?" Reese asked, puzzled.

"A girl. Someone special. You know . . ."

"No," he said, too quickly, remembering all the women he had known, especially the ones who had died. It seemed as if they had all died, at least the ones he knew by name.

"Never," he added, almost as an afterthought.

Sarah paused, surprised. "You mean, you never—"

Reese turned back to the window, his fingers tightening around the gun involuntarily. "There was little time for that. I was in a war. If they were old enough for . . . that, then they were old enough to fight. They were just other soldiers—nothing more."

The gray and endless loneliness of his life struck her then, and the little Sarahs felt the hot wind of outrage and despair, then something more painful and yet more wonderful than that coming after—something that twisted them around and made them face a new part of Sarah so that they wept and held each other. "I'm so sorry," Sarah said, and impulsively touched a raised, poorly healed slash under his shoulder blade. "So much pain . . ." Tears came out of her then, rolling hot down her cheeks, tears for him as he sat rigid under her touch, seemingly oblivious of her fingers caressing an old wound.

"Pain can be controlled," he was saying, his voice flat.

"Pain is a tool. Sometimes, when it is irrelevant, you can just disconnect it."

"But then you feel nothing."

Reese held on to John Connor's words. He replayed the briefing over and over at high speed through his memory, clamping down on his emotions, which were boiling over and out of him. He tried to block them, tried to seal the cracks, but the feelings were under enormous pressure, and her fingers felt so soft and good.

Sarah felt Reese's muscles ripple under her fingers now, and his breath caught in his throat. Then he spoke very quietly, as if she were a priest and he were giving confession. "John Connor gave me a picture of you once. I never knew why. It was very old. Torn. You were young, like you are now. You had a faraway look in your eyes, and you were smiling, just the slightest bit, but somehow it was a sad smile. I always wondered what you were thinking. I memorized every line, every curve."

He choked off the last. No way was he going to continue, but he couldn't stop, because now he was blasted open. Everything held inside was spurting through the gaping breach, and his mouth went on, and his voice grew strong with conviction as he said, "Sarah, I came across time for you. I love you. I always have."

*There now. All said. Now go back inside and cement over the breach and everything will be fine.* But he couldn't find his way back, because he was staring at Sarah's luminous eyes. She was looking at him in shock, her eyes moist, and he wasn't certain anymore of anything—not his training, not his duty, and especially not her feelings toward him. But he knew that he had loved her and that nothing would ever kill her. Not a man, a machine, or anything else would ever come near hurting her again, because he would destroy a world to save her. He would cut himself in two. He would cease to exist so that she might live, not for mankind now but for her.

Sarah saw all this on his face and in his eyes, and it was his expression more than his words she believed. What shocked her the most was the revelation that she had, after all, inspired the Look, more profoundly and painfully than she ever imagined anyone ever could. Reese was giving her the Look, and it was so intense it burned her, but she wasn't going to look away. She wanted him to look at her that way forever. And as she wanted that, time began to slow down, and it became very hushed in the small dark room.

Sarah touched his face. The skin over his cheekbone was so soft. . . .

Suddenly, Reese remembered the way back. It was dark and cold and hard, but it was important that he start toward it now if he really loved her. Wrenching himself to his feet, he walked away from her.

"I shouldn't have said that," he hissed through clenched teeth. He stood over the table and began methodically packing the pipe bombs into the nylon bag. For a moment Sarah went weak with disorientation. He was moving like a machine, like a cyborg. He was hiding in the machine from her.

This she could not bear, and she came to him, pulled him around, embraced him, kissed his neck, his cheek, his mouth. The rush of feeling seemed to flow through her arms and mouth into his body and melt his rigidity. Reese knew the way back was lost forever.

He let out a soft whimper as a part of him died and another part grew stronger. He pulled Sarah tighter into his arms, crushing her to his chest, and drank from her mouth.

Somehow they were on the floor by the table. He couldn't feel it. There was nothing around him but Sarah, and he wanted her and pulled her closer and closer.

She was kissing his scars. She was taking away the pain and altering the purpose of his life. She was a thief, and he was a willing victim. She was moving above him now, hovering like a tender antithesis to the Aerial H-Ks, and he reached for her even though she was already as close as he could get her without crushing her to death.

Sarah felt his need rage through his body and resonate all through hers until she was hungrily devouring him. For a timeless stretch, it was like that, mindless clutching and gasping, without plan, both of them drowning in the first powerful wave of their love.

But then Sarah began to emerge and see that he was lost now, undirected, wallowing in confused need for her. She led Reese to the bed.

Once there, she helped him get out of his pants, then guided him over her body, putting his hands on the places that had seemed asleep because they had never been truly awakened. They awoke now to his touch and cried out for release. Soon both of them were naked, making a new environment of togetherness, an environment that had never been before and would never be again. And now time did stop.

They alone beat out a measured thrust of time as their bodies met at the tender, pulsing center of a grim cosmos.

### Tikki Motel
### 11:28 P.M.

Sarah opened her eyes and watched the light patterns shifting on the wall.

Reese was asleep next to her, his chest rising and falling with deep satisfaction. His face was so sweet in repose. Thinking back on the whole thing, she realized what a child he was and how much this experience had changed them both. Before they found each other, she had been a waitress locked inside her own insecurities. He had been a child-soldier, making only war his life. But now that they had collided and become one, they were both new persons.

The solemnity of this thought made her heart almost stop. She rolled to Reese and held him tightly in her arms. He stirred but did not awake. This was a triumph of sorts. He was safe in her arms. There was an impenetrable bubble around them now, and nothing, not even a terminator, could break through.

She kissed his face gently, and he moaned. He had kept death away, and she was giving him life. They were both teachers. The knowledge was equally important to their survival. Love and war. Pleasure and pain. Life and death. And endurance. Yes . . .

But they were not alone in the universe. Sarah became aware of the noise of civilization outside their door. Traffic. Murmurs from the room next door. The high whistle of a military jet passing overhead. A dog barking. Endurance was necessary when you were being tailed by an unstoppable machine bent on your destruction. That was the kind of life that lay before them. Running from something that would never give up searching, that would keep coming after them until they were both dead. It gave the word relentless an almost-physical dimension. The dimensions of a terminator.

She knew that they must change their strategy. Reese evidently was simply here to prevent Terminator from killing her, keep her well hidden until the war, and help her emerge with her son and rally the resistance movement to turn the tide. But how could they survive as long as Terminator was in the world? Reese had tried to destroy it before in Tech Noir. The police had riddled it with bullets. And still it came after them.

Now they had the pipe bombs. And they had something more powerful than simple, animal cunning. They had a feeling so strong it would fire their will and perhaps make it possible now to turn around and wait for Terminator. To prepare a special welcome and then obliterate the bastard. There must be a way. Reese would know.

She sat up and started to awaken him, but his eyes were already open. He was concentrating on something very far away.

"Listen to the dogs," he said, and the tone of his voice sent shivers like icicles through her. She faced the window and heard the distant barking of dogs. Two, then three. Another howled. They were blocks away, some maybe half a mile away, taking up the alarm from backyards and porches, their body chemistry rubbed raw by what they smelled in the wind. A dog, sensing a world we don't see, could look into a man's eyes and know if what looked back was human. Then the German shepherd chained outside the hotel took up the alarm.

Whatever it was, it could not pass canine check, and it was coming toward them. As they lunged for their clothes simultaneously, time rapidly began to speed up.

Terminator walked past the office toward the target, ignoring the snarling creature, restrained only by the snapping chain, lunging at it, each step bristling with increased energy as microprocessor circuits fired up to attack speed. The details of its environment became crystal sharp and so dense with information that no human brain could have retained it all. The weight of gravity. The texture and temperature of the asphalt. The distances of all objects relative to it. The wind velocity. The ocean of sound washing over its sensors. The movements of heated bodies behind the stucco walls. The exact dimensions and qualities of everything within Terminator's field of contact were measured, clocked, and entered into the constantly updated equation of motion and mass.

They didn't have a chance.

Terminator stood before their door and raised the AR-180. With one snap of its leg, the door caved in, exploding into three large jagged planks.

The machine stepped into the room and sprayed it efficiently with automatic fire. Bullets thudded into the bare table—collapsing it, splunked through the easy chair —geysering chunks of wadding, and found the bed, ravaging it until the smoking carcass of mattress and metal frame could hold no life.

Terminator reloaded, then looked around.

An error had been committed. Terminator's digitalized view of the interior revealed every object in stark relief, every object but the target. Room number doublechecked. Option? Reroute. Negative. Scan farther.

The cyborg rapidly strode into the room and looked around. It saw the open back door and heard the running footsteps simultaneously.

Herb Rossmore had slowed the Bronco and gazed up

sleepily at the glowing Tikki Motel sign. He needed to get some sleep before he went out like a light on the freeway and bought himself some divider fence. By mistake, he had turned one apron early and come to a stop in the rear parking lot, facing the back doors of the rooms. Cursing under his breath, he had jammed the stick shift into reverse and was about to release the clutch when what he saw caused him to stall out the engine.

A couple slipped out the back door of one of the rooms and moved quietly but rapidly along the wall. They were both barefoot, and the guy was still shrugging into a long overcoat, with no shirt on underneath. The girl had her jersey on inside out and was carrying a heavy-looking nylon bag.

Snapping his head up, the guy spotted Herb and started running barefoot across the lot right for the Bronco. Herb reacted quickly when he realized what was going to happen next. He slapped the door lock, then grappled with the window crank, desperately trying to get something between himself and this lunatic. But Reese was on him then, ramming his hand through the space between window and door and closing iron fingers around Herb's throat. Herb battled ineffectually at Reese's arm, then acquiesced when he saw the pistol in the other hand. He unlocked the door.

There was the sound of a loud crash from the far side of the building, followed quickly by the stuttering cracks of Terminator's AR-180.

"Sarah!" Reese screamed as he flung Herb to the pavement. She was on the other side of the Bronco, already piling in, terror distorting her face. Reese clicked the key in the ignition just as Terminator strode through the door.

Herb had only a moment to roll out of the way as the madman in his vehicle churned the V-8 engine to a high whine and dropped the clutch.

Herb heard the crunch of metal with confused disdain as the Bronco struck something head-on and mashed it against the motel building.

It was a man.

Horrified, Herb cowered as his Bronco screamed with burning tires and lurched backward out of the parking lot. It spun in a circle and growled mechanically as it crunched into first gear, then roared off into the night. That was pretty bad, Herb thought, but what was worse stood up nearby.

The big man who had been flattened against the building, who should have been dead, quickly retrieved the dropped weapon, noted the direction in which the Bronco had headed, then turned and fled through the ruined back door.

A moment later, Herb heard a motorcycle explode into hi-revs. Two seconds later, he saw it being wheeled down the sidewalk at the end of the motel. It tore off down the street after the stolen Bronco. As Herb stood on trembling legs, he was overcome with one single sane conclusion in a whirl of chaotic thoughts—he wasn't going to get his Bronco back. And he was right.

They had almost died.

Sarah was gripping the Bronco's dash, her heart hammering as the pinpoints of streetlight blurred by, experiencing a soul-wrenching déjà vu. They had almost died naked in each other's arms. The machine had tried to extinguish them, blindly and stupidly, for no reason, as far as it was concerned, except instructions from another machine. And now she could see it coming on after them, a single headlight growing steadily larger in the rearview mirror, almost as if it were growing there like a tumor to explode into the Bronco's cab. She hated it.

Reese was breathing in and out in a mechanical, regular rhythm to get his body under control. He yanked the wheel, and Sarah slammed into the door as the Bronco broke contact with the road and described a rude-angled arc onto the freeway on ramp. Then she was slammed back as Reese bottomed out the accelerator.

The chase was so different this time. She was watching Reese operate now with a mixture of fear for him, and pride. He maneuvered the Bronco into the fast lane in an instant.

Traffic was light this far down the coast at this hour. A few lumbering eighteen-wheelers and even fewer cars, heading south to San Diego. Reese wended through them masterfully, as though they were stationary objects.

But then, so did their pursuer. In fact, Terminator was continually gaining ground, moving closer in agonizingly small increments, like the inexorable and regular movement of a clock. Sarah stole a glance backward and started. Terminator was right behind them, looming closer now that it was not artificially distanced by the distortion of the mirror. The thing was tucked over the handlebars to reduce air resistance, throttle rammed open, and now it was unslinging the assault rifle. Against the blast of wind, the cyborg raised the weapon in a one-handed grip. The barrel was rock steady, aimed directly at her.

"Down!" Reese shouted as he saw the gun coming up, but Sarah was already ducking. A second later the back window of the Bronco shattered from the impact of the bullets. One stray shot ricocheted around the cab, embedding itself in the dash above Sarah. Close.

Reese swerved the Bronco, diving for cover around a tractor trailer.

Terminator leaned hard, right behind them, relentlessly closing the gap, missing the rear of the trailer by millimeters.

Reese ripped the tires from the surface of the road by weaving wraithlike through the slow-moving traffic.

People barely had time to register the objects that streaked around them. It was utter madness. And it got worse.

Tires squealed as the back of a moving van loomed up. Synthetic flesh and metal knee ground into the road, maintaining balance in a thirty-degree lean.

Reese feinted right, then left, sliding toward a Greyhound bus in a four-wheel drift.

Terminator fired the assault rifle again. This time the bullets struck the guardrail where the Bronco had been. A clear miss!

The Bronco slipped around two parallel trucks and sped through the narrow space left by a night crew working on the divider fence. Terminator saw that it would have to throttle back and change lanes to follow. It did not want to slow; it wanted to accelerate, so it choose a different path.

It wrenched the cycle past a Winnebago down an off ramp, and without slowing, ran a red light at the intersection and climbed back up the on ramp. There was some wreckage in the cyborg's wake as cars swerved into each other to avoid hitting the insane motorcyclist. None of it mattered. It was just Terminator and Sarah.

Reese saw Terminator roaring onto the freeway, the cyclopian glare of the Kawasaki's headlight bobbing back and forth in a tight pattern that would lead to the Bronco.

"Change places!" Reese screamed over the hammering pistons of the V-8. She slid under him as he kept the pedal glued to the floor. She grabbed the wheel and slipped her foot over the accelerator.

"Don't slow down!" Reese said.

"I won't," she answered, and there was conviction in her voice, a tone that was new to her and somehow very comforting. For an instant, Reese and Sarah locked eyes, and time froze.

But then the Bronco grazed a Datsun 240-Z tearing off its side-view mirror, and time exploded into howling fragments. Sarah steeled her arms and turned the wheel the way Ginger would have done, getting the Bronco back on track. Reese began digging in the nylon bag for weapons. He trusted her to drive. Their lives were in each other's hands, literally.

Terminator shot through an open pocket of traffic and fired a short, disciplined burst at the Bronco. Bullets thudded into the rear panel. One took a chunk of rubber off the left rear tire, but the steel bands held. Sparks exploded and died. Terminator gunned the cycle.

Reese got the first pipe bomb out and held a Bic lighter under the fuse.

Sarah yawed the truck onto the divider shoulder, inches away from the fence, grimacing as she fought to hold the Bronco on an even track, as Matt would have. For the first time in her life, she was controlling her own fate—at ninety-eight miles an hour.

Reese got the fuse lit and leaned out the passenger side. He watched the fuse sputter and smoke in the wind until it fitfully burned down to the end cap, then tossed it onto the road.

Right into Terminator's path.

The road erupted, geysering flame and smoke abruptly. For a moment, nothing happened. Then, almost simultaneously, the concussion blew back Reese's hair, and Terminator roared out of the rising cloud, undamaged. Too soon.

Reese got another bomb.

The AR-180 chattered again, tearing up the Bronco.

Sarah feinted left, then right, her stomach protesting every radical move.

Reese leaned out and waited for the fuse to burn down half an inch above the end cap. Then he let it go.

It clattered on the pavement and rolled like a crazed bowling pin—past the cyborg. There was another explosion, well behind Terminator, which succeeded in terrifying the drivers in the wake of this impromptu urban combat. A black Corvette spun out, stopping crossways in its lane, only to be blown into splintered Fiberglas by a fishtailing truck.

Ahead, traffic was thinning out. That was bad. Less cover.

Terminator slung the AR-180, using its free hand to grope for the last magazine. In one rapid movement, it shoved the clip into the assault rifle and whipped the weapon back into firing position.

Meanwhile, Reese groped for another bomb.

The Bronco sped around a chromed semi milk tanker and accelerated into a long, tiled-lined underpass. As they entered the fluorescent-lighted tunnel, Reese lobbed another bomb. It clattered and bounced up into the air, slowing rapidly. The explosion thundered in the enclosed space. A wall of smoke formed behind them. They could hear the startled dinosaur howling of the semi's air horn, a chorus of tires screeching, and then a motorcycle punched a hole in the smoke. Terminator fired at them. The side mirror exploded. Bullets furrowed along the Bronco, whining ominously. Two found Reese.

He grunted, surprised, as the twin clubs of pain smashed into his chest and arm. The pipe in his hand dropped, fuse unlit, useless. Ironically, it end overed into Terminator's leg, tearing a chunk of flesh off the calf. Reese slumped over the door, half in and half out of the cab.

"Kyle! Oh, god, no . . ." Sarah lunged for him, dragging him back onto the seat, in the process slamming the Bronco into the far wall of the tunnel. Instinctively, she took her foot off the gas and went for the brake. Instead, Sarah fought the wheel and rode the wall for a moment, sanding off the paint past the primer coat, showering sparks. Sarah, listening to a new voice born of her union with Reese, smacked the accelerator again, the V-8 sucked fuel, and Sarah was slammed back as the Bronco churned out into the road, climbing quickly back to ninety. But it was already too late.

Terminator had not slowed; it was thirty-eight feet behind them. It aimed the AR-180 directly at the back of Sarah's head and depressed the trigger.

The bullets did not shear off Sarah's head at the neck, because the AR-180's clip was expended.

Without pausing, Terminator dropped the assault rifle. Before it hit the ground, Terminator had pulled the little nickel-plated .38 revolver from its jacket and triangulated on the back of Sarah's head and fired.

But Sarah chose that moment to feint left. The bullet demolished the mirror on her side, showering her with shards. Flinching, she lost control. The Bronco weaved right and left, beginning to drift; then Sarah got it straightened out in a rush of controlled panic. But now Terminator was coming alongside, aiming the huge pistol at her through those dark sunglasses, the bared eye pulsing red beneath the lens. It fired again. The bullet clanged through the cab and tore past her ear before shattering the windshield.

Terminator was her enemy. It had shot her lover. It wanted her death. And the fear inside Sarah was suddenly blown out by the blast of anger that erupted now, coursing into her arms. A very human expression of murderous rage distorted Sarah's face as she lifted her foot off the gas; slammed it down on the brake and cranked the wheel.

The Bronco slammed the motorcycle into a guardrail. It went down in an instant, smacking pavement, bouncing back up, toppling end over end, then dropping into a slide. Somewhere in there the cyborg let go.

The Bronco and the cycle shot out of the tunnel at eighty miles an hour. Something followed more slowly, rolling out of control and then going spread-eagled to stabilize: Terminator. Sarah was trying to see where it was when she drifted into the divider, locked the wheel in the wrong direction, and flipped the truck.

The world upended, cartwheeling around the cab as Sarah and Reese were pressed against each other and the roof of the cab. Sarah's fear returned, but her scream was muffled by the crash of the Bronco slamming back to concrete and rolling onto its back.

Terminator hit a guardrail post and backflipped over the center divider. It hit the other side, rolling to a stop in the shadow of an overpass. Its leather jacket was smoking, and patches of skin had been scraped raw, as if it had been dragged over a cheese grater. But the machine stirred, then sat up.

Terminator turned at the demon roar of an air horn. Then it was struck by a Kenworth tractor trailer, which slammed into it at seventy miles an hour like an enormous flatiron. The cyborg disappeared under the truck even as the air brakes began to scream. The trailer wheels locked in clouds of smoke as Terminator tumbled, ricocheting viciously between the chassis housing blurring above it and the pavement beneath.

The driver hadn't seen anything in his lane. The absolute shadow of the overpass had hidden the man-shaped mass there until his headlights were upon it, and by then it was too late. He was on the brakes in an instant, cutting in the jake and feathering the pedal to prevent the big rig from jackknifing so that his load of six thousand gallons of superunleaded wouldn't wind up covering an acre of freeway. His partner was thrown forward, waking up with a nasty start.

"Son of a bitch!" they bellowed, not quite in unison.

The two tanker trailers slewed and fishtailed like a derailing train.

*Shit, I'm losing it,* the driver thought.

The body came up for a sickening instant before falling back to the pavement. They could hear it thunking up underneath, slamming around, and could *feel* the thuds as what they thought was bone smacked the undercarriage. They heard and felt all this over the high-pitched squeal of locked tires on asphalt, over the shuddering rumble as the truck ground to a halt.

The two men let out their breath slowly, daring to believe that somehow the driver had managed to get the wild machine stopped. They looked at each other, the color gone from their faces; 6,000 gallons of superunleaded—fuck!

"Stay here," the driver said, and dropped out the driver's door. His partner just stared straight ahead, gripping the dash.

The driver didn't want to look. *But you never know,* he thought. *Maybe the guy is still alive.* Oh, god, wouldn't *that* be horrible—an agonized, pulverized basket case *he* had made. As he reached the second tanker trailer, he slowed down. It was up ahead on the road. A blood smear. And was that a lump of clothing, or flesh?

Momentum carried him past the end of the second trailer and into the cyborg's hands.

When Terminator had been struck by the tanker, it bounced up under the cab and shot an arm onto the low-hanging exhaust pipe, then was dragged along for a moment before letting go. It aimed itself strategically and correctly estimated the bounce angle. When it ricocheted underneath the truck, it grabbed the drive-shaft casing, and hand over hand, the man-machine made its way back toward the connecting disc behind the cab. But the truck suddenly braked, and the momentum caused an error in calculating the next outreach. Terminator was torn loose, bounced back, smacked the bottom of the first tanker, and then rolled to a stop near the rear trailer's tires.

It immediately crawled out and surveyed the vehicle. Considering its options, it decided to commandeer the truck to continue the pursuit. As it started forward, its internal screen displayed damage reports. Backups started kicking into the battered hydraulics, but nothing could be done about the pivot joint in the left ankle. It was mainframe damage that would require full attention later, if necessary. But actually all it did was cause the machine to limp. And it could no longer sprint up to twenty-two miles an hour. But it could walk. As it came around the last tank trailer, it collided with and immediately terminated the driver. Terminator's powerful fingers tore out the man's throat, then started for the cab, letting the limp body melt onto the pavement like a mass of Jell-O and broken sticks.

The partner had been sitting on the passenger side in the cab, trembling with shock. The horror of what had happened was only just beginning to sink in when a grisly apparition opened the opposite door and sat behind the wheel.

The partner shrank back at what he saw: the face gouged open by the road, flesh hanging down in a raw flap, a torn-open eye socket with something demoniacally glowing inside, like an alien eye, a blood-pulsing slash along the powerful arm.

It stared down at the controls in the dash and seemed to be thinking about them. Then it looked up and into Wayne's eyes and spoke. "Get out."

He didn't have to be asked twice. He bashed his door open and leaped to the pavement, cracking his shin, then ran, limping, as fast as he could go away from the dead thing they had killed that had stared him in the face.

Terminator scanned the layout of controls in the big cab, cross-referencing with memory on the make of truck, shift pattern, transmission configuration, and engine specifications. When its bloody fingers closed over the shift knob, it felt the massive transport machine as if it were an extension of itself. It shifted into low second and let out the clutch.

Terminator spun the wheel and gunned the diesel engine. Slowly, the tanker lumbered in a wide circle. The machines were coming back to Sarah.

Sarah came up from claustrophobic semi-consciousness. When she fought for a breath and began to see images, the world came back to her in slashes of light and intermittent flaps of reality. They were upside-down in the cab, lying on the roof, staring up at the pedals. Reese was under her, limp and still. She tried to get off him, but their legs were entangled. Finally, she got clear and looked back at him. There was new blood on his chest and his arm. His face was like milk, and his eyes had dark circles under them. A slight blue tinge began to hue his pallor, and she realized in a shock he must not be breathing. She grabbed his collar and shook him.

"Reese!"

A black void opened up before her as she saw him being slowly torn out of her life. She tried to pull him back from the brink, to drag his lifeless being back into existence. She kissed his face. She wept, she coddled, and she urged sweetly, then finally, reaching a pragmatic behavior by default, blew air into his lungs. She noticed how it bubbled in red froth out of a hole in his chest. Instinctively, she slapped her palm over it and continued. He coughed and opened his eyes. Raising a bloody hand, Reese weakly pushed her back, trying to rise. Trying to protect her. To continue the mission. It would be okay if he could just—if he could— He fell back, gasping.

Then Sarah looked up and saw Terminator killed. She watched the tanker slide to a halt about seventy-five yards down the road and squinted as the driver stepped down and walked to the rear of his truck. She gasped as a shadowy figure limped into the pool of streetlight and murdered him and blinked with incomprehension as the thing looked calmly toward her, then to the cab, got in, and began making the long, slow death arc back toward her.

The truck ground through three gears, lurching up to forty-eight miles an hour, then veered into the divider fence, smashing it flat and thundering across into Sarah's side of the freeway. The nightmare wasn't going to end. Instead, the nightmare had swollen to the size of a tanker truck, its headlights stretching out, licking at the overturned Bronco, bleaching the interior, growing brighter by the second, its engines rattling the night.

Sarah snapped into action, kicking the bent door open and yanking on Reese's body, trying to get them both out of the cab before the truck flattened it.

But Reese was hanging on to the rim of life by his fingernails and needed every ounce of strength to stay there. He couldn't help her at all.

Sarah grunted and then came out of the Bronco and slipped her arms under Reese's. He was so heavy!

The headlights bored into her, and the engines screamed mortality. She was blinded, and her ears rang. She couldn't see Reese. She couldn't hear her own scream. She could only feel him in her arms. She pulled.

His leg was caught. That was the problem. Somewhere in the cab Reese's leg was caught. She turned his body, and his leg came loose, but now the truck was so near she could feel its thunder, and she looked away so that the only sign it made in her head was the two suns glowing onto the pavement behind her. Sarah was out of breath and strength. Gravity did the rest. She fell backward into the street as the tanker struck the Bronco.

Metal slammed metal, and rigid steel was instantly ripped and crushed into new shapes. There was no explosion, just sound—a thunderous crash and screech as the Bronco folded across the front of the tanker's grille, hesitated as long as the laws of energy conservation allowed, then rebounded into the air just as Sarah fell back—and Reese's legs cleared the cab.

A moment later Terminator locked the brakes, and the tanker backed up on itself, the full load of petroleum compressing into the forward sections of the tankers, bulging the metal there. The Bronco had been blasted into a high arc, and when it came back to earth, it flipped four times, then rocked on its side and lay still. In an instant, it had graduated from vehicle to modern sculpture.

Sarah looked back as the big truck lurched to a stop and then turned. The headlights were crawling across the landscape, spinning around, searching for her.

She heaved Reese to his feet in one exhausting pull. He was murmuring something in her ear.

"Go on without me. Go on—"

She slapped his face, hard. It was a reflex. Everything she was doing was reflex now, because most of her had been put on hold. The little Sarahs had nothing to say; they'd been ripped and thrown away. She struck Reese again. His eyelids snapped up. The stinging pain cut through the dull ache in his chest and arm. There seemed to be two five-ton weights in his body, and he could barely move, but when Sarah slapped him, he could put all that into perspective, focus on her face, see the headlights reflected in them simultaneously with the fear, know that she was going to die unless he came with her, and since he did not want her to die Reese took a step. It was a major triumph. But it was all out of scale with the juggernaut bearing down on them. One step was a drop in the bucket.

They had to run.

Sarah threw his arm around her shoulder, and they began to move.

The truck was gaining speed, roaring on.

Reese was searching for some reserve strength to get his legs moving. He thought of Sarah dead and bleeding and found it.

They ran.

Slow, uneven strides but better than walking and certainly better than shuffling, but the truck went into fourth gear, engine racing, hitting forty-eight miles an hour.

Inside the cab, Terminator estimated point of contact in eight seconds.

But Sarah was pulling Reese down the side of the freeway toward the border fence. Terminator made adjustments in contact estimation. It yanked the wheel and then squealed into another arc, now assuming point of contact at nine seconds.

Sarah saw the rig bouncing over the edge of the freeway and thundering down the ivy-encrusted slope toward them. She heaved Reese up over the fence, all but flinging him into the bushes on the other side. The headlights lighted the way ahead, tantalizing and mocking as they closed on the pair. But Sarah was now leaping the fence and pulling Reese to his feet.

Terminator lost traction, and the truck began to slip on the wet ivy. It crashed through the border fence about four feet away from Sarah and Reese.

The truck crashed through the chain-link fence and tore through bushes, then rolled onto a residential street. By the time Terminator got the transmission back into first and was gunning the truck around, Sarah and Reese were about fifty yards ahead, running into a parking lot.

Terminator and the truck gained speed, sideswiping a row of parked cars.

Sarah and Reese staggered and ran down the street toward the only cover nearby—an industrial park. As they were running down the driveway apron, they heard the bellowing engine of Terminator's tanker truck not far behind.

Reese knew his legs were giving out. He couldn't go much farther. His entire body was closing down for the winter, the long cold winter, but before that happened—

"Go ahead!" he yelled at Sarah. She shook her head violently until she saw the pipe bomb in his hand and he brutally pushed her onward.

She understood and acted, running on, moving more slowly into the middle of the lane between several parked cars. The truck rumbled after her. She could see Reese fling himself into a deep shadow, scrabble forward, and shove the bomb into the tailpipe of the passing tanker.

Terminator was shifting gears and highballing through a parked car only forty yards behind her, rapidly closing the gap. Sarah dodged around a tree and broke into a leg-pounding run, springing all out, head tilted back, charging out of death's open jaws, but the truck was bearing down, splintering the tree, and howling pistons were screaming for her blood.

She ran faster—thirty yards.

She ran faster—twenty-five yards.

Her legs were blurs. Her lungs were dying. Twenty—

Sarah reached the corner of a building as a wave of light and heat flared behind her. She threw herself to the ground and rolled. Looking back, she saw the most beautiful destruction she could ever have imagined: a fireball grew from the tailpipe to the cab, rolling in bright yellow waves of superoxygenated gas, the liquid furiously releasing its energy. An ocean of flame enveloped the entire tanker truck, and it jumped forward into the air, angrily self-destructing at high speed. Sarah lay back behind the corner of the building as a concussive shock wave hit her like a slap, driving the breath out of her lungs. She could hear rending metal as the traumatized remains of the truck crashed back to the pavement and rolled to a stop. She had to see the thing frying in the wreckage, had to *know* it was finished once and for all. She leaned out around the building.

Flames surrounded the truck, geysering up in flickering sheets, blotting out the stars with thick clouds of roiling smoke. Something moved in the twisted cab: Terminator. It pushed out of the bent debris, charred, mishappen, lunging down to the ground. It fell and rolled onto its back, a moving torch. Could it feel pain? Sarah shielded her face from the heat, looking through her fingers. Even at this distance it was like looking into a steel smelter. The pavement was melting and bubbling around the burning wreckage, catching fire itself. Terminator continued to crawl without apparent pain. It was tangled in the twisted debris, the hair and clothing already gone and its remaining flesh sizzling like bacon on the griddle of its own superheated endoskeleton.

Slowly, reluctantly, the thing in the flames stopped moving until only its head turned, locking into position so that its eyes were facing her. Even in death it watched her. Sarah knew then she would live out the rest of her days.

She had survived. But that blackened skull of a face would haunt her every night of her life. She watched it burn for a long time until it was obscured by settling wreckage. A dim sense of triumph welled up but was quickly extinguished when she remembered Reese.

Scrambling to her feet, Sarah forgot about Terminator burning in the debris. She staggered into the searing air, moving around the truck, trying to see past the flames to the dumpster on the far side. But the fire was in her way. And the heat was a physical wall she could not penetrate. Her face was stretching taut, baking off the moisture.

"Reese!"

Then she caught a glimpse through dying flames of the dumpster. Burning gas had made a finger of light to it, and now it was surrounded by smoke. Had Reese gotten out? She needed to know if he was alive more powerfully than she wanted to live. She started to walk into the flames when Reese called her name.

He was there, lunging through a momentary pocket in the blaze, held back, as she had been, from breaking through. Now they came into each other's arms. There was smoke pouring off Reese's clothes. Blood caked his skin. He groaned weakly when she embraced him, but she could not be gentle now. Her body was still reacting, almost of its own volition, crushing him to her breast, kissing his face, murmuring her love.

They sagged to their knees on the pavement, locked in an embrace before the raging truck/cyborg inferno.

"We got it," Sarah said, rocking him now, making time slow down, closing off the heat with her body, protecting him now from the flames, from his own mortality, if possible, returning the favor of his love and protection. The lovers clung to each other and so did not see the debris stir, did not notice the clang of metal as twisted steel was pushed out of the way. Did not see Terminator rising like a phoenix from the fire.

The machine had shut down temporarily to allow maximum heat shunting. As the flesh burned away and the superalloy of its chassis began to glow red, it came back on line, its internal power growing in rapidly multiplying increments. It was using the fire to strengthen its energy reserve, waiting for the ruined covering of flesh to be purged so it could continue the mission with more freedom of movement.

And now it rose up, smoking, purified of the outer skin, more clearly revealed for what it was—a chrome skeleton with hydraulic muscles and tendons of flexible cable.

Sarah saw the cyborg now over Reese's shoulder. She lifted him, pulling him toward the building. Terminator followed on a ruined leg. If the ankle joint had not been damaged under the tanker truck, it could easily have overtaken them.

Sarah reached the door. Locked. She groped on the ground for something and found a chunk of hot metal. Terminator, coming relentlessly on, was only twenty paces back. She swung the metal at the door and was dismayed when it clanged off the tempered glass without breaking it. She swung again, putting all her 106 pounds behind it, and the glass exploded inward.

They stepped through the shards, entering a corridor. Terminator was drawing nearer, the tempo of his clank-scrape metallic limp increasing.

Sarah slammed the hall door behind her and led Reese past partitioned cubicles. Terminator hit the door hard, blasting it off the hinges, and staggering through to spot them as Sarah dragged Reese around a long glass wall that separated the offices from a more industrial-looking hallway.

There was a large metal door at the far end of the hall. The rest of the rooms were either doorless or featured cheap wooden ones—useless barricades against their pursuer. Sarah made for the metal door. Terminator clanked after, gaining speed, an engine of destruction.

Sarah reached the fire door and pushed it open. Reese had all but collapsed in her arms as she pulled him through.

She fought against the weight of the fire door, but it wouldn't move fast enough. The machine reached out for her. Reese fell against the door and heaved, slamming it into its frame. He slapped the bolt across the door, locking it an instant before the cyborg impacted on the other side.

Sarah and Reese staggered back. They were in a factory. Dim hulking shapes of assembly robots rested, the assembly line shut down for the night. It seemed almost fully automated. Terminator crashed into the door behind them, and it rocked as Reese staggered to a large breaker panel, clawing it open.

"What are you doing?" Sarah screamed.

"Cover," he shot back as he threw all the switches. Then she got it. When the cyborg got through the door, as it would, its hypersensitive hearing could detect them in the dark labyrinth.

One by one, the machines came to life. The conveyer belt whined into motion. Rollers squealed, robot arms clutched futilely at the air, and mechanical pincers gyrated, conducting an orchestra of computor-controlled brutes in a cacophony of grinding noise. "The terminator can't track us!" she yelled.

He nodded, grabbing her hand, and they moved into the cavernous room. Ducking a swinging steel arm, they ran down aisles of eerily animated mechanisms.

Again the door behind them thundered as the thing on the far side used itself like a battering ram. Once more, and the door shuddered, the sheet metal bulging inward under the tremendous force.

When Reese stumbled and collapsed, Sarah bent over him.

"Reese, get up!"

His body disobeyed. His mind screamed to go with her, but his flesh had been driven past agony to numbness. Her only chance would be to go on alone, leaving him here in a delaying action.

Terminator tore a hole in the door with a screech of tortured metal. Light shot into the factory and fell on the machine above their heads. Sarah looked toward the source and saw Terminator reaching into the slit, probing for the bolt latch.

She tried to lift Reese again, but he was going slack

and heavy with death. The cyborg was ripping off the bolt and coming through. Sarah put her mouth to Reese's ear and shouted, "Get up, soldier! Move! Move your ass! Move it, Reese!" And somehow he responded, almost completely on reflex, to the words and tone of command. He thrust aside heaviness and beat back the stupor of shock to clutch Sarah's outstretched hand. They moved on into the machines.

Terminator thrust the ruined fire door aside and strode into the room, scanning. Its optics were unable to use infrared, which had completely overloaded in the fire, so it used a slow pan scan with enhanced clarification.

There was movement everywhere, but none of it fit target profile. It walked past the assembly line, completely merging into the hissing, gleaming texture of the factory, brethren to the blind mechanisms around it but oblivious of the irony that these moron robots were its primitive antecedents.

It scanned methodically, patient unto eternity.

Sarah and Reese moved in a crouch along a slightly raised catwalk, lost among the tangle of pipes and control panels. Reese picked up a short length of stout pipe from a worktable. Moments later, as Sarah clambered over an exhaust duct, her knee accidentally hit a red push button on a small black panel alongside it. With a sudden roar, the stamping plate of a massive hydraulic press slammed down an inch from her hand. Startled, she tumbled onto the catwalk.

Terminator's auditory sensors had filtered out all arrhythmic sounds and identified their patterns as vermin, water dripping from bad pipe fittings, and the target moving in the machinery up ahead. It swiveled its head on precision bearings and moved toward the sound.

Reese and Sarah ran to the end of the catwalk, only to face a locked door. Cursing, Reese about-faced and headed back the way they had come, Sarah rapidly following.

Terminator strode around a compressor unit, blocking them, a skeletal silhouette in the roaring darkness. Sarah staggered back. Reese raised the piece of pipe, holding it two handed, like a baseball bat, though his left arm was almost useless.

"Run!" he shouted to her, shoving her back.

"No!" Her voice was a scream, hysterical, unable to accept what was about to happen.

Terminator advanced. The male human had only one good arm and a four-centimeter pipe as defense. The man/machine took its time, ducking a swing and backhanding Reese's jaw, shattering it. Reese flew back against a protective grille but rebounded with the bar swinging. It caught Terminator in the chromed temple. The cyborg's head rocked back, then snapped toward Reese without expression. The skull's metal teeth were gleaming, however, in a perpetual grimace of hate.

Lashing out with lightning speed, it rammed a fist into Reese's bad arm. That woke Reese into the most lucid alertness he had ever experienced. All the rest of his life had seemed like a dream compared to this agony. He fell back, screaming. Terminator stepped forward to finish him off, then proceed to the unprotected primary target, whose figure it kept in view. She was backed against the catwalk railing, about four feet off the ground. There was nowhere to go but into the next life. Reese was trembling with the last awful internal explosion of energy he would ever know. He fumbled in his coat for the remaining pipe bomb, shielding it from the cyborg's line of sight. The Bic lighter was slippery in his ruined hand but lit immediately when he struck the flint. A breathless moment later, the fuse was burning, and Reese rolled on his back, using all his strength as the cyborg bent toward him.

"Sarah," he yelled, "get down!"

She saw the lit bomb in his hand and realized in one hyperreal instant that he had no intention of throwing it. Crying out in blind animal torment, she turned and ran.

Terminator had its fist drawn back to drive into Reese's skull when it felt the pipe charge jammed under its thoracic plate. It groped for the thing, but it was too late. Sarah hit the railing at a run and flipped over it, plummeting toward the concrete as Terminator exploded.

She struck the floor and rolled. Chunks of heated matter flew past, some hard, some soft. The concussion from the blast slammed her down, and she blanked out for an endless second. When she swam desperately back to the surface of awareness, she saw that Terminator was in pieces all around her. A leg there, hydraulic piston here, and over there a foot. Steaming particles of charred cable and oily chunks of alloy peppered the floor. Scrap metal.

It was over, finally.

She sat up and screamed. Pain shot through her leg, and she reached blindly for it. It was twisted beneath her, the calf punctured, oozing thick blood. Something had buried itself in her leg. She dragged the limp appendage out from under herself and saw that it was a sharp piece of Terminator that had been blown directly into her calf muscle about halfway between ankle and knee. Even in death the cyborg had tried to kill her. It was in her now, invading her flesh, in a kind of cold rape. She wanted it out and pulled. That hurt worse, but she doubled the pressure, and in a sudden sucking pop, the chunk of steel came free. She dropped it and gasped. When the pain began to subside a little, she opened her eyes and saw Reese.

Before she had a chance to register an emotion, she knew he was dead. The blast had flung him into a wall, and now his body was slumped on the floor, eyes staring at her but not seeing. There was a strange expression on his face. One he never could have had while he lived, because even asleep he never looked this peaceful. The soldier had completed his mission.

Sarah pulled herself across the floor toward him. She passed a large chunk of metal and didn't realize until after it reached out and grabbed her ankle that it was Terminator. Or what was left of it.

It pulled itself upright as Sarah looked back and screamed. Cables dragged behind it from the gaping hole at the bottom of the spine where the hip joints used to be. But it had two arms, a torso, and a head. The eyes locked on target, and it began to pull itself toward her. With her free, uninjured leg, she kicked at the thing, writhed, and broke free. It crawled after.

She couldn't move the broken leg, so she pulled herself along the floor. But she couldn't get away from it, because they were equals now, mutual cripples dragging themselves through chunks of debris, the hunter and hunted, enacting their roles.

She pulled herself onto a moving conveyer belt. The machine followed suit, rolling onto it about ten feet behind her. They both rested as it carried them along, eyeing each other, seeking strategic gain.

Then Sarah rolled off onto the floor, and it reacted much more slowly than usual, toppling after her about twelve feet away. She had the advantage now and crawled toward *her* target, a target newly acquired.

Terminator calculated her trajectory and angled off to intercept. It didn't know what she was moving toward and didn't care.

Sarah realized it was going to get to the catwalk stairs about the same time she was. She could turn away and seek another path, perhaps even outcrawl it to safety outside. Maybe. But she wanted to end it. *She*. Not anyone or anything else. She heard the rhythmic, constant scrapes of steel on metal as Terminator followed. She climbed off the catwalk into a dark jungle of machinery. She could hardly move there, wedged between two vast rectangles of metal. Her skin was covered with sweat, and she slipped repeatedly, losing ground. Terminator crawled in after her.

Sarah saw the target up ahead and heaved herself forward. The clattering, scraping, and whirring behind sped up. She felt its metal fingers rake her feet and sucked herself in, recoiling from the thing. It must be very close now, but she had no more time to look back, only ahead.

Sarah came to the far edge of the crawl space and threw herself out onto the catwalk. Her legs followed her upper body more slowly, melting after in slow motion as a metal arm clutched at them. She reached up for a sliding-steel gate as Terminator crawled to the edge and groped for her. The gate crashed down and locked with a clang. The cyborg thudded against the safety gate, a hammer reverberating a massive bell.

Sarah fell back, gasping, staring up at the man-machine as it pressed against the barrier. It was working the arm through the narrow space between the bars. Terminator locked its eyes on Sarah, triangulating on her pulsing neck, then fired its bicep hydraulics. Steel screeched in protest as the arm shot out for her throat, the fingers extending, flexing, eager for contact. Sarah backed as far as she could go against the confining machinery. The cyborg rammed its shoulder against the gate, and its fingers nicked her collarbone.

She reached up for the control panel she had seen before, extending her arm as far as it would go. Her fingers waved in the air a quarter inch from the button.

Terminator strove forward, tightening its grip on her. She screamed in rage and frustration and all-consuming terror, then lunged up, slamming her hand onto the button. The red button.

Time stopped.

In the sudden silence, Sarah clearly saw Terminator looking up at her and felt the icy fingers closing on her windpipe just as the hydraulic press slammed down with forty tons of pressure and ground the cyborg between the slabs of metal. With great satisfaction she watched the press slowly closing the space in which Terminator was caught.

The cyborg reached out, transferring all available power to that arm and hand. The eyes burned into hers, and its chassis-sensors recorded sudden deformation on a major scale. Even the hyperalloy could not resist the full weight of the press, which screeched steam and heaved, mindless and relentless, like a terminator.

The torso was slowly collapsing, and the highly protected circuits there began to crumble into silicone dust. Power was interrupted everywhere and splashed into alternate routes that were then disrupted. The microprocessor brain overloaded, distorting Terminator's awareness. The last thing it saw as the press flattened one of its optics and its fingers closed around the target's neck was her expression of agony and fear give way to utter, savage, and very human triumph.

When the press ground to a halt just shy of its automatically preset distance, the remaining cyborg eye flickered, then blinked out forever.

"You're terminated, fucker," Sarah said grimly.

# DAY THREE

**Leucadia**
**7:45 A.M.**

Sarah had blacked out then. When she came to, the factory machines had been shut down, but there was still noise. Sirens. Screeching tires. Excited murmurs. She was being lifted onto a gurney and gently strapped in. She felt pain, but somehow it was muffled and distant, disconnected. Faces swam into focus and out again. Attendants. Police. Onlookers. As they put her in the ambulance she saw a black van nearby. The word Coroner was printed on the side, and a bag was being loaded into it as if it were a sack of flour. She knew it was Reese. Before she had time to mourn consciously, the doors of the ambulance clanged shut and sent her reeling back down into the blessed darkness.

As the ambulance pulled away, Greg Simmons hiked up the itchy collar of his leisure suit and turned to go into his office. What a way to begin a day. But he was intercepted by his assistant, Jack Kroll, a compact, hyperactive kid with a genius I.Q. and the street smarts of a cocker spaniel.

"Look at this, Greg!" he shouted enthusiastically, and thrust a small electronic chip the likes of which Greg had never seen before into his palm. It was maybe thirty-five millimeters in diameter and laced with imprinted circuitry that made absolutely no sense whatsoever, although it seemed to be very efficiently connected. For what purpose?

"Where'd you get this?"

Jack indicated the assembly line in the back of the building. "I wasn't supposed to, but I crossed the police line, because this thing was—"

Greg clamped his arm around Jack's shoulder and pinched his arm, hard. Jack howled and tried to break free until Greg nodded toward a patrolman standing about six feet away. They walked into the parking lot away from the knot of coworkers and officials.

Jack told Greg he had found the chip on the floor in the middle of a lot of strange-looking debris. Greg kept turning it over and over in his hands, puzzled and getting more and more excited. "Did the boss see this?"

Loyal Jack looked wounded. "No, Greg. I brought it right to you. Nobody knows I have it."

Greg nodded happily. "Let's keep it that way."

"Huh?" Jack said, confused. "Don't you want to take it down to R and D?"

"What for? So old man Kleinhaus can get the credit? We're on salary here, pal. Design techs for hire. They give a shit about us. Why make them rich?"

"What are we going to do?"

Greg looked into his foolish friend's eyes. Jack was his treasure, an undiscovered artist in electronic engineering. Everyone else saw the package. Greg saw the contents. That was his advantage. He and Jack would go into business for themselves. A small office with little furniture. Just a front for the lab in back. He'd mortgage his house, his car, his wife and kids, and sink all Jack's savings into this project. Once they figured out exactly how to exploit what must have been some kind of new microprocessing circuit, they would figure out what it should be used for.

It took them longer than Greg originally thought it would. Sixteen months and four days to be exact. Their gamble paid off. They got a bank loan, patented the circuit, and waited to get sued. They didn't. *Nobody* knew what the hell it was. As though it had dropped into their laps from another planet. But it was just beginning to make them wealthy beyond their wildest fantasies. In another two years, they had their own company, bigger than the one they had suddenly quit after finding the chip. One of the most difficult tasks they faced in those years was coming up with a name for their fledgling company. All the other design corporations had already used up every possible combination of tech-sounding syllables. One day Jack walked into their office with a big shit-eating grin on his face and announced that he had found the right name. Greg agreed, and within days they had incorporated under the legal title of Cyberdyne Systems.

Thinking back on the whole serendipitous, mysterious train of events that led to their good fortune, Greg had to admit . . . it was fate.

# DAY
# ONE TWENTY-SIX

**Buenaventura, Mexico**
**7:46 A.M.**

The flat scrubland was already heating up for the midday snake roast as the sun crested the ragged outline of mountains in the distance. And yet the air was thick with moisture. The weather was confused, as it often is in Mexico. Sarah took little notice as she drove the open jeep along what passed for a highway, the wind blowing her hair like a chestnut flag. She was wearing sunglasses and was pregnant. Below the small, sweet swelling that would one day become John Connor was a .357 Colt Python revolver nestled safely in her lap. It was loaded, and she had learned how to use it. Very well.

Pugsly Junior sat next to her, yawning. It was an eighty-three-pound German shepherd, attack trained to kill anyone remotely unlike Sarah, should they make threatening gestures. It could be gentle, but Sarah never truly considered it her pet. It was a weapon.

She had been driving all night, moving in the relative safety of moonlight, as she always did these days, although she knew that should another terminator come through time—which was a possibility she could not discount—the night would not protect her. *She* was her best protection.

But she stayed low profile more out of a sense of paranoia that chance accident might destroy all she and Reese had fought for. No inane traffic accident, no idiotic plane crash, no random act of violence, must claim her life now. It was vital that she live.

She had changed.

It wasn't just the pregnancy, although her body had changed, with a not-unpleasant heaviness in hips and breasts. She felt somehow richer in appearance because of it. The major alteration was internal, behind her eyes. She had been able to measure the full distance of the gulf between what she once was and had become when they told her in the hospital that her mother had been murdered. She had felt the whole exploded jigsaw of those horrible three days falling into place. Along with that had come the grief, fed by all the other life-shattering tragedies, but she had channeled it in such a way so that it did not drown her. Then she jammed it into a metal box and welded it shut.

Later, when she was stronger, she would take it out from time to time and let it wash over her. And then, by extrapolating from it, she could mourn in advance for the world that would be utterly lost. Taking that emotion, so real and wrenching, taking it to the nth limit, she could catch a glimpse of the future, with its loss so vast that it would forever defy all but the most abstract comprehension. And that made her stronger yet. Because hate is a powerful emotion, too, and so much more effective.

And so she began the Plan. When she was discharged from the hospital, she emptied her meager bank account, collected her mother's life insurance, bought the attack dog, the .357, and the jeep, then set out on the road. South. All the way to the bottom of South America, maybe. Get into the birth and raise John Connor and prepare him for the war. Where it was safe from nuclear attack. Where it was serene and beautiful and windblown and—

She was low on gas. Better fill up before going into the

mountains. She pulled into the ramshackle gas station in the dusty bowl of land alongside the highway.

She turned off the cassette recorder on the dash. She had been dictating the next section of the Book, the survival guide for her son. She was trying to get it all down in case something happened to her before she could raise him to maturity and to concretize it on magnetic tape before she forgot the details. Already a lot of what had happened was fading away, refusing to be brought back, because that would have also brought back the old Sarah, and you could not bring back the dead. In a way, Terminator *had* killed her.

Just before pulling in for gas, she had been saying, "Should I tell you about your father? That's a tough one. Will it change your decision to send him here, to his death? But if you don't send Kyle, then you can never be."

Once in a while, when she faced this kind of paradox, she would grow dizzy and faint with time vertigo. You could go just a little mad thinking about it.

She stopped the jeep's engine, slipped the gun under the seat, and got out of the vehicle to stretch her legs. They were plumper now, even more pretty, and the scar had almost healed. The pin was there, holding together the bone Terminator's debris had shattered, the same pin Terminator had been fruitlessly searching for in the legs of those other Sarah Connors. Those poor women. Sometimes she felt an irrational guilt, as if those innocents had died for something she personally had done. In a way, they had. She just hadn't done it yet.

How strange, she often thought, to be making history and all the time know it and know the impact. It made her feel significant but then insignificant, simultaneously. Almost as if she were a cog, a puppet of fate, a mere link in the causal chain.

She knew there was more to it than that, of course. Her rage to survive, to will herself to survive, had determined the outcome. Which then made that aspect of her character merely another element in the design. The snake eats its tail, and it always will.

Pugsly growled softly and lowered his ears as Sarah scanned the gas station. Chickens clucked and fussed around the jeep's big tires, flustered occasionally by the rising wind. The station was an oasis of junk in the wasteland, about two kilometers beyond a town that had been little more than a momentary widening of the highway.

Here, surrounded by joshua trees and not much else, was a tired little building in the center of what looked like a junk-car farm. Rusting pickups rested on blocks, wheelless, their glass gone. There were mottled and dented vehicles of all descriptions, waiting apparently for others of their kind to die so the necessary parts could be salvaged to repair them. Some sleazy *piñatas* swung and twisted in the bursts of wind, their bright colors mocking the apparent lifelessness of the place.

Finally, a figure appeared in the doorway. An old man, stooped and weathered, detached from the shade and shuffled toward her. He might have been full Yaqui, and his eyes were red rimmed from too much of the cheap local *mescal*. Sarah saw his eyes and felt a momentary chill. She suddenly had the absurd feeling that he could see into the future. It passed immediately, replaced by an even stranger thought. *She* was the seer. It was she who could see beyond the horizon, and like those throughout history who were touched by visions, she wished it were not so.

The attendant nodded politely. Sarah groped for the pronunciation of *Llena el tanque*, but the leather-skinned proprietor cut her off. He spoke a little English and was overwhelmingly proud of it this far south of the border. He assured her he would "fill it up, *sí*."

Sarah got back into the jeep, for the wind was picking up, whipping hot sand in her face. She had a thought and hit the record button on the machine.

"I suppose I'll tell you about your father. I owe him that. And maybe it will be enough if you know that in the few hours we had together, we loved a lifetime's worth."

She was struck then by how inadequate those words

were. They could never convey the strength of emotion or the rightness of it.

A snap-whir startled her, and Pugsly sat up, alert, but it was only a little Mexican boy, maybe on the near side of ten. He was holding a camera, an old and dented Polaroid he must have "liberated" from a passing *turista*. A photograph was rolling out the bottom slit.

The boy spoke to Sarah too rapidly for her to understand. When the attendant came up, she asked him to interpret.

"He says you are very beautiful, *señora*, and he is ashamed to ask five American dollars for this picture, but if he does not, he says his father will beat him."

Sarah eyed the scrawny, grinning kid in his holed T-shirt and then said, "That's a pretty good hustle, kid. Four. *Quatro*."

The boy gave her the photo, snatched the money out of her hand, and danced away, happy to have found another sucker among the infrequent *turistas*.

Sarah watched the image form with a sense of her own future coming together. The eyes that solidified out of the white void on the Polaroid surface were her own. She watched the rest of her face darkening, a slow fade-in on the Sarah that was now. *Older,* she thought. But it wasn't a physiological change, only a new set to the old mild features. There was a faraway look in her eyes, and she was smiling just the slightest bit, but somehow it was a sad smile.

Sarah set the picture aside, tossing it casually on the passenger seat among the hand-labeled tapes of her journal. As she reached for the ignition key, the photo was already almost forgotten. Pugsly sniffed it once, leaving a moist noseprint, the first of many abuses that would age the plastic rectangle before it would rest lightly in the palm of a soldier's hand as he crouched in the thundering darkness the hellfire of the machine Reich raging above him. Sarah would have given it to John, and he would then give it to Reese. This was the beginning of the circle. But of course circles have no beginning or end.

Sarah paid the attendant for the gas and started up the jeep. Wind tore at her and rolled tumbleweeds across the highway. The boy was chattering behind them and pointing toward the mountains.

"What did he say?" she asked the old man.

"He said there's a storm coming in."

Sarah looked toward the sky and the gathering clouds. Sheet lightning fired behind them like giant strobes.

"I know," she said quietly, and put the jeep into first gear.

Out on the road, she thought about Reese. And time. And history. And most importantly, destiny.

# TERMINATOR 2: JUDGMENT DAY

## *Randall Frakes*

*'I'll be back'*

In THE TERMINATOR, a cyborg from the future was sent back in time to 1984 to kill a seemingly innocent woman who was destined to give birth to a child, John Connor, who would one day lead the human Resistance against the machines. It failed.

Now, in TERMINATOR 2: JUDGMENT DAY, a second Terminator has been sent back in time. Its new mission is to strike at John Connor himself, while he is still a child. As before, the Resistance is able to send a lone warrior as a protector for John. It's just a matter of which one will reach the boy first . . .

# ARNOLD
## The Unauthorised Biography of Arnold Schwarzenegger

### *Wendy Leigh*

'Some day the world is going to know who I am – just by hearing my first name'

That day has long passed. For years he's been 'Arnold' to millions of fans around the world. Bodybuilding legend. Box-office superstar. Kennedy family member. But until now the real story of Arnold Schwarzenegger has never been told ...

Wendy Leigh delves deep behind the public image and, after two years' research and scores of interviews with Arnold's friends, family, lovers, colleagues and rivals, she emerges with some startling facts. She explores his troubled boyhood in an obscure Austrian village, his tortured relationship with his Nazi father, his sexual exploits, his political ambitions and his lifelong penchant for often cruel practical jokes. The portrait that emerges is of a complex, intelligent, sometimes ruthless and often manipulative man who has allowed little to stand in the way of his meteoric rise to success.

# ARNOLD:
## The Education of a Body-Builder

*Arnold Schwarzenegger
with Douglas Kent Hall*

*A super-man's programme for super-fitness*

ARNOLD is the long-awaited book by Arnold Schwarzenegger, his bestselling autobiography and fitness plan. In its pages the superstar of PUMPING IRON tells you how he became the most successful bodybuilder of our time. With the aid of vivid photographs and a step-by-step programme, the man who became Mr Olympia and Mr Universe lets you into the secrets of his astonishing success – what to eat, what to wear, how to expand your normal exercise routine into a championship-level workout. A special four-day gym programme includes specific exercises to develop specific muscle-groups, with each exercise illustrated with photographs of Arnold in action.

Fascinating and inspiring both as an autobiography and as a fitness guide, ARNOLD: THE EDUCATION OF A BODYBUILDER will show you how to enjoy better health and increased relaxation through the disciplines and rewards of bodybuilding.

# ARNOLD'S BODYBUILDING FOR MEN

## *Arnold Schwarzenegger with Bill Dobbins*

Arnold Schwarzenegger won his sixth Mr Olympia title in 1975 and decided that competitive bodybuilding was too easy. He needed to keep really fit in his new career as an actor and author, even though he didn't have time for four hours of intensive training every day. Now he makes time for a daily workout – even if it means starting at 11 at night – and has put together a complete health and fitness programme for even the busiest man.

Arnold's programme will make you look great *and* feel great! There are special sections for teenagers, older men and professional bodybuilders as well as the basic three-level exercise programme for individual body conditioning, increased stamina and advanced training. Full descriptions of all the exercises, equipment, warm-up and warm-down routines in the unique Schwarzenegger method – plus hundreds of photos of Arnold and other bodybuilders in action – make this a really complete programme for total fitness.

# PUMPING IRON

## *Charles Gaines and George Butler*

Who are these men who dedicate themselves to building bodies like Greek statues? And why do they do it; travelling across the world, competing for grandoise but publicly uncelebrated titles like Mr Universe and Mr Olympia, their lives rigidly defined and regulated by their obsession, completely without the public acclaim that accompanies athletic achievement?

Novelist Charles Gaines and photographer George Butler spent two years trying to find out. They followed the bodybuilders from competition to competition, trying to capture the essence of their strange, joyful and exotic world. A fascinating and compelling look at a resonant and enthralling subculture.

# STARK

## *Ben Elton*

Stark has more money than God and the social conscience of a dog on a croquet lawn. What's more, they know the Earth is dying.

Deep in Western Australia where the Aboriginals used to milk the trees, a planet-sized plot takes shape. Some green freaks pick up the scent. A Pommie poseur, a brain-fried Vietnam Vet, Aboriginals who lost their land . . . not much against a conspiracy that controls society. But EcoAction isn't in society; it just lives in the same place, along with the cockroaches.

If you're facing the richest and most disgusting conspiracy in history, you have to do more than stick up two fingers and say 'peace'.

# SHARKY'S MACHINE

## *William Diehl*

1944: Three American soldiers, killed on a bizarre mission behind German lines, sprawl dead beside an Italian lake. At the bottom of the lake: four million dollars' worth of gold...

1976: Sharky, ace undercover cop busted to the Vice Squad for being too damn sharp, listens to some outrageous erotic tapes that catapult him into the murderous world of financial manipulation, top-level political intrigue and sexual corruption spawned by that wartime bloodbath.

Soon Sharky and the team he calls his 'machine' are headed for the storm centre of the most lethal conspiracy America has ever known...

*Sharky's Machine* sweeps from Nazi-occupied Europe to the deadly opulence of Hong Kong's brothels, from the steel-and-glass fortress that houses one of the world's mightiest financial empires to the depths of the criminal underworld and on to the most shattering climax in modern thriller fiction.

| ☐ Terminator 2: Judgement Day | Randall Frakes | £3.99 |
| ☐ Arnold | Wendy Leigh | £5.99 |
| ☐ Arnold: The Education of a Body Builder | Arnold Schwarzenegger | £10.99 |
| ☐ Arnold's Bodybuilding for Men | Arnold Schwarzenegger | £11.99 |
| ☐ Pumping Iron | Charles Gaines/George Butler | £9.99 |
| ☐ Stark | Ben Elton | £4.99 |
| ☐ Gridlock | Ben Elton | £4.99 |
| ☐ Sharky's Machine | William Diehl | £4.50 |

Warner Books now offers an exciting range of quality titles by both established and new authors. All of the books in this series are available from:

Little, Brown and Company (UK) Limited,
P.O. Box 11,
Falmouth,
Cornwall TR10 9EN.

Alternatively you may fax your order to the above address. Fax No. 0326 376423.

Payments can be made as follows: cheque, postal order (payable to Little, Brown and Company) or by credit cards, Visa/Access. Do not send cash or currency. UK customers and B.F.P.O. please allow £1.00 for postage and packing for the first book, plus 50p for the second book, plus 30p for each additional book up to a maximum charge of £3.00 (7 books plus).

Overseas customers including Ireland, please allow £2.00 for the first book plus £1.00 for the second book, plus 50p for each additional book.

NAME (Block Letters) .......................................................

................................................................................

ADDRESS ......................................................................

................................................................................

................................................................................

☐ I enclose my remittance for _____

☐ I wish to pay by Access/Visa Card

Number | | | | | | | | | | | | | | | | |

Card Expiry Date | | | | |